HIS HANDS WERE QUIET

HIS HANDS WERE QUIET

ZACHARY GOLDMAN MYSTERIES #2

P.D. WORKMAN

pdworkman

ALSO BY P.D. WORKMAN

Zachary Goldman Mysteries

She Wore Mourning

His Hands Were Quiet

She Was Dying Anyway

He Was Walking Alone

They Thought He was Safe

He Was Not There

Her Work Was Everything

She Told a Lie (Coming soon)

He Never Forgot (Coming soon)

She Was At Risk (Coming soon)

Kenzie Kirsch Medical Thrillers

Unlawful Harvest

Auntie Clem's Bakery

Gluten-Free Murder

Dairy-Free Death

Allergen-Free Assignation

Witch-Free Halloween (Halloween Short)

Dog-Free Dinner (Christmas Short)

Stirring Up Murder

Brewing Death

Coup de Glace

Sour Cherry Turnover

Apple-achian Treasure

Vegan Baked Alaska

Muffins Masks Murder

Tai Chi and Chai Tea

Santa Shortbread

Reg Rawlins, Psychic Detective

What the Cat Knew

A Psychic with Catitude

A Catastrophic Theft

Night of Nine Tails

Telepathy of Gardens

Delusions of the Past

Fairy Blade Unmade

Web of Nightmares

A Whisker's Breadth (Coming soon)

High-Tech Crime Solvers Series

Virtually Harmless

Stand Alone Suspense Novels

Looking Over Your Shoulder

Lion Within

Pursued by the Past

In the Tick of Time

Loose the Dogs

AND MORE AT PDWORKMAN.COM

To shock those who didn't know
and acknowledge those who have been shocked

Mira Kelly put the pictures of her son down on her kitchen table, one at a time, like they were precious treasures she thought Zachary might try to run off with.

Photographs were Zachary's passion. Ever since Mr. Peterson, his foster father at the time, had given him a used camera for his eleventh birthday, he'd been taking pictures. It was that passion that had eventually led him to his profession. Not a department store photographer or a wedding photographer, but a private investigator. It gave him the flexibility to set his own hours, even if many of them were spent sitting in a car or standing casually around, waiting for the opportunity to catch a cheating spouse or insurance claim scammer in the act.

Zachary ignored the lighting and framing issues in Mira's pictures and just looked at the boy's face. He was a teenager, maybe thirteen or fourteen. Still baby-faced, with no sign of facial hair. Dark hair and pale skin, like Zachary's. Quentin's hair was a little too long, getting into his eyes in uneven points. Zachary couldn't stand hair getting in his face and ears and kept his short. Not buzzed like foster parents and institutions had always preferred, but still easy to care for. The first few pictures of Quentin didn't give a clear view of his eyes. His eyes were closed, hidden by his shaggy hair, or his face was turned away from the camera. Then Mira put one down on the table that had caught his eyes full-on, looking straight through the camera. Blue-gray. Clear. Distant.

Mira kept her fingers on the photo, reluctant to release it to him. "Quentin was a beautiful baby," she said. "Everyone always said how beautiful he was. Not cute or handsome, *beautiful.* He could have been a model. But he didn't smile and laugh when you smiled or tickled him, like other babies. He laughed at other things; the sunlight filtering through the leaves of a tree, music… I didn't realize, in the beginning…" She wiped at the corner of her eye. She'd been resisting tears since she had first greeted Zachary.

Isabella Hildebrandt had said that Quentin had been autistic when she asked Zachary if he would meet with Mira. The boy had been living at the Summit Living Center, some sort of care facility, when he had died suddenly. 'Died suddenly' was a euphemism that Zachary particularly hated.

Mira was convinced that Quentin's death couldn't have been suicide. "He wouldn't have done that," she insisted again, looking at the picture that showed Quentin's eyes.

"Why not?" Zachary asked baldly.

He could see that his bluntness surprised her. She was used to people talking about her son's death in veiled terms. Coming at it sideways and trying to comfort her. But that wasn't Zachary's job. Zachary's job, if he took the case, would be to find out the truth about Quentin's death. And if he was going to do that, he needed Mira to speak plainly instead of soft-pedaling euphemisms.

"He… he couldn't." She stumbled over the words, looking for a way to explain it. "That just… wasn't something that he would have been capable of."

"Physically, you mean?"

"No, he was healthy physically, mostly, but… he had autism. He didn't have the ability… mentally… to decide to do something like that, and plan it out, and follow through." She shook her head. "The idea is ridiculous."

"Because he was mentally handicapped."

"No… not handicapped. I just don't think… I don't think he could have understood what it meant, to kill himself. And I don't think he could have planned it out. There is other stuff that can go along with autism… His executive planning skills…"

Zachary wasn't sure what that meant. He looked at the other angles of the case. "Was he depressed?"

"He was happy at Summit. It was a good place for him. The only place that had been able to manage his behavioral issues."

Zachary looked at the haunting eyes that looked up from the photograph. "This is a recent photo?"

"Yes." Mira looked down at him. "I know he's not smiling for the picture. But he never smiled for pictures. He *was* happy at Summit. They were able to get him off of all of the meds that the other places had put him on. So that he could be himself and not a drugged-out zombie."

"Sometimes depression isn't obvious. People are often taken by surprise by suicides." Zachary looked away from her uncomfortably. Other times, depression was obvious, and friends or family members did everything they could to head it off. Like with Isabella Hildebrandt, when her mother had hired Zachary to look into her son Declan's untimely death, hoping to bring Isabella some peace. They'd been unable to prevent her suicide attempt. Only luck and quick-acting professionals had been able to bring her back. As they had done for Zachary in the past. "When you say they took him off of his meds… did that include antidepressants?"

"No, he was never on antidepressants. He was on other medications to keep him quiet. I couldn't have him at home anymore, because he was too much of a danger to my younger sons. And me."

There was a snapshot on the fridge of Mira with two younger boys, maybe eight and ten. Mira was a slight, small woman. The ten-year-old was almost her height. There were no pictures of her with Quentin, but Zachary suspected he was taller than she was by a few inches. Even though Quentin had a slim build, a child in the midst of a meltdown could be very strong. Looking down at the pictures of Quentin on the table, Zachary saw another child in his mind's eye.

Annie Sellers had also been autistic, and well-known for her rages. He had watched, through the narrow observation window of his detention cell, as several members of the Bonnie Brown security staff had tried to bring her under control. She was slim and small, but even three guards together could barely hold on to her to get her into a cell.

Zachary blinked, trying to focus on the case at hand. Annie was in the distant past. He couldn't do anything for her. No one could.

"How long had Quentin been at Summit?"

"Two years. They turned him around completely. He was not the same child."

"And you hadn't noticed any changes in behavior recently. Anything at all."

Mira bit her lip. She was a strawberry-blonde with a pixie cut. She kind of reminded Zachary of a forty-year-old Julie Andrews. The same shape to her face. But there were fine lines that told the tale of a hard life. There was no sign of a man in the house. Raising three boys as a single mother was not an easy job, especially when one of them had behavioral issues. Summit was a good two hours' drive from Mira's house, which meant that she wasn't visiting him daily.

"He'd been agitated the last few times I went to see him," Mira said finally. "They said it was probably just hormones, and they were increasing his therapy sessions to address it."

Zachary scratched a note to himself in his notepad. "What do you mean by agitated?"

"More... anxious... more... behaviors..."

"Describe to me what that looked like. What exactly was he doing?"

"Picking at his skin... flapping... He was voicing and didn't want to sit down to visit with me. He wanted to walk around to visit, but they said… his therapist said he needed to work on sitting quietly to visit. When they forced him to sit down, he started banging his head or got angry, and they had to take him out and cut our visit short."

Zachary wrote down each of the behaviors. "He didn't usually do those things?"

"No, he'd been pretty good at Summit, they could usually suppress them."

"Is there something that triggers them? When he lived at home, did he do them all the time, or just sometimes?"

Mira ran her fingers through her hair. There were bags under her eyes, camouflaged with makeup. She looked exhausted. She probably wasn't sleeping.

"Yes, when he was frustrated about something… Before he died, I felt like he wanted to tell me something. But it's difficult for him. If I'd been able to walk around with him, talk with him some more, I might have been able to figure out what it was. But they said he had to go back to his room."

"So he *could* talk…?"

"He was mostly nonverbal. He had a few words. He would take my hand to show me something or ask me to do something for him. But Summit said I needed to force him to use speech." Mira sighed heavily. "They said that if I ignored his nonverbal communication… he would use words more…"

"Oh." Zachary nodded. "Then he could, if he had to?"

Mira frowned and tugged at a lock of hair. "Well… it was hard for him. They said that if he could speak some of the time, then he could speak all of the time, if he just worked at it. When he was at home, we would use pictures, gestures, whatever we could." She wrapped the lock around her finger. "It wasn't like he was just being willful or lazy when he wouldn't speak. That's what Dr. Abato says, but I always thought… Quentin was doing the best he could, and that we should let him use PECS or signs or whatever he needed to communicate…"

"That makes sense," Zachary agreed, giving her a nod of encouragement.

"They said that I was just babying him. Keeping him from progressing. They said if he was ever going to get out of Summit, maybe on a work program or something, he would have to be able to speak. To get along in the real world and be treated like everyone else, he needed to be able to speak."

"And it was working? You said that his behavior had improved at Summit. Did that include his speech?"

Mira picked up one of the photos from the table and stared at it, her eyes shiny with tears.

"Scripted speech," she offered finally. "They were very proud of how well he was doing with scripted speech."

"What's that?"

"I would come to visit him, and he would say, 'Hi, Mom.' And I would say hi to him. He would ask me how I was doing, and I would tell him and ask him how he was. He would say, 'fine' or 'happy' or 'well.' But that was it... if I asked him what he had been doing, or who his friends were, or anything like that, he would fall apart. He would cry and mope and shake his head at everything I said. Then when it was time go, and I would say goodbye and hug him, he would pick up the script again. He'd say, 'Bye, Mom. Love you. See you next time.' They'd taught him how to say hello and goodbye..." Mira's voice cracked. "But they had just trained him to say the words. He still couldn't have a conversation. He still didn't have a script for what came between hello and goodbye."

"Maybe that would have come."

"Maybe... but conversations are complicated. I don't know how many different scripts he could have learned. There are so many different pathways a conversation could have followed."

Zachary looked at the yellow envelope at Mira's elbow that she had not yet opened. She was assiduously ignoring it.

"Do you want to take a break?"

Mira looked relieved. She let out her breath. "Yes. How about some tea? Can I get you a drink?"

"Tea would be great," Zachary agreed. He was not a tea drinker, but it was a soothing ritual for those who were. It would help Mira to calm down and move forward again.

She got up from the table and moved around the kitchen, putting the kettle on and rattling the cups and saucers and other bits. She opened the kitchen window a crack, letting in a breath of fresh, cool air.

"How long have you known Isabella?" Zachary asked her.

Isabella, *The Happy Artist*, beloved local TV personality, had connected the two of them. Zachary had been the one to investigate her son Declan's death and, in spite of the hell she'd been through as a result, she seemed to be grateful to Zachary.

"I've known Isabella a long time. Since we were both in school. We weren't really close friends. But I watched her when she started painting on TV. Quentin loved to watch her show. I knew Isabella had used a private investigator, so I called her…"

Zachary nodded.

Mira set their cups on the table and filled them. Zachary stirred his, not really interested in drinking it.

"I can look at those when I get home," he said, nodding to the unopened envelope. "There's no reason you have to look at them again."

Mira hesitated, considering his offer, then shook her head. "No. I can do this."

She took a couple of determined gulps of piping hot tea and picked it up.

2

O

h, that poor boy," Kenzie sympathized.

It wasn't the first time Zachary and the attractive brunette had looked at photos of dead bodies together over dinner. Being attached to the local medical examiner's office, Kenzie had a strong stomach, so things that would have made a normal woman queasy didn't bother her one bit.

Not that Quentin Thatcher's photos were gruesome. Strangulation was bloodless, and his body wasn't bloated and swollen like Declan Hildebrandt's had been. But they were still stark and depressing.

"His mother saw these?" Kenzie asked. "She's a stronger woman than I would be. I could never look at photos of my dead child like this."

"She had a pretty hard time with it," Zachary said. "But yes… she's strong."

"The poor woman."

Zachary had a sip of his soft drink and nodded. "I feel bad for any mother who has lost a child."

Saying it brought back painful memories of his break-up with Bridget. The loss of the child he had expected to raise with her.

Kenzie looked at him, her brows drawing down. "I hear a 'but' in there somewhere…"

"No, no, not at all. I do feel sorry for her."

"Okay."

They were silent for a couple of minutes until the waiter brought their meals. Kenzie poked at her phone, not speaking to him, and he got the feeling she was waiting him out, trying to force him, by not asking questions, to say what was on his mind. Just like Mira had been told to ignore Quentin's nonverbal communication so he would be forced to use speech.

Zachary cut into his steak, pretending that he was checking to make sure it had been cooked to his specifications. It had been, of course, and he really wasn't that picky as long as it wasn't bleeding. He just wanted to look at something other than Kenzie, patiently waiting for him to spill his guts. Outside, it was raining, the intermittent traffic passing the restaurant with that familiar swish of wet roads.

"I guess she just irked me a little," he admitted. "She did what the institution said to, even though she didn't think it was the best thing for her son."

"But they are the professionals."

"Sure… but I've dealt with a lot of doctors. They're not always right. In fact… they are frequently wrong when they're dealing with messy stuff like mental illness. Or autism and the other conditions that go with it. They have so many patients to treat. They only have a few minutes to spend on each case. But Quentin's mother only had to deal with him. She raised him for the first twelve years. She knows him and what he needs better than they do."

Kenzie twirled her fork through spaghetti marinara, her movements smooth and dexterous. "But she doesn't have the training. The doctors and therapists have studied the best way to treat kids like this. All of the latest research. All of the different methods. The mother doesn't have that."

"Maybe not… or maybe she does. Parents have a lot of

resources available now. Internet, support groups, millions of books. They can spend hundreds of hours researching what's best for their particular child." He paused, chewing a couple more bites of steak. "But… I don't get the feeling she ever did any of that. She just let the institution dictate what she should do."

"Do you think the doctors were doing something wrong, or do you just not like his mother toeing the line?"

"I don't know yet. I'm trying to go into it with an open mind." Zachary looked down at the pictures of Quentin still on the table, the dark bruises around his throat. "If nothing else… they didn't stop him from killing himself."

Kenzie nodded. "He should have been closely supervised. They should have known if he was suicidal and have had him on a watch."

Zachary took another sip of his cola, wishing that he had something stronger. When he started to get anxious, like the case was already making him, he liked something to take the edge off. Kenzie watched him put the glass down. He wondered whether she could tell what he was thinking, whether she knew that he was craving a real drink. He breathed out, long and slow, trying to release the knot in his belly.

"She feels guilty for institutionalizing him," he told Kenzie.

"Of course. I'm sure every parent who has a child like that does. But she did what she had to do."

Zachary laid down his fork, unable to pretend that he was interested in his steak anymore. "She also said that when she took him there, when she had to go home and leave him behind… she felt relieved."

Kenzie looked at Zachary, her eyes traveling over his face like she was reading a book. "That sounds pretty normal too. He was probably exhausting to take care of. Getting bigger and harder to control. Maybe even violent."

"Yes. He was. She said she feared for her other children."

"And herself, even if she didn't say so. Even a child can hurt you when they're in a rage. More so when it's a teenager who doesn't understand how much damage they could do."

"Yeah." Zachary looked down at his plate. He picked up his napkin and dabbed at his mouth, covering up the grimace he couldn't check.

"What is it?" Kenzie asked, when a few minutes passed in silence.

"Nothing. It's nothing."

"I think I know you well enough by now to tell you're upset about something. Why don't you tell me about it before it builds up into something worse?"

He tried to swallow a lump in his throat. Kenzie let him sit and stew for a while longer. Her eyes went to the photos and she picked through them with two fingers, moving them around. She didn't point out anything suspicious.

"My mother," Zachary said finally. "I told you that she didn't want me. She had me put… into a place like that."

Kenzie put her hand over his. "Oh, Zachary…" She shook her head. "I still don't understand how she could have done that. I really don't. I don't think that any child deserves to be locked up for making a mistake. And that's what it was. A mistake."

"I did things I knew were wrong. I knew, and I went ahead and did them anyway. I wore her ragged. She couldn't manage all of us. It wasn't just her. I never lasted long in any foster family; no one could manage me. No matter how many meds they put me on, no matter how much therapy I did, I always ended up back at places like that."

"But you made it. You're okay now. You turned out alright. You might have had the childhood from hell, but you're not a child anymore. Everything turned out okay."

He wondered if she really thought that he was okay. Whether he could pass as normal to her. His past always plagued him, floating in his peripheral vision, clouds of darkness that threatened to overcome him the moment he let his guard down. People could tell, even if they didn't understand what it was about him. They could always tell that he was different.

He swallowed hard. "I just couldn't help wondering, when Mira said that, how my mother felt when she told the social worker to put me away. I always wondered if she regretted it. If she ever felt the least bit sorry about breaking us up. Abandoning us like that. But what Mira said she felt..." Zachary struggled mightily to keep his cool and not allow his voice to crack, "...was relief."

Kenzie's hand squeezed his more tightly. "I'm sure she felt all of the other things that Quentin's mom felt too. Guilt. Regret. Sadness. No parent wants to institutionalize their child."

"*She* did."

"She said she did. But I'll bet she cried."

Zachary thought about this. She thought about all of the times she had screamed at Zachary or his siblings. Hit them. Punished them unfairly. She hadn't been exaggerating when she told the social worker she was at the end of her rope and couldn't do it anymore. He had done that to her. Had she regretted it? Had she cried, once she was out of sight? Once it was all over and she could let down her guard? He honestly couldn't picture it. The last thing he had seen of her was her unrelenting anger.

"I don't think she cried," he said finally.

But Mira had.

3

After parting ways with Kenzie with a friendly peck on his cheek and nothing more, Zachary headed back to Mario Bowman's apartment. All was quiet; Bowman had left the light on for Zachary in the living room and had already gone to bed.

Bed.

Zachary's mind was a storm of thoughts and questions about the case, impressions from the evening, and the intrusive flashes of memory from his own past. There was no way he would be able to go to sleep without help. In the bathroom, Zachary took out his prescription bottles one at a time and set the pills in a neat row. Two sleeping pills. One anti-anxiety. One antidepressant. His hand hovered over the non-prescription bottles as well. An over-the-counter antihistamine? Stress vitamins? Valerian?

The reason he hadn't had anything to drink at the restaurant was because he had known what was coming. He had known that he wasn't going to be able to settle down for bed. That his emotions and the memories had all been stirred up and there was no way he was going to be able to sleep without an aid. Several aids.

He left the rest of the bottles. He would go with the pills he had already selected. He knew that he could take all of them together. He had before. And the combined punch would, he hoped, let him forget Quentin's haunting face and get a few precious hours of sleep before he was again pacing the room.

He swallowed the pills dry and checked the time on his phone. He would give his body half an hour to start to absorb the pills before lying down. Then he would be able to sleep, or get some semblance of sleep. He went back to the living room and turned the TV on, volume low, and tried to lose himself in a sitcom. But he didn't even know what he was watching, much less follow the jokes. He just stared at the screen filled with silly, joking people, and tried to let it all expand to fill his brain and push out all of the other pictures and impressions that crowded in vying for his attention.

At the half hour mark, he did as he had planned and lay down on the couch, pulling the blanket up over himself and closing his eyes.

For a long time, he lay staring at the back of his eyelids, amebic red and black, searching for peace. He could feel the sleeping pills working, slowing his heart rate and breathing, dulling the thoughts but not silencing them. The knot of anxiety loosened, and he tried to push himself the last few inches toward sleep.

Then he was dreaming. He saw himself in a cell at the institution Mira had put Quentin into. The Summit Living Center. He had never been there, but he had been enough places like Summit that his brain filled in the details. A bunk attached to the wall, immovable. A stainless steel toilet affixed to the wall, equally immovable. No sink. No desk or counter. No lamp, just the bright fluorescent overhead lights. No windows. Only the narrow rectangular window set into the heavy steel door that kept him locked in the cell. Zachary went to the window. Except he wasn't Zachary. He was Quentin. Zachary wasn't sure how he knew the difference, but he knew he was not in his own skin. He was in Quentin's body, at Summit, looking out into the hallway.

At first, he closed his eyes. He didn't want to look through the narrow window. He knew what he was going to see. But the dream went inexorably on and he was looking out the window, into the hallway, watching as they brought another resident to the cell next to his. It was a girl. A young girl, blond and pretty. Or she would have been pretty if she hadn't been a kicking, screaming, spitting ball of arms and legs thrashing to get away from the guards.

Her screams went on and on. He didn't know how she could keep screaming her throat raw like that. The noise hurt his ears and he covered them up, trying to block it out, groaning himself with the pain of the noise drilling into his head. And then the noise stopped abruptly. He rose to his feet. He hadn't realized that he had been crouching low to the floor, waiting for the assault of the noise to pass over him. But then it was gone, and he was drawn back up to look out the window of the door, as if he were a puppet on a string.

The girl was on the floor. She lay face down, unmoving. One of the guards was hitting her with a balled-up fist, and the other was sitting on her. Her hands were cuffed behind her back, but they still continued to assault her as if she were fighting back. He reached for the door, wanting to hammer his fists against it and shout at them to stop. But the door was too far away. He couldn't find it with his fists. And when he tried to shout, he was voiceless. Nothing came out. He had to tell them to stop it. To leave her alone. Didn't they see that she wasn't moving anymore? Even the rise and fall of her breath had stopped. He raised his head and howled wordlessly, soundlessly, impotently.

The voiceless scream was so violent that it woke Zachary up. He clutched at the cushions of the couch underneath him, trying desperately to feel them. To ground himself there in the apartment, on the couch, instead of far away in the institution, helpless in a detention cell, powerless to help himself or anyone else.

He knew the girl's name. Knew because he had seen her before, almost thirty years previous. He had watched the police take her down. Seen them beat her into submission, manacle her wrists, kneel on her until she was silenced and no longer fought against them. She had been no older than he was. Ten or eleven. No threat to the security and police.

In real life, they had realized something was wrong. They had gotten up, rolled her over, and made sure that she had started breathing again before taking her away to the police station to be booked for assault after biting one of the guards.

Annie.

Like Quentin, she had been autistic. That had been how she was differentiated from any other Annie. Not as Annie Sellers. Not as blond Annie or little Annie. But as autistic Annie. It had been her title and her identity at the home. And everyone knew about her tantrums and behavioral problems. They knew how difficult she was for the staff to control. Maybe she didn't belong there. Maybe she should have been in some specialized treatment facility instead of a home for unwanted children. Bonnie Brown was a stopping place between foster care and juvenile detention. They didn't need a judge or a conviction to lock the children up. Zachary, Annie, and dozens of other kids whose crimes ranged from ADHD to autism to psychosis and sadism.

"Annie." Zachary said it out loud. It had been a long time since he had dreamed about her.

He'd never forgotten her, but he had been able to banish her from his dreams for a number of years.

But she was back, and he was vibrating, shaking with anger and impotence over the way she had been treated. He *had* pounded on the door all of those years ago. Pounded on the door and screamed and gotten himself a beating for misbehaving.

She had started breathing again.

That time.

When Bowman came out in the morning, Zachary was pacing up and down the living room rug.

Mario Bowman, balding and potbellied, not yet in his police uniform, leveled a look at Zachary. "You're going to wear a path in my carpet."

"Yeah, sorry… I just couldn't sleep."

"Do you ever sleep? You're up when I go to bed. You're up when I get up. That's if you're here and not out on surveillance. You've heard how important sleep is to your health, haven't you?"

Zachary sighed. "You know I would if I could."

"I know, bro. That's why I worry about you."

"I got in a few hours last night."

"A few being…?"

"I don't know. Three hours, maybe."

"Not enough."

"So, I'll sleep better tonight. That's the way it works, isn't it? You're short on sleep one night, so you are tired and get a better rest the next."

"I'd agree if I hadn't actually seen your sleep habits over the past few weeks."

Zachary entered the kitchen ahead of his friend and pressed the button on the coffee maker. They both stood watching it while it pottered and bubbled away, a thin stream of coffee eventually starting to fill the pot.

"You were out with Kenzie last night?" Bowman asked, smothering a wide yawn with the back of his hand.

"Yeah. Had dinner at Old Joe's. It was good."

"The two of you sharing anything more than photographs and medical examiner's reports?" Bowman suggested, giving him a sly, sideways look.

Zachary shrugged uncomfortably, watching the coffee pot as if it were the most important thing in the world. "We're going slow. She's… well, Bridget kind of spooked her. And we've had… a few other rocky places. I don't think she's ready for a serious relationship, and I'm not really the hit-and-run type." His face heated up. Zachary scratched the back of his neck, turning away from

Bowman slightly to hide his flush. "So right now… it's mostly business. Friendly, but professional."

"I think she'd go for you, if you were willing to work at it a bit."

The coffee maker was finally dripping its last and Zachary moved in with his mug. He filled both his and Bowman's, while a few stray drips hit the hot plate and sizzled. Bowman was the guy who knew everyone's likes and dislikes and how to get things done by sending a little sugar—or caffeine, or alcohol—the right direction. If he thought Kenzie might be swayed in Zachary's direction, there was every possibility he was right.

"I'm willing to work," Zachary said cautiously. "If it's actually going to go somewhere."

"Did you at least get through dinner without being interrupted by Bridget?"

Zachary nodded. He took a sip of his coffee, still too hot for him to drink. "Yes. Thankfully."

Bowman grinned. "A date always goes better if the ex doesn't show up raging. Even if it is just a business date."

Zachary blew on the surface of the coffee. "You have no idea."

4

———

The morning was clear and refreshing and Zachary had enjoyed the highway driving. He was sorry to arrive at his destination and have to get down to work. Sitting in the parking lot, he studied the building before entering. It looked like a hundred other facilities. Like a school or a small hospital or Bonnie Brown or one of the other places that he had gone for school or therapy or to live for a few months. A squat red brick building, sprawling as different wings and phases had been added on. Dr. Abato's assistant had given him driving directions and instructions as to how to find the visitor parking and the right door to enter so that he wouldn't be wandering around clueless for an hour. It was a good thing, because he suspected he could quickly be lost in the twists and turns of the building. That would not help his investigation.

There was a tap on his window, and Zachary turned to see a security guard standing there looking in at him. His heart immediately started pounding like he'd been caught doing something he wasn't supposed to. He'd had experience with security guards at places like Summit. They hadn't been pleasant. Zachary rolled down his window.

"Sorry, am I in the wrong place?" he asked. "Dr. Abato's secretary gave me directions, but if I ended up in the wrong parking lot…?"

"No." The guard shook his head like Zachary was an idiot. "But you've been sitting here in your car for a long time. Thought something might be wrong. Do you need assistance?"

"No. Sorry. Just thinking and getting myself prepared." He pulled out his key, opened his door, then realized he needed to roll his window back up. He reinserted the key into the ignition, feeling a warm flush on his cheeks. He rolled the window up.

The guard stood over him as if he might be trying to get away with something.

"Sorry." Zachary wasn't sure what he was apologizing for. He wasn't doing anything wrong by sitting in his car.

"We get some real kooks around here," the guard said, one hand still resting comfortably on the butt of his taser. "People who don't think there should be facilities like this, that people with disabilities should all just be at home somewhere." He *tsked* and shook his head. "Not like these kids have anywhere else to go."

Zachary tried to swallow the lump swelling in his throat. "No," he agreed.

The guard hitched up his heavy utility belt and watched Zachary lock the car. He walked beside Zachary toward the double doors Dr. Abato's secretary had directed him to.

"You a reporter?" the guard asked.

"No." Zachary mentally assessed himself. What would make the guard assume that he was a reporter? "No, I'm just here for a tour."

The man grunted. "Most of the strangers I see back here are reporters. You're obviously not a parent." He chuckled.

Again, Zachary considered himself as if he were standing in front of a mirror. What about him said, 'not a parent?' He was certainly old enough. At forty, he could have a child of any age up to twenty. He was still wearing his wedding ring; the guard had no way of knowing that he was divorced. What was there about him that said he wasn't a father?

"No," he admitted, "no kids."

The guard stopped at the doors and nodded to Zachary. "Well, enjoy your tour, then."

Zachary went in. He couldn't restrain a backward glance once he was through the doors, and saw that the guard was still standing there watching him. Making sure he got where he was supposed to be going. Zachary walked up to the reception desk and introduced himself to the sour-faced, middle-aged woman in a nurse's smock that was sitting at the computer.

"He's expecting you," the woman acknowledged. She picked up her phone and pressed a button. After a short pause, she announced Zachary's name, then hung up. "He'll be right out."

Dr. Abato was a younger man than Zachary had expected. He had dark, well-groomed hair and wore a dress shirt and tie under his white lab coat. As Zachary got close enough to shake the doctor's hand, he saw that the man's lean face was faintly lined; older than he looked at first glance.

"Mr. Goldman, a pleasure to meet you," he said pleasantly. "I'm always happy to accommodate anyone who wants to learn more about the facility. We're quite proud of the work we do here."

Zachary nodded and pulled back from the handshake. Dr. Abato was just a little too jovial and held on a little too long. It felt false. Like a camouflage. He wasn't sure if Dr. Abato remembered the reason that Zachary was there to tour the facility. That he wasn't a reporter or the parent of a prospective resident, but a private investigator looking into a death that had occurred there. Could Abato have forgotten something like that?

"This way," Abato invited, touching Zachary's arm for a moment to direct him out of the lobby into one of the adjoining hallways. Zachary noted the security locks on the door they passed through. Abato wasn't punching a number into the PIN pad or swiping a security pass, but Zachary had a feeling that if he had turned around to test any of the doors that they walked through, they would all be securely locked.

The walls were painted in bright colors and were liberally sprinkled with framed posters of cartoon and movie characters. The initial corridors that they walked through were well-maintained. No dented, scuffed, chipped walls. But Zachary supposed they were still in the administrative area, which would be easier to maintain with no access by residents. Abato was looking sideways at Zachary, watching him for his reaction.

"It's very bright and cheerful," Zachary obliged.

"We take great pride in making this a happy place, a place children can enjoy being."

Zachary nodded. Some of the hospitals he had been in had made an effort to decorate with cheerful themes, but it didn't fool anyone into thinking the patients would choose to be there instead of home. It had never made Zachary feel any better about being in some psych unit instead of being well enough to function on the outside.

Rather than making him smile, the glossy, colorful posters at Summit made him feel anxious and trapped. He focused on breathing deep and slow. Pushing his breath out completely before taking in another lungful of air to ensure he didn't start hyperventilating. The oxygen would make him feel less anxious. Breathing slowly would keep his heart rate down. It would keep his autonomic nervous system calm, so he didn't dissolve into a panic attack.

In theory.

Dr. Abato was talking about the facility, motioning in random directions as he talked about their various features and programs. Zachary tried to focus on what he was saying to process the words, but he couldn't. The words were English, but Zachary couldn't string together the thoughts. He just kept smiling and nodding so Abato wouldn't notice his reaction.

"Residents come to us from all over the country," Abato said. "Summit's programs are unique, it's one of the only facilities of its kind."

Zachary nodded again. Abato opened a door and motioned

for Zachary to go through ahead of him. Zachary walked through the door, transported from the silent, peaceful hallway into a chaotic, noisy carnival of flashing lights and arcade games. He froze, senses overwhelmed by the change in the environment.

Abato's hand was on the small of Zachary's back, walking him the rest of the way through the door so that he could shut the security door behind them. He laughed at Zachary's reaction.

"It's quite something, isn't it?" he said proudly.

Zachary looked around. There were children of various ages playing electronic games. There was a ball pit, a climbing wall, and what looked like hamster-tubes to crawl through. The theme of bright colors and cartoon posters continued.

"What is it?" Zachary asked.

"This is a reward room. When a student is able to reach the goals that his team has set to moderate his behavior, he is allowed a 'big reward.' They get smaller rewards for every good behavior, of course, that's how we are able to teach them. But we have found that they are far more motivated, especially the higher-functioning kids, when they have that big 'Disneyland' reward to work toward."

Abato motioned Zachary forward. Zachary tried to focus on the details and shut out the assault of the noise and lights and bright colors. It was not as busy as he had thought at first. Not theme-park-busy. The residents were quiet and well-behaved, mostly playing separately rather than in clusters. Abato's 'kids' ranged in age from around nine years old to teenagers and young adults, with a couple who were obviously in their forties or fifties. Each resident had a staffer standing nearby or helping them with what they were doing. Most of them had on school backpacks. Zachary noticed that the aides had small boxes hanging from their belts with pictures of the residents they were responsible for. Maybe for meds, schedules, or emergency protocols.

"This is our store." Abato pointed out a glass-fronted retail store where Zachary saw girls' frilly dresses, handbags, snacks, magazines, and other sundries that a commissary or gift shop might have. "Those who want to can earn tokens that can be redeemed for items in the store. So they can save up for things that they want, learn how to budget, and other important life skills."

Zachary nodded. "That's cool."

He had been places that used token economies to allow kids to make purchases, and had always found it humiliating and dehumanizing. You made your bed? You got a token. Eat with your fingers at dinner? You don't earn your meal token. Participate in class? Token. Ask too many questions and irritate the teacher? No token. And after weeks or months of bowing and scraping and being forced to do every little demeaning task the staff asked him to, he would be able to buy a chocolate bar, or writing paper, or a key chain with a cartoon character on it.

There were a couple of girls looking at purses in the rewards store, shaking their heads at each other, whispering, and looking frequently over their shoulders at the supervisors.

A boy was walking toward Zachary and Dr. Abato. He had pink cheeks and a sunny expression. He was probably eleven or twelve, but had the open, guileless expression of a much younger child. He was walking directly toward Zachary, eyes on him.

"Walk on by," the male aide with him instructed. "Don't bother the doctor. He has a guest."

But the boy gave no indication that he heard. He continued to move directly toward Zachary and the doctor. The aide reached out and nudged the boy's shoulder, steering him off to the side. The boy opened up his arms as if to envelop them both in a hug. The aide grasped one arm and jerked him away, pulling him forcefully away from them. Zachary slowed, opening his mouth and turning to look. But Abato pressed him forward.

"Don't stop and give him attention. That would be rewarding bad behavior. He needs to learn how to behave appropriately and to listen to his aide when he is told something. Just keep going and don't even show that you saw him."

There was a yelp from behind them, and despite Dr. Abato's

stricture, Zachary looked back at the boy, who was starting to cry, his arms bent and hands close to his face, shaking.

"He's fine," Abato said. "Just part of the learning process."

He directed Zachary around a corner. "The games can be over-stimulating for some of the kids. Some of them are uncomfortable with the noises and flashing lights, or just with being around so many other students. So there are quieter reward rooms as well."

Zachary peeked into the rooms that they walked by. A pool table in a room with dim lighting. A shelf of books and a couple of beanbag chairs. Computers in study carrels so that the user was not distracted by the others sitting close to them.

"We have an incredible success rate," Abato bragged. "We have succeeded in improving the behavior of some of the country's most intractable students. They can learn! Even those who refuse to talk. Who refuse to toilet or take care of themselves. We can teach them at Summit. And you can see how they love it here."

All around, Zachary saw quiet, cooperative children who, despite being taken away from their families and institutionalized, appeared to be happy and thriving. There was little physical inter-vention, with staff members hovering nearby or giving verbal instructions and rarely having to physically redirect the residents. Maybe it wasn't the kind of place where Zachary had lived, where he'd had to be vigilant all the time to avoid being victimized. Maybe a child like Annie could live happily at Summit.

Dr. Abato gave an expansive smile. "You're looking at the best place in the world to send your special needs child. The very best of the best."

Zachary gave a brief nod, not sure what to say to this. They walked into a bright, sunlit room. An arboretum of some kind. Big skylights, tall trees, bushes, flowers, the sound of trickling water. There were a few children there, standing quietly or walking around looking at the ground. One of them, a boy of about seven-teen, looked up through the branches of the trees at the blue sky, moving his fingers rapidly back and forth in front of his eyes. The staffer standing close to him said something to him. The boy made no response. He just continued to shake his fingers in front of his eyes, letting out a delighted laugh. Dr. Abato looked at Zachary and checked his watch. "I'm sure you'd like to linger here, but I have other appointments, so we need to move on. There are other things I would like you to see before our time here is up."

Zachary nodded, turning away. He heard the aide prompt the boy again. He turned his head to look back. Suddenly the boy let out a shrill yell. He clenched his hands, his face an ugly grimace, his back arched. He shrieked something incomprehensible. The other children in the arboretum were looking his way, their faces white and anxious, eyes wide. One of them started hitting his forehead with his fist. The teenage boy's aide moved in and took him by the arm, speaking in a low, firm voice, and escorted him toward a door the opposite direction from where Zachary and Dr. Abato were going.

Zachary was shaken. The boy had seemed to be perfectly happy and then had suddenly started yelling. Was he angry or upset about something? Was the mood shift simply part of autism? Zachary knew that Annie had been prone to tantrums and meltdowns. Mira had said that Quentin had been violent. So he assumed it was just part of the behavior that one expected with autism.

"Nothing to be concerned about," Dr. Abato said, reading Zachary's face. "If the students cannot control their behavior in the reward rooms, they will be taken back to their units. You can't expect perfection. They are still learning."

Zachary nodded. "I just wondered... if there was something specific that triggered his outburst. If he was upset or... something happened...?"

"Sometimes we can identify the antecedent, and sometimes we can't. The more we can identify about what triggers outbursts or bad behaviors, the better we can do at eliminating inappropriate behaviors."

"Sure. That makes sense."

The talk of eliminating inappropriate behaviors made him

uncomfortable. He couldn't count the times in the past that someone else had been passing judgment on his behaviors without understanding why he acted the way he did. Sometimes Zachary himself hadn't been sure why he acted the way he did. But sometimes… he just felt like the adults in his life were being unfair. They stood at the periphery, uninvolved in his life except to decide when he was behaving and when he was not behaving, punishing him according to their arbitrary decisions.

"Does he talk?" Zachary asked, motioning to the boy who had been taken away.

"Justin? No. He's completely nonverbal, despite our best efforts to find his voice." He made a gesture toward where the boy had been standing. "Other than yelling, that is. We've tried to help him to find his words, but he's very resistant. Very stubborn."

"So you can't ask him what it is that sets him off."

Abato looked at Zachary for a moment. "No, he can't tell us what it is that bothers him. But even if we could ask him to explain it to us… I doubt it would be of any help. These children tend not to be very self-aware. Even the higher-functioning and non-autistic kids that we get… asking them to explain what's going on in their minds doesn't make much difference to the therapy. They lie, they don't know, they are manipulative. Sometimes it is actually the lower-functioning kids who are easier to treat. They can't argue with you." Dr. Abato gave a little laugh and shake of his head at the irony.

Zachary just looked at him.

"We want our students to be happy," Dr. Abato said. "But it's up to us to figure out what is going to make the child happy. Not the child himself."

5

They headed down a long corridor and took a turn. "We are leaving the reward rooms, and entering the treatment wing," Abato explained. "You've seen what it is that the children are working toward, what their goal is as they work with our therapists. Now we get down to the nitty-gritty, and you see what exactly it is that we do here."

"Great."

The new corridor they entered was lined with rooms with viewing windows. So they could look into the various therapy rooms to observe what was going on without being seen by the child being treated. Zachary bit his lip. His stomach turned. He felt like a voyeur. The thought of someone else watching and listening to him during any kind of therapy session was repellent. He'd been through many different treatments and therapies as a child and as an adult, and he had always been told that what went on between him and his doctor or therapist was private. No one else would ever see or hear what he said or did. But at Summit, the residents were on display. Not just to other doctors or therapists, but to anyone who happened to be touring the facility during their session.

Zachary thought at first that they would just walk quickly

past, catching a glimpse of the kind of work they did. But Dr. Abato looked down at the clipboard he was carrying with him and picked a room out. They didn't stand at the hallway observation window, but went into an anteroom to the therapy room, where there was another window and they could sit down, turn on the speaker to hear what was going on, and watch the session as if it were the latest in reality TV.

Abato motioned to a chair and sat down himself. There was nothing Zachary could do but sit beside him, looking for a way to voice his discomfort.

"This is Raymond Maslen," Abato introduced. "Age five. He has been coming here for about a year. He is not a full-time resident, but comes here for our day program. He is in therapy for forty hours a week and goes home to his mother and his family in the evening."

"What kind of therapy?"

"What we do here is almost entirely ABA. That's Applied Behavioral Analysis. It's a system of reinforcing positive behavior and ignoring or imposing a consequence for negative behavior."

Abato threw the switch to turn on the speaker so they could hear what was going on in the therapy room. Raymond had wavy hair, reddish brown, a bit on the long side, and the face of an angel. The woman who was working with him had masses of blond hair. She wore a purple smock and was just a bit on the heavy side. Raymond was laughing as she played a game with him, blowing his face with a red toy she held in her hand. Every time she blew his face and hair with it, he squealed with delight. She put the toy down on the table and looked at Raymond with a very hard, intense stare.

"You're doing really good, Ray-Ray," she said in an encouraging voice. "You're having a good therapy day today, aren't you?"

He looked at her as if he weren't sure what she was talking about, then gave a nod of his head, sort of a diagonal lowering of his head that could be taken as a nod, but might equally have been a shake.

"You're having a good day today," the blond woman repeated. "You are, right? You nod your head." She nodded her own head emphatically.

The little boy gave a more certain nod, but it was still somewhat sideways, as if he really weren't sure and wanted some way out of it if challenged.

"Nod for Sophie," the woman instructed. She straightened Raymond's head so that it was perpendicular, and pressed his chin, encouraging him to nod. When that didn't work, she put one hand under his chin and the other on the top of his head and put him through the motion of nodding straight up and down. "Good, Ray-Ray! That's right!" she praised. She patted him on the cheek and tickled him under the chin. "Good boy, Ray-Ray."

He clapped his hands excitedly. Sophie caught his hands and pressed them down to the table gently, stilling them. Raymond tried to clap again, and she pressed them more insistently to the table, held together. "No. Quiet hands," she insisted. "No clapping. You can clap if we play a clapping song. Otherwise, keep them still."

She held them for a moment longer, then lifted her hands off of his. He kept them still.

"Good boy, Ray. Good quiet hands." She kept her voice soft. Raising her voice would, Zachary figured, just get him excited and clapping again, which, for some reason, was forbidden.

"Now, listen to what Sophie says, okay? I want you to follow me and do what I say. Can you... touch your nose?"

Raymond raised one hand off of the table and looked at it, then looked at her, evaluating whether this was something he was allowed to do.

"Touch your nose," Sophie repeated. She did not model the behavior, but waited for him to follow her verbal instruction.

Ray-Ray curled his other fingers in, leaving his index finger in a pointing position. He looked at her to see if he was doing okay so far. She didn't give any indication whether he was doing well or not. The little boy raised his finger and very slowly moved it toward his face, eventually touching the very tip of his nose.

"Good job!" Sophie praised. "That's right! You can have one lick of your candy." She picked up a lollipop from a bowl next to her and held it out to him, allowing him to touch his tongue to it. Then she pulled it away and put it back down.

"Now touch your ear. Touch your ear, Ray-Ray."

He moved more confidently this time, raising his index finger to touch the tip of his nose.

"No!" Sophie said so sharply that not only did little Raymond jump, but Zachary did too. She pulled his finger away from his nose and leaned closer to him, clearly into his personal space. "No, Raymond! I didn't say nose, I said ear!"

His smiley face was gone, crumpling up like he was going to start bawling.

"No," Sophie warned. "No crying. I want you to touch your ear. Do it now."

His face froze. He looked at her for a moment, hovering on the edge of tears.

"Touch your ear," Sophie repeated.

He again made a pointer finger with great concentration. But he didn't touch his ear or his nose.

"Your ear," Sophie said. She reached out and pinched Raymond's earlobe. "Touch your ear."

Ray-Ray still hovered, hesitant.

"Touch your ear." Sophie grasped Raymond's little clenched fist and raised it up beside his face, touching his fingertip to his earlobe. "Good!" she praised immediately. "Touching your ear. Good listening, Ray-Ray. Have a lick." She picked up the sucker from beside her and held it out to Raymond, allowing him one lick.

The stricken expression had disappeared from his face, and he was cheering up. Sophie put the sucker back down in the bowl.

"Now, touch your ear."

The little boy ran his fingers through his hair, tousling it and winding a lock around his finger. Sophie waited.

Ray-Ray raised his finger and touched his earlobe a second time.

"Good boy, Ray-Ray!" Sophie praised. "Good job." She tickled his neck and offered him a lick of the lollipop. "One more time, and you can play with the toy. Okay?"

He started to clap, and Sophie pressed his hands back down to the table again.

"Ready? Touch your nose, Ray-Ray."

He made a pointer finger and touched his ear.

"No!" Sophie slapped her hand down on the table.

Ray-Ray burst into tears.

Zachary realized he was gripping the sides of his chair, his knuckles white. He looked over at Abato.

"It's okay," Dr. Abato assured him. "He's fine. He'll calm down in a minute."

"Isn't she being pretty harsh with him? He's just a little guy and he hasn't done anything wrong."

"We need to be very clear when he is giving the right response and when he is not. There can't be any confusion. He needs immediate, clear feedback."

When Zachary didn't respond, he explained further.

"It's like training a dog," he said logically. "When the dog sits, you give him a treat, right? And when he jumps up, you tell him 'no' and push him down. He learns to do the things that earn him a treat, and to avoid the things that cause an unpleasant response."

Zachary was uncomfortable with Ray-Ray being compared to a dog. It might sound like a logical course of action, but he was a child, not an animal.

"But teaching a child, especially one as disabled as the kids we treat here, isn't as simple as training a dog," Abato said. "He doesn't just need to sit and stay. He needs to learn complex language, behavior, social skills, life skills. If that little boy is ever going to be independent and contribute to society instead of being a drag on it, he has a lot to learn."

Zachary looked at the little boy, already starting to settle down and wipe his tears away. "He doesn't seem that… different," he said. "He seems like any other… neurotypical kid."

"Does he?" Abato considered Raymond through the glass. "That just shows you how well we are doing with him. How far he has come since he started with us. When Raymond was first evaluated by our staff, he couldn't sit in a chair. He flapped and clapped his hands all the time. He couldn't follow a single instruction. He chattered constantly about his favorite show. Top Gear."

Zachary couldn't help but smile at that. Maybe Ray-Ray would grow up to become a mechanic. It was a useful skill. If he'd already started learning about car engines at age five, he'd be an expert by the time he was an adult. Fixing his mother's car. Maybe all of the cars on the block.

"You may think that's cute behavior," Dr. Abato said. "But it is dysfunctional. And when he's seventeen and aggressive and won't be dissuaded from his pet topic, it stops being cute. He won't be able to make friends, get a job, or have any productive interaction with his community. If we don't break him of it. How functional is it for him to be able to tell you how to put an engine together if he can't tell the difference between his nose and his ear?"

"Well… okay," Zachary admitted. "He needs to learn those things. Or whatever he can."

"Kids like Raymond have to be explicitly taught how to function in society. They don't pick it up by just watching other people. We have the ability to make him indistinguishable from his peers, if we have enough time with him. That's the goal here. Not just learning to touch his ear or his nose. But to break down every skill he needs to know as a functioning human being, and teach them to him, one step at a time. We'll repeat the same exercise a hundred times. A thousand times. Ten thousand times. Whatever it takes for him to learn it."

"Wow. Okay."

They turned their attention back to Sophie and Ray-Ray. Ray-Ray was no longer crying, but still looked miserable. His hair was more untidy than ever. He motioned to the toy on the table. "Play time?"

"No, Ray-Ray. It's not play time. No toys if you can't do what you're told."

He looked around the room. His gaze lingered on a cupboard mounted on the wall. It was out of the boy's reach, and a padlock hung through the eyelet of the latch, keeping it shut. The padlock wasn't locked, but perhaps if Raymond had been older and taller, it would have been, to keep him away from whatever was in there. Zachary's heart went out to the little guy. He remembered having nothing as a foster child. Having only his clothes and toothbrush in a plastic shopping bag and having that taken away from him by a foster parent. Having them act as if it were their own property, to do with as they pleased. As if Zachary himself were another piece of their property, to acquire, use, and dispose of as they pleased. Sophie and Dr. Abato thought they had every right to treat Raymond as they pleased. To take away his possessions and lock them up. To train him to do what they wanted him to. Because he was just a child. A broken child who needed to be fixed.

"Go home?" Ray-Ray asked.

"No. It's school time. You need to work hard. If you do what I tell you to, you can play with a toy. And you'll go home when we're all done."

He flapped his hands beside his face. Sophie pressed them to the table. "Quiet hands."

Ray-Ray held his hands together on the table, his expression pained. Sophie went on with the session.

"I want you to come give me a hug, Ray-Ray."

Zachary was taken aback. He looked over at Dr. Abato to see if he would put a stop to this, but he didn't. Sophie waited.

"Stand up," she instructed eventually.

Ray-Ray sat there, looking at the toy on the table and at his hands held quietly on the table in front of him. When he didn't respond, Sophie stood up herself. She reached around the little table and pulled Ray-Ray to his feet.

"Give me a hug," she told him again.

The boy stood there like a statue for a moment, then started to shuffle toward her, inching his feet forward, until he was close enough to press his body against hers. He didn't reach up and put his arms around her.

"Give a hug," Sophie prompted again. She reached down to grab Ray-Ray's arms and wrapped them around her body. She held them there for a moment, then let them go, praising him. "Good hug, Ray-Ray. Hugging is nice, isn't it? Hugging makes people feel good." She grabbed the lollipop to give him a lick.

Zachary ventured another look at Abato, still waiting for him to step in and intervene. Abato gave him a supercilious smile. "Hugs are a necessary a part of our social construct as shaking hands," he informed Zachary. "We hug our friends and family as a greeting, to comfort each other, to initiate a romantic relationship… we can't get along in life without human touch, no matter what sensory defensiveness we might have. Don't you think Raymond's mother wants to be able to hug him when she says hello or puts him to bed at night? Wants him to be able to hug his grandmother when she comes to visit? Wants him to grow up and meet a nice girl and have a relationship? Of course she does. All parents want those things for their children. And that's our job here. To teach kids all of those little things, so that they can be comfortable and make friends and function normally."

Zachary looked back at the therapist and her charge. Sophie continued to put Raymond through the paces, requesting hugs, making him hold her tighter or longer, until he was responding on command each time.

Let's see how he is able to generalize this skill," Dr. Abato suggested.

Zachary frowned, not sure what the doctor meant. Dr. Abato stood up and Zachary followed his lead. The doctor smoothed back his hair and went to the door of the therapy room. He checked to make sure that Zachary was following him and let himself in.

Sophie looked up to see who was interrupting her session and gave Dr. Abato a plastic smile. "Doctor."

"Raymond." Dr. Abato waited for the boy to look at him. "Come give me a hug." He opened his arms in invitation.

Ray-Ray looked at Dr. Abato, then back at Sophie, waiting for her instruction. She remained silent, not giving him any indication one way or the other what he should do. A few seconds of silence ticked by. Then the boy moved slowly to approach Abato and give him a hug. He barely touched Dr. Abato, then withdrew again quickly. Abato reached around him and gave him a squeeze, holding on to him firmly. Ray-Ray squirmed to get loose.

"Good job," Sophie praised when Dr. Abato released him. "Doesn't it feel good to get a hug?" She tousled Raymond's already-messy hair and offered him another lick of the lollipop.

"Now give Mr. Goldman a hug," Dr. Abato instructed, waving a hand in Zachary's direction.

"Oh, that's okay," Zachary protested. "He doesn't know me. I'm just here to observe…"

"He needs to generalize instructions," Abato said firmly. "And he needs to learn that a hug is normal, non-threatening contact so that he doesn't overreact defensively to them in the future. We know what we're doing here, Mr. Goldman." He looked at Raymond again. "Give Mr. Goldman a hug."

Ray-Ray turned toward Zachary. To his surprise, the boy didn't shuffle and approach him reluctantly as he had done with Sophie and Dr. Abato. He threw himself at Zachary, wrapped his arms around him, and clung to him tightly. Zachary looked down at him, not sure how to react, then put his arms gently around the little boy and rubbed his back gently. "There," he said gently. "There, that's okay."

Dr. Abato chuckled. "Okay, let him go now, Raymond."

Raymond continued to hold on to Zachary, his grip not loosening. Zachary wasn't sure what to do about it, continuing to rub Ray-Ray's back soothingly. But Sophie wasn't waiting for anyone else to act. She strode across the small room and grabbed hold of Raymond, peeling his hands away from Zachary.

"You need to listen," she chided.

The boy struggled, striking out blindly with fists and feet, letting out a howl of protest. Sophie took him back to his chair and dropped him back into it.

"Proper sitting," she told him, holding him in place. "You know what to do. Show me proper sitting."

He gradually stopped struggling and sat still. Sophie went back around the table to her seat and looked across the table at him.

"Look at me, Ray-Ray."

He sat there with his face blank and his eyes distant, not acknowledging that there was even anyone else in the room.

"Raymond. Look at me. Eye contact."

He didn't budge.

"This kind of defiant behavior is not acceptable," Sophie snapped. She reached across the table, holding Raymond's head between her hands, and centered his face directly in front of her own. She leaned forward, just inches away from his face, eye-to-eye.

Raymond started to howl as if she were hurting him. He clawed at her hands and spat at her, trying to pull away.

"No," Sophie said firmly. "Stop. I'm not letting you go until you listen. You make your body quiet and show me good eye contact, then I'll let you go. I can't talk to you until you show me eye contact."

He continued to struggle for what seemed like an eternity. Zachary stood there, his whole body rigid, wanting to rescue the little boy. But Sophie and Dr. Abato were silently insistent. With no other options, Raymond finally stopped trying to get Sophie to let him go and looked into her eyes with his tear-filled brown eyes. He whimpered and sniffled, but didn't struggle. Sophie let him go. Ray-Ray's body immediately slumped.

"No," Sophie warned. "Proper sitting."

He was coaxed into an attentive sitting posture, shoulders back, feet flat on the floor.

"Hands on the table," Sophie instructed. "Show me quiet hands."

With a great effort, as if he were holding bowling balls in them, Raymond arranged his hands on the table, both of them cupped slightly, one hand resting in the other. Sophie nodded.

"Good hands," she approved, and stroked his messy hair. "That's a good boy."

Zachary was exhausted as Dr. Abato led him out of the therapy room. All he had been doing was observing, yet he'd been so tense and rigid, his heart pounding so hard, he felt like he'd just had a huge fight.

Dr. Abato smiled at him cheerfully, as if he'd been energized rather than drained.

"He's come such a long way," he told Zachary. "If you'd seen Raymond when he first came to us, you would not believe he was the same child." He looked at his watch, frowning. "It did take a long time, though. I have time to take you to Quentin's room, and that will have to be it. I have other things I need to do today, I just can't spend the whole day talking to you."

"Okay. Lead the way." Zachary was relieved that there was only one more thing to do; then he could go home and veg for a while and get his energy and his perspective back again. Even with all of the brightly-painted, well-lit rooms, the institution felt oppressive. It reminded him too much of all of his hospital and institutional stays. He couldn't help feeling like if he stayed there too long, they would lock him up again. They would see through his thin veneer of civilization and realize that he too needed to be properly trained before he could function on his own in the real world.

The doctor continued to patter away as he led Zachary down the halls, out of the therapy wing and into living quarters. Zachary barely heard a word he said. It was probably in all of the online information on the institution's website anyway. Zachary could review it later, when he was at home and could concentrate on the words without being distracted by his own demons.

Abato stopped at a door and opened it for Zachary. "This was Quentin's room."

Zachary looked around. He wasn't sure what he had expected. A pool of blood? Quentin's sheets still on the floor? An untouched crime scene?

It was just a small, square room. A bunk attached to the wall. A small, drab, institutional dresser with four drawers. A little closet with no doors and no hangers on the rod. Painted semigloss institutional white, scuff marks and chips here and there. They would repaint it and put another boy there.

Zachary rubbed the back of his neck. "Were you here when they found him?"

"It was early morning, I wasn't on yet. We do have medical personnel on staff. Of course, we have to, dealing with residents who are violent or self-injure. Nonverbal residents can't always communicate that they're sick or hurt and can be seriously ill before we find out something is wrong. Even if we're just dealing with day-to-day colds and flus, we need someone on staff. Epidemics can run rampant in places where so many people are in such close contact."

"So someone on site was called? Who was it that found him?"

"One of the unit supervisors, when he didn't come out for breakfast."

Zachary could visualize it. The reveille or breakfast bell rang, and everyone lined up for their food. Someone noticed Quentin's absence. A supervisor went to find him, discovering he had died in the night.

"The photographs show that he was on the floor instead of on the bed," Zachary said, sketching out the location of the body in the cell with his hands and evaluating the view angle from the observation window set in the door.

"Yes. That's right."

"Is anyone checking on the residents at night? Are the doors locked or unlocked?"

Dr. Abato pursed his lips. "Most of the doors are unlocked. If a resident is prone to wandering or is a danger to others, they are locked. But most of them, no, not locked."

"And was Quentin's?"

"Quentin could be violent. If he'd had any episodes during the day, his door would probably be locked. But I'd have to get someone to check the records. See if it was logged."

"There's not a rule that it has to be recorded? It might not have been?"

"No, there's not a specific rule about recording locks. But everything out of the ordinary is supposed to be logged. We keep detailed records on therapies, behaviors, how many times a child has to be prompted… all of that. If his door was locked, I expect someone would have made a note of it."

"Wouldn't the supervisor who opened his door be able to tell you? Whether she had to unlock it or not?"

"No." Abato smiled. "We all have proximity keys." He showed Zachary a plain bracelet around his wrist. "When you reach out to open a door, it unlocks. She wouldn't notice whether it was locked or unlocked, because she would be able to open it either way."

"Oh." Zachary nodded. "That's cool." He thought about it. "They're all individually programmed? So different staff would have access to different areas."

"Yes, of course."

"So who would have had access to Quentin's room?" Zachary made a gesture to indicate his surroundings.

"Anyone with an administrative or high-security rating. The unit supervisors and security staff. His therapists."

"Why would his therapists have access to his room?"

Abato raised his brows. "So they could come and get him when it was time for a session."

"A supervisor or guard wouldn't just open it for them?"

"Why, when we've got this system that allows personalized access? No need to bother anyone else, they just collect the kids they need."

Zachary felt a sudden wave of cold. He rubbed his arms. "Are all of the unlocks logged? So you know who has been in and out?"

"I don't know. I suppose they're probably recorded in the system somewhere."

"What if a child disappeared? You would need to know who had gotten them out."

"We don't have children disappearing," Abato said slowly, his brows drawing down. "We've never had an issue like that."

"All it takes is one."

"Well… I'll certainly take a look into that. I'm sure the unlocks must be logged somewhere."

"Can you find out who accessed Quentin's room in the twenty-four hours before he died? Didn't the police ask you for that?"

"No. They just asked about how he was discovered. When anyone last saw him alive. How he had been."

"What did you tell them?"

Abato shrugged. He looked around the little room. "Let's walk and talk. I need to get you back to your parking lot and get to my meeting."

Zachary was reluctant to leave the room so soon, but it was obvious there was nothing hidden there. The police forensics unit wouldn't have missed anything. If they'd even been there. The room was completely bare.

He followed Abato out to the hall. "Can I take a quick turn around the unit? Just to get a feel for it…?"

Abato took an impatient look at his watch and nodded. They walked briskly around the unit loop. Bedrooms like Quentin's and a few small gathering rooms along the outside. An administrative desk or nursing station, storage and utility rooms, and restrooms on the inside. Typical for any hospital or institution. Abato nodded to the staff members as he escorted Zachary through the unit but didn't stop to make introductions. He had already made it clear that he was out of time. It felt like he had been there for at least half the day.

Abato jerked his head to the left as they exited the unit and led Zachary down a blue corridor.

"We'll take a shortcut here."

"You never said what your answers were to the police's questions."

"What?" Abato looked at Zachary vaguely, seemingly distracted by something else. "Oh. No one had noticed anything unusual about Quentin's behavior, no. Of course, we asked every-one. And even with hindsight, we couldn't identify any behavior that might have been concerning. Nothing to indicate that he was depressed. But then… he didn't have a lot of words. He wouldn't have been able to tell us much, even if he had been inclined to."

"He didn't try to communicate with the staff?"

"No. Do you know the derivation of the word 'autism,' Mr. Goldman?"

"Uh…" Zachary shook his head. "No. I thought it was just a diagnosis…"

"It was a word used by both Kanner and Asperger to describe one of the key facets of the disorder they were observing in the children they were treating. Auto, from the Greek word for 'self.' Children who were withdrawn into themselves, who kept separate from other people, who lived in their own realities. It was a word that had been used to describe people with schizophrenia, but they noticed a qualitative difference from schizophrenia. These were not children who lived in a fantasy world, but they lived in the world of themselves, didn't naturally reach out to others. So, no. Quentin did not try to communicate whatever emotional issues he was having with the staff. Like most autistic children, Quentin did not seek out contact with other people. He just wanted to be by himself. That was his normal."

"Okay. What about their other questions? When he was last seen alive? There were no bed checks?"

"He was last seen alive when he went into his room to go to sleep. No one… no one noticed anything unusual or of concern during bed checks." Abato frowned to himself, walking faster so that Zachary almost had to run to keep up. Anything other than a normal-paced walk still felt awkward to Zachary since his car accident, and he was worried about tripping and falling flat on his face. Abato looked around, noticed Zachary lagging, and slowed a little to continue the conversation. "They didn't go into his room to check on him. Just looked through the window."

"But he was on the floor, not on his bed."

"Kids like Quentin can be unpredictable. It's not unusual to find one curled up asleep under his bunk or hiding under a table."

"So they *did* see him on the floor?"

"Yes, of course. It is my understanding that the guard who was doing the bed checks that evening has been let go. We are not asserting any negligence, but for Summit's optics, it was best for him to find other employment." Abato took a deep breath. "Quentin died by his own hand, Mr. Goldman. It's tragic and we all feel horrible that we weren't able to prevent it. But in the end… maybe it's for the better."

Abato stopped walking and turned to Zachary, speaking in a low, confidential tone.

"Quentin was never going to be able to leave here. He was never going to be able to be independent and live a life outside of an institution. Maybe if his mother had gotten him into our program when he was young, like Raymond, instead of waiting until he was twelve, violent, and intractable, we could have done more for him. But once a child passes ten or twelve… we can't always turn them around. All we're doing is trying to make things tolerable for their families. They want their kids off of meds, being taken care of by someone else, somewhere they can go and visit once a week or once a month and pretend they're living a happy, meaningful life."

"So you knew Quentin wasn't happy."

"We do our best to make our residents happy. And he was probably happier here than he was anywhere else. But it was obvious that we were not going to succeed with him. He was never going to be able to pass as normal. He was going to be here for the rest of his life. We just didn't realize how short that would be."

They started to walk again, at a slower, more thoughtful pace.

"I saw some residents who were older in the reward rooms," Zachary said. "But I haven't seen a lot of them around. You have mostly teenagers and young adults?"

"The older adults tend to be in self-contained units. They unfortunately tend to have shorter lifespans than non-autistic adults. Much higher incidence of cancer and other diseases. They don't have the self-awareness and communication skills to seek treatment early on. And in most cases, the family members choose not to prolong their suffering."

His words made Zachary feel physically sick. Abato was eager to show off the successful children and teens in his program, the ones who might someday be able to 'pass as normal,' but he seemed like he was just dressing up the fact that they were just warehousing the older adults, waiting for nature to take its course.

Quentin was *not* better off dead.

He didn't need to die so that someone else could take his place in the program; someone who was more likely to 'succeed.'

His mother, at least, hadn't wanted him to die.

7

Dr. Abato walked Zachary back out to the reception area where he had first arrived. He held up a hand to indicate that Zachary should wait for a moment, while he talked to the receptionist in a lowered voice. He nodded his thanks and then joined Zachary again.

"We've got some protesters outside the grounds today," he informed Zachary. "Your best route out of here is to turn a left out of the parking lot and circle around to the freeway entrance. The protesters know that they're supposed to stay off of the grounds and are not allowed to block traffic, but they have been known to do it in the past. Just keep your car crawling forward and don't make eye contact, and you should be able to get out of here alright. If you do get stuck, stay in your car with the doors locked. Our security will do their best to get them out of your way, but your best bet at that point is to dial 9-1-1. The police will be far more likely to respond to your call that you feel threatened by the protesters blocking your way than they would to a call from us. Just a matter of police officers identifying better with an individual citizen than to a big corporate entity."

Zachary felt overwhelmed by it all, but he nodded his understanding. "Okay. Thanks."

"You will be more of a target if a guard escorts you out, or I would have someone walk you to your car. You'll be alright?" Abato leveled a piercing look at him. Zachary felt like Ray-Ray being forced to look Sophie in the eye.

"Sure. Thanks so much for your hospitality. I'll call you with any follow-up questions? And you'll get back to me on the security lock logs?"

"Of course."

Dr. Abato shook Zachary's hand, his grip too tight for comfort, and Zachary was happy to be able to get away from him, to get away from everyone in the oppressive place and get back to his car. Sitting in the driver's seat of his new Civic, Zachary just breathed for a few minutes, trying to calm the shakiness in his thighs and his abdominal muscles and to re-center himself. He had known it would be a rough day. Not just because he was investigating a child's death, but also because of the institution itself and his own past. Because of Annie and his other memories of places like Summit.

But now that part was done. He'd seen what he needed to there. He would finish reading the medical examiner and police reports and deal with any further questions over the phone or email. Unless there were further details that required him to return to Summit, he was finished there.

Taking one last deep breath, Zachary pulled the car out of the parking space and at the exit of the parking lot, turned left. There was a small cluster of protesters. He remembered Dr. Abato's advice not to make eye contact, and avoided looking at their faces. He focused on the road ahead of him and tried to pretend they weren't even there.

He got past them, and it wasn't until then that he looked at their signs in his mirror and saw Quentin's face.

Bowman was off of his shift when Zachary got home, exhausted from the drive to and from Summit, from the tour and the anxiety that plagued him there, from thinking about it, and from trying not to think about it.

"You look like death warmed over," Bowman observed. "What exactly did they do to you in that place? Put *you* in the rubber room for a few hours?"

"It was just… a tiring day," Zachary said, trying to brush it off and not allow any images of detention cells to bubble up from the past. "All of the driving and everything."

"Have you had anything to eat?"

Zachary was trying not to put Bowman out by expecting him to supply all of the meals while Zachary was living there but, once again, he had forgotten to provide for himself and had gone home empty-handed, without groceries, fast food, or even a thought about meals.

"Uh… it's fine. I'm not hungry," he said truthfully. "You don't need to make anything."

"When I say anything, I mean anything. Did you have breakfast? Lunch?"

"Uh… no. Just… coffee this morning."

"You said you were going to grab something on the road. On the way there."

"Yeah… I guess I got distracted. I forgot."

"It's no wonder you're so skinny! Did Bridget ever get you eating three meals a day when you were living with her?" Mario readjusted his belt, lifting his belly and patting it ruefully. "I could never forget to eat."

"Well… some of the meds I take kill my appetite. I don't really get hungry." Zachary tried not to think of Bridget and the life with her that he had lost. The heartache was more than he could handle.

"I'm having dinner, so what do you want?"

He swallowed. "Whatever you're making is fine."

"Burgers and fries?" Bowman suggested.
"Yeah, sure."
"Alright. I'll throw them on."

8

Ray-Ray held the cold, hard metal of his piston to his face, trying to be still. Mommy said he had to stay in bed, and he was trying, but he was uneasy. He turned onto his side, and the weighted blanket shifted and settled back over him, soothing. Like the man's hands when he had hugged Ray-Ray.

Ray-Ray's brain was a motor that ran all the time. It didn't stop when it was bedtime, and it didn't stop while he was asleep. Mommy said he slept like a windmill, when he finally slept. A windmill was a big fan, like in an engine, and she meant that his arms and legs were always moving, not that they went in circles. When Mommy slept, she was still, like a car that had been parked in the garage at night.

But Ray-Ray's motor kept running. When he didn't have something else to occupy his attention, like watching Top Gear, his brain replayed the events of the day over and over again. Examining them from all angles. Analyzing his mistakes and everyone's scripts. Top Gear was a TV show, and that meant it followed a script, Sophie said. One that was written ahead of time so that everyone knew exactly what to say and do next. Real life had scripts too, but they weren't all written out ahead of time, you had to pay attention to figure out which one to use. Ray-Ray wasn't very good at figuring out which one to use. The word that came most easily to his tongue was 'no,' and that just made Sophie angry.

It made everyone angry. He was not supposed to say 'no.'

Usually.

Ray-Ray hadn't seen the man before. He didn't usually see new actors at Summit. He saw Sophie, Mrs. Beale at the reception desk, the doctors, and a scattering of smaller parts; other kids who went there for school, their teachers, other aides and staff whose bodies and voices and movements had become more familiar to him. But the man was someone new. Ray-Ray was sure, as his brain reviewed every other day he'd gone to Summit, that he'd never seen the man there before.

Mr. Goldman.

'Hug Mr. Goldman,' Dr. Abato had said. So the man's name was Mr. Goldman.

He looked different from the other people at Summit. He came from somewhere else. He smelled like another place. Coffee, sweat, a chemical smell that new kids at Summit sometimes had. Mr. Goldman didn't smell like home and he didn't smell like Summit.

And it was like he had a light inside him, shining out through his windows and headlights. A light that shone on Ray-Ray and made him feel safer, like he'd felt when the man put his arms around Ray-Ray and told him, 'There, that's okay.'

He'd felt okay for a few seconds. Safe and warm and protected. Like he felt with Quentin. And then Sophie had pulled him away and made him do proper sitting and quiet hands and eye contact, until he felt so small and far away that he didn't know who he was.

Ray-Ray pressed the piston against his cheek again, feeling the cool, smooth metal and inhaling the smell of machine oil.

9

Zachary fell asleep sometime after supper. He and Bowman ate in front of the TV and, with his blood sugar stable, his mental exhaustion from the day at Summit, and physical exhaustion from not sleeping, it wasn't long before Zachary's eyes closed, and he fell into a restless sleep. He knew he shouldn't go to sleep early, or he wouldn't be able to sleep at night, but his brain and body were too overwhelmed to get up and do something else. He kept prying his eyes open for a few seconds, only to be overcome and drift back off to sleep.

At some point, Bowman got up and went to bed, leaving Zachary in the living room with the TV droning on. Bowman knew from experience that if he turned the TV off, Zachary would be instantly awake and unlikely able to get back to sleep again all night, so he just left it playing.

Zachary's tour of Summit had stirred up a lot of memories of Bonnie Brown and other institutions, hospitals, and group homes he had been in. The memories were fluid, time and place shifting and flowing from one to another.

There were hands on him, gripping his shoulders tightly. A male voice. "You were asked to go to the common room, Zachary."

"I don't want to," he protested, trying to pull away.

"I didn't ask if you wanted to. That's where you're supposed to be."

"Only if I want to. I don't want to watch some stupid movie."

"It's not optional."

Zachary tried again to pull away. Usually, he was allowed to stay in his bunk if he didn't want to join in on the planned activities. The man dug his thumb into the nerve in Zachary's shoulder, making his legs buckle with the sudden pain.

"You're coming."

Zachary didn't have it in him to argue any further. It was all he could do to keep from crying. He wasn't going to be seen in tears in front of the other residents. He didn't resist as the staffer steered him toward the door. He couldn't even raise his voice to ask why he had to go.

He wasn't going fast enough for his escort, which meant he was manhandled further, a strong hand on his arm hustling him forward, making him stumble over his own feet. When he got to the common room, he pulled away and looked around to decide where to sit.

"There," the man told him, pointing to an empty seat.

Zachary shook his head. That would put him next to Roddy Rodriguez, and he had no desire to be within arm's reach of Roddy Rodriguez.

"Sit there." The instruction was accompanied by a rough nudge toward the seat.

"No! I can sit where I want."

"You can sit where I tell you to," the man growled. "There."

Zachary angled toward an empty seat along the wall. The man grabbed him, moved him closer to the seat beside Roddy, and when Zachary didn't comply by sitting down, brought a hard forearm down into the hollow of Zachary's neck and shoulder, forcing him down into the seat.

Fury blossomed in Zachary's chest, but he was helpless to defend himself. A slight preteen, he had no chance of winning against the big, burly staffer. He saw Roddy laughing at him. Roddy was a ruthless bully and Zachary had even less defense against him. He erupted from his chair, swinging at the guard. Let them put him in a detention cell. Let them knock him around and leave him in handcuffs. At least he'd be safe from Roddy and he wouldn't have to sit through whatever teachable moment the staff was trying to coordinate.

Zachary saw red, and then black, and then he was awake, on the couch, staring at the TV screen like it was the enemy.

Zachary swore and tried to catch his breath and relax. He closed his eyes, still on the edge of sleep. If he didn't wake himself up any further, he'd be able to find sleep again. Maybe more restful this time.

He flowed into another dream. Innocuous. Relaxed. *Not in a facility this time. He was in a department store. Bored. Walking with a woman who had to be a foster mother.* There had been too many to remember so many years later. Her name was something musical. Lyra? Viola?

"Quit dawdling," she told him, looking back over her shoulder.

Lyra. Definitely. Zachary sped up a little, not really making much of an effort. When she stopped looking at him, he dawdled again, looking around at the merchandise.

They stopped in the boyswear department. Zachary started looking through t-shirts with licensed cartoon characters on them. He never got to buy new clothes. It was always hand-me-downs from other foster children, or uniforms, or something from the thrift store that looked like it had been left on the side of the road.

"Oh, cool," he paused at a Spider-Man shirt. "Can I have one of these?"

"No," Lyra said flatly. Non-musical. No inflection.

Zachary looked at her, trying to discern what her objection was. Price? Something the school wouldn't allow? There were no swear words, no blood and gore. He let go of the shoulder of the Spider-Man shirt.

"What can I have?"

"I'll decide what you can have."

He waited for further direction. But she didn't offer any enlightenment. She went to a wall of drab, dressy shirts. Zachary wandered through the racks, looking at other clothes. Daydreaming and imagining what he would buy if he could have anything he wanted.

"Zachary!" Her voice had a snap in it. "Get over here."

Zachary located Lyra and moved back through the racks to where she stood.

"You are not to wander off. You're supposed to be right here at my side. Understood?"

"I was just looking over there—"

"Is that right by my side?"

"No."

"Then that's not where I said you need to be, is it?"

"No," Zachary muttered, low, angry.

"What?"

He raised his voice, eliminating all traces of emotion. "No, ma'am."

"I need you to stay right here by me."

He grunted and stayed put. She grabbed him by the shoulder and turned him around to hold a shirt up to his shoulders in the back. When she draped it over her arm, he turned back around.

"Could I have a blue one?"

"No."

He looked at the wall of shirts, and looked sideways at her. "Can I have another color?"

"No." She nodded to the olive drab shirt she had draped over her arm. "This is fine."

"Won't I need more than one?"

"I'll get another one if that fits you. After you try it on."

"In another color?"

"No."

Zachary ground his teeth. "Why not? Is there a school uniform?"

"No. This is what you're getting, and I don't want to hear anything else about it."

He'd never been able to choose his own clothes before, so Zachary wasn't sure why it should bother him so much that he didn't get to choose the color he liked. But he was there, standing in the department store, able to express his opinion. And there was more than one color. They were all the same price. It wasn't a uniform. So why couldn't he choose a different color?

"Are we getting pants?"

She looked at him. "Yes, we're getting pants too."

"Which ones can I look at?"

"You can stand here with me. I'll pick out what we are buying."

"Can't I look?"

She didn't answer, which Zachary supposed was as good as a 'no.' He bit the cuticle of his thumb. It hurt, but it distracted and calmed him. He didn't care about clothes. Why worry about it? He should be happy that he was getting new clothes. He didn't know when the last time was that he'd had new clothes. Maybe when he was a baby. Or maybe even then his family had been too poor to buy new and had picked up what they could find at the thrift stores. It would be a new experience to put clothes on his body that had never been on anyone else's.

"Stop fidgeting."

Zachary dropped his thumb from his mouth and tried to stand still. Lyra held a pair of black pants up to his hips, frowning.

"You're so thin," she complained. "And I suppose you'll hit a growth spurt as soon as I buy you anything."

And, of course, he had. They changed around his meds, she was a good cook, and in a couple of months he'd put on twenty pounds and shot up three inches. Then it was back to thrift-store clothes and hand-me-downs, with his barely-worn new clothes being stored away in closets and boxes for the next skinny boy who happened to need them.

Zachary rolled over. The light from the TV was bothering him, but he was too tired to get up and turn it off. If he did that, he would wake himself up and he wouldn't be able to get back to sleep again.

The low murmur covered up the noises of the building and made him feel like he wasn't alone.

So he pulled his blanket up over his face to block out the light from the TV screen, and closed his eyes, seeking sleep again.

He should have known that trying to go back to sleep a third time would undo everything. He wanted to go to a more peaceful place. Like when he had gone from the dream about Roddy Rodriguez at Bonnie Brown to the dream about shopping with Lyra. But instead of finding a happier memory, he found himself in the detention cell at Bonnie Brown, his face pressed to the window, watching Annie die while he screamed and banged impotently on the door.

***

Zachary waited until mid-afternoon to call Kenzie. She sounded happy to hear from him and ready to take a break from her work.

"Zachary! I've been wondering how your case is going. Did you get in at Summit? Or are they blocking you?"

"I went there yesterday. Spent a few hours there, touring the facility, seeing what it is they do. Saw Quentin's room where it happened."

"Well, what did you think? What did they seem like?"

"It's a lot to go over," Zachary said slowly. "Do you want to get together for supper again? I don't want to take you away from your work for too long."

She made a little groan that communicated she would like to get out of there sooner. But Zachary knew she was diligent about her hours and wasn't going to sneak off just because there was something more interesting to do.

"Yeah, let's do that," she agreed. "Where do you want to go? We haven't done the buffet for a while."

"Sure, that's good for me. Just give me a call when you're off, and we'll head over."

That way, whether she left early or had to work late, they wouldn't be waiting on each other. Kenzie agreed and, after muttering a bit more about her work, told him goodbye and got back to it. Zachary hung up the phone and sat there looking at it for a few minutes, wishing she would call him back and say that she was just going to take off, and she would make up her hours later. Or maybe someone else would call him, just to chat and cheer him up. But there weren't a lot of people who would call him just to chew the fat. New clients, current clients asking for progress updates, insurance agents, but not friends.

He sighed and got back to work, signing on to his new laptop and waiting while it connected with the cloud, where all of his documents were now stored so they couldn't be destroyed in a house fire. Or an office fire. Or a hard drive breakdown. He'd learned the hard way and he wasn't leaving his data at risk again.

The time passed slowly, but eventually Kenzie called to say she was done and on her way to the restaurant. Zachary packed his laptop and notebook into a slim portfolio and headed out to meet her. He thought briefly about Bowman's comment that Kenzie would be interested in a relationship if Zachary would work on it. But he wasn't sure what the next step would look like.

So the meal followed their established pattern. A bit of small talk about the weather and how things were going at the medical examiner's office, a few jokes about the stiffs she worked with. Dishing up their meals from the buffet and sitting down to discuss the nitty-gritties of Zachary's case. Kenzie was ready the minute she sat down and stabbed a baby corn-cob with her fork.

"You look about bursting to tell me all about it," she said, "so go for it. What did you find out?"

Zachary tried to keep his narrative chronological, to explain what he had seen, in the order he had seen it, but he was easily distracted and quickly segued completely to the therapy session with Ray-Ray. Kenzie listened carefully, nodding in understanding.

"That all sounds about right," she said. "I mean, it all goes back to Pavlov, doesn't it? Conditioning them to give a certain response to a certain stimulus? Getting more complex, of course, but when you break it all down, that's what they're doing."

Zachary nodded. He rubbed the bridge of his nose, up to his forehead. Trying to smooth out the frown lines he could feel there. He ate a few bites of the random foods piled on his plate, trying to come up with a response.

"I just… I guess I'm having problems with treating people like animals," he said. "Like you say about Pavlov… training them like dogs. Like they aren't thinking, feeling human beings."

"It may not look like they care, Zachary, but I'm sure they do. All of the therapists that I've ever dealt with have had loads of empathy for their patients. But you can't necessarily let that dictate how you deal with them. Right?"

"If you had seen… it felt abusive. Not giving him any breaks, shouting and making loud noises and threatening him when he made a mistake. Grabbing him and forcing him to do what she wanted him to…"

"If she had been doing something wrong, the doctor wouldn't have let it go on. He would have interrupted the session to make sure that Raymond was safe and pulled the therapist out or corrected her in how she was administering the treatment. But he didn't, right?"

"No. He sat there watching… said that Raymond was okay… kept bragging about their program, how many people wanted to get into it. From all over the country… I can't imagine how parents would actually want their kids to go through that, if they knew what was going on."

"I'm sure they do know," Kenzie said. She speared a length of asparagus and cut it neatly into several pieces. "They would have gone through an orientation. Watched videos. Gone through training of their own. Because the kids that go home are going to need consistency when they're not at Summit. They need to be getting the same responses no matter which environment they are in."

Zachary thought about Ray-Ray's face crumpling when he was corrected after giving the wrong response. The idea of Ray-Ray's mother treating him the same way as Sophie had, taking away the things he loved, yelling at him, forcing his hands and his body to obey, made Zachary's stomach tighten. He took a deep breath and let it back out again. He wasn't investigating Summit's therapy methods. Not unless those methods had led to Quentin's death. He was there to determine if the police were right and Quentin had committed suicide. He wasn't there to stop them from making Ray-Ray cry.

"They physically restrain him," Zachary said, jumping right back into it. "What if that was what happened to Quentin? What if someone put him in a choke hold because he wouldn't do what they wanted him to, and accidentally killed him?"

"It's a big jump from restraining a five-year-old's hands to choking out a fourteen-year-old. You didn't see them physically harm the little boy, did you? They didn't do anything to hurt him?"

"No… they were rough, though. A lot rougher than I think you need to be with a child who is so small and defenseless."

Kenzie gave him a warm smile. Zachary wasn't the stereotypical hard-boiled detective of pulp fiction. He wasn't the rough-and-tough, beat-the-hell-out-of-suspects type that got all of the pretty girls on TV and in paperback novels. But Kenzie seemed to like that about him. She didn't act like she was disappointed that he had a soft heart instead of a hard fist. That he didn't carry a gun. That most of his work was tedious computer research rather than sweating suspects. That all seemed to be okay with her, and even won him a soft smile and hand-holding when he got all sentimental about someone.

"Sometimes therapy can be uncomfortable," she said. "You've had physiotherapy, right?"

Zachary nodded. Most recently, he'd had physio to get him back on his feet after the accident, to retrain him to walk after the spinal cord injury that had left him temporarily paralyzed. And long before that... he could remember the therapy he'd had when he was ten, after the fire. He was glad that she'd referred to physical therapy rather than to the years of visiting all manner of counselors, psychologists, and psychiatrists. He could look more dispassionately at physio and talk about it. "Yeah. A few times," he agreed.

"Did it hurt?"

Zachary raised his brows, surprised by the question. "Well... yeah, it did." If she thought that physiotherapy was all roses, she should think again.

"In fact, it can be pretty brutal, can't it?" she prodded.

"Yes."

"I've had friends who have done physio. Friends who have done boot camp and said that physio is worse."

Zachary nodded.

"But that's not abuse, is it?" Kenzie went on. "Even though they push you really hard, and it hurts, even makes you cry, that's not abuse."

Zachary could see where this was going, so he didn't answer immediately. Kenzie had a sip of her drink, and looked at him, eyebrows raised.

"It *can* be abusive," Zachary stonewalled.

She cocked her head, considering. "I suppose so. They could take it too far. Reinjure you. Push you to do something painful just because they wanted to see you sweat. But that's not the norm. I think usually they're pretty good at knowing where to stop. Exactly how far they can push each patient."

"Yes. Usually."

"Well, that's my point. That just because it's painful, that doesn't mean it's abuse. It's like... debriding a burn. In order for the burn to heal properly, you need to scrape all of the dead skin away. They say it's very painful. But it has to be done."

Zachary caught his breath and held it. All of a sudden, he was ten years old and back in the hospital. After the fire that had burned his house down and ruined his family forever. It was more than just remembering what it had been like, he could feel the burns all over again. Most of the burns had been on his arms and legs, and inside his throat from breathing in the superheated air. He'd been lucky not to have more of his body burned. At the hospital, they had put him on heavy painkillers, but even with opiates in his IV drip, debriding the wounds had been excruciating. It had taken several nurses to complete the process, some of them holding him down while the others took turns scraping the wounds clean. Zachary screamed, cried, and threw up, but they still had to do it.

"Zachary."

Kenzie was far away from him. He could hear her, but he wasn't in the present anymore. He was far in the past, trying to fight off the nurses who tortured him. Lashing out like an animal, screaming with pain.

"Zachary." Her fingers moved from his hand to his wrist, gently resting over his pulse. "Come back to me, Zachary. You're okay."

There was another murmured voice, but Zachary couldn't make it out. He was barely holding on to Kenzie's voice; he couldn't see or hear anyone else.

"No. We're fine. Just give us some space." She touched Zachary's shoulder. His cheek. "I'm sorry, Zach. Are you okay? Come on. Just talk to me. Tell me about it."

Her hand went back to his wrist again, first taking his pulse and then stroking the white scars across it.

"Have a drink. A nice cold drink." She guided his hand to his glass, and Zachary automatically closed his fingers around it.

Brought it up to his mouth. Took a few sips of the ice-cold soft drink. The restaurant started to resolve around him.

He wasn't in hospital. He wasn't having his burns treated anymore.

That had been years before. Decades.

"Better?"

He could see Kenzie, her dark curls and bright-red lipstick. He could see the fine lines around her eyes as she studied him, worried. Zachary took another sip of the cold, sweet drink. He held it in his mouth while the bubbles fizzed on his tongue, then swallowed it down.

His throat was fine. Not sore. Not burned.

"Sorry," he croaked out.

She wrapped her fingers around his and gave them a little squeeze. "Tell me about it. What happened?"

She knew so much of his sordid past. The really bad stuff. Yet he was still embarrassed to show this weakness in front of her. To have to explain it.

It could have been worse. She'd seen him collapse in a panic attack before. Helpless as a baby lying in a heap on the frozen sidewalk. And she still chose to go to dinner with him. Having a flashback wasn't as bad as *that*. And he didn't have to tell her the whole thing. She already knew most of the story.

How he had been the one to light the fire. How he had ended up destroying everything.

"A flashback," he said softly, breathing out and in and out again. It seemed like it had been a long time since he had breathed last.

Years.

Decades.

"Yeah, I thought so." She rubbed his shoulder soothingly. "What about?"

"The fire… but afterward. The… debriding."

"Oh!" Her mouth was small, her eyes wide. She swore. "Oh, I

didn't think. I didn't know… I didn't realize you were burned that badly. You never said…"

"I don't like to talk about it. It's not your fault."

Zachary unbuttoned the cuff of his right shirtsleeve and pushed it up. He showed her the scars on his arm. Old, pink, stretched scars.

"Oh, Zachary." She touched it. Like she didn't really believe what she was seeing. "Oh, I'm sorry. You never said it was that bad. I wouldn't have used debriding as an example if I'd realized."

"You're right, though," Zachary tried to get the focus off of himself and back onto Summit and Raymond and the therapy program. "Therapy can be painful. Physically. Mentally. And I'm not a professional, so what do I know? How can I judge whether they're doing it right, and how soft or hard she should be with him? They're the experts. Dr. Abato kept telling me how advanced their program is, better than anyone else's. He kept telling me how they succeed where everyone else fails. What do I know, walking in there for the first time?"

Kenzie nodded. She let go of him and went back to eating her supper as if nothing had happened. He appreciated the gesture. She didn't spend the whole night treating him like a baby. She didn't ask him why he wasn't on a medication that would stop the flashbacks and anxiety. She just went back to what they had been doing and acted like nothing unusual had happened.

Zachary was getting looks from the diners at nearby tables and some of the wait staff. Had he been that obvious? Caused a scene? He didn't think he had shouted or cried, but he couldn't be sure. He thought that he had just withdrawn, gone back in time in his mind, but that shouldn't have been noticeable to people sitting at the other tables. Zachary poked at his meal, looking for something appetizing. He didn't feel like eating anything more, but he knew he needed to. He'd learned that he had to eat whether he was hungry or not. He needed to take care of himself. He didn't want Kenzie seeing him as a sick, broken person.

"What did you find out about Quentin?" Kenzie asked. "Nothing out of place in his room?"

"No. Well, yes and no. I'm still looking for some more answers. Who saw him last. If they did bed checks. If anyone went into his room."

"Do you think they were negligent?"

"When they found him, he was on the floor. Not on his bunk. The medical examiner's report said he'd been dead for four to six hours. If he was on his floor for six hours, shouldn't someone have noticed?"

Kenzie considered, nodding slowly. "Unless that was normal behavior for him."

"Abato said some kids hide under their beds. Sleep on the floor. That it wouldn't have been out of the ordinary."

"But was it out of the ordinary for Quentin? Did he usually sleep on his floor or on his bed?"

Zachary pulled his notepad out of his case and added the question to a list of other similar ones. "I wish I'd been able to spend more time talking to the people who were in charge of his unit and less time on the tour. Dr. Abato didn't know much about Quentin's habits or what had happened the night before they found him. He didn't even know if they had computer logs of when Quentin's door had been opened. They're all electronic locks. So there must be a record of when they went in there."

"Only if it was locked."

Zachary stared at her, realizing that she was right. Dr. Abato had said that the door would only have been locked if Quentin had been involved in an incident earlier in the day. And if his door had been left unlocked, there would be no security log of who had opened the door.

"If it was locked," he agreed. "And Dr. Abato couldn't tell me whether it had been. One of those questions that I'm supposed to be getting answers to later."

"They must have had to answer them for the police too."

"I'm not sure. I get the feeling that the police investigation was pretty… cursory."

"They're required by law to investigate any homicide, including suicides. But if everything looked like suicide, I'm not sure anyone would be wasting their time digging down deeper."

Zachary nodded. He took a bite of red Jell-O gelatin. There was a bit of ranch dressing on it, but just on the edge. He sucked it around his mouth, liquefying it like he used to when he was a kid. Jell-O had always been a favorite. As long as they didn't put anything weird in it. Peaches were okay. But not carrots or cottage cheese.

"I would talk to his therapist," Kenzie said. "Not a behavioral therapist, but a psychotherapist or counselor. Someone who would know whether he was depressed."

"His mother didn't think he was depressed. But she said he was…" Zachary strained to remember her exact words. "Agitated. They were increasing his therapy sessions."

"So find out who he talked to. Find out what they thought was wrong."

Zachary nodded. "I will… but I don't know if they will be able to tell me anything. He didn't really talk, so how would they know?"

"They're trained professionals. They would notice changes in his behavior. His demeanor. Even if he couldn't speak, he must have had other ways to communicate."

"His mom said that they wouldn't let him communicate any other way. They wanted him to speak, so they wouldn't pay attention if he tried to communicate another way."

"His therapy or counseling would have been different," Kenzie assured him. "If something was bothering him, they would have worked with whatever communications method he had."

"Okay. I'll find out, then."

"A lot of people with autism deal with depression or self-harm. I'm sure they'll have protocols in place to evaluate their residents, even if they're non-verbal."

"But if he was depressed, you don't think it was because of anything they were doing at Summit."

Kenzie cocked an eyebrow. She shook her head. "No, not at all. Like I said, it's very common. And Summit has a sterling reputation."

"The police report said that they've had other deaths. I haven't looked into the details yet, but doesn't that make you suspicious?"

"People are going to die there. At any institution. But not violent deaths…?"

"I haven't looked them up yet," Zachary repeated. "The police didn't seem to think they were anything to be concerned about."

"But it's your job to look at it all again," Kenzie said, giving a melodramatic sigh. "It's your job to be suspicious. I get that. But how many deaths are we talking about? If it was anything out of the ordinary, it would have been in the news, and I don't remember hearing anything like that."

"I don't know. Half a dozen, I think."

"Half a dozen? In how long? This year? Five years?"

"Since it opened."

Kenzie laughed. It wasn't a mocking laugh, but genuine amusement. Zachary shifted uncomfortably, staring down at his plate.

"Since it opened, Zachary?" Kenzie repeated. "They've been operating thirty, forty years. Six deaths in thirty years is nothing. Probably just natural causes."

"No, I think those are deaths that were investigated. Suspicious deaths."

"Even so, one death like Quentin's every five or six years? You'll see more than that in any municipal jail."

"You think so?"

"Absolutely. I'm sure it's a shock to the parents when something like this happens, but kids commit suicide at home, too. The institution can't prevent every death. It's just not possible."

10

The following day, Zachary spent some time re-reading the police reports in the small hours of the morning, until he was sure he had taken in every word and sorted out all of his questions. He still didn't have all of the answers he wanted from the staff at Summit, and a couple of polite emails and voicemail follow-ups had not produced any results. By the time Bowman got up, Zachary had decided to go back to the institution. He needed to talk to the psychologist who had been treating Quentin. To the supervisor of his unit and the person who had discovered the body. The night staff who hadn't noticed anything was amiss. And if he were there in person, Dr. Abato couldn't put off his questions in the hopes that he'd just stop asking.

"Where are you off to so early?" Bowman asked after a few gulps of scalding-hot coffee. Zachary had put his into a travel mug and was waiting for it to cool.

"Back to Summit Living Center."

"More questions to be answered?"

"Yes… I've gone over everything I can, but there are still holes in what the doctor over there told me and what was in the police reports. It doesn't seem…" Zachary tried to word it tactfully, "like it was… investigated very deeply."

Bowman shrugged. "No skin off my nose. It's not our police department. And suicides… they're not investigated the same way as other homicides. If there's nothing on the surface that's suspicious, the police don't spend months sifting through the details. Why would they? Ninety-nine percent of the time, if you walk into the room and it looks like a suicide… it was. It's only on TV that murderers try to cover up a killing by making it look like suicide. Or Victorian murder mysteries. In real life, if someone takes a bottle of pills, or slits their wrists, or hangs themselves… you walk in, you do your scene survey, talk to the family, forensics does their bit, and you wait until the lab comes back with all of the details confirmed. The medical examiner makes his ruling, you write your summary, and the case is closed."

Zachary nodded. That pretty much confirmed what he'd read on the file. Very high-level, superficial. "If it looks like a duck…"

"Exactly," Bowman agreed. "Even in cases where the family didn't know the person was depressed… it's not usually that big of a surprise. After the initial shock wears off… they admit that they knew there was a problem. Addiction, depression, a series of traumas… when someone commits suicide, there's usually been a long lead-up."

Zachary pretended to take a sip of his coffee, even though it was still too hot for him, just so he could hide any changes in his expression. Bowman didn't know much about Zachary's own history. He didn't know he was talking to a self-qualified expert on suicide. Zachary cleared his throat.

"You're probably right," he said. "It probably was. But his mother is paying me to investigate, so if anything doesn't fit… I'll find it."

Bowman grinned. "You're a good investigator. That's why she hired you. I wish you all the luck."

He looked down at his watch. Without looking at his, Zachary took the hint. "I'd better be heading out. Got some driving and thinking to do."

Bowman gave him a little salute. Zachary grabbed his soft-sided briefcase and headed down to his car.

Unlike the previous day, it wasn't clear and fresh, but pouring rain and dark due to the thick clouds. A miserable day to be caught outside, but he was warm and dry in his car. Once he was settled and on his way in the Civic, Zachary called Mira and gave her a brief non-report.

It was a lengthy commute to Summit, but Zachary found it easier to think in a moving vehicle. He didn't know the psychology of it, whether his ADHD restlessness was satisfied by a constantly changing horizon, that he had something to occupy his hands, or whether it was the soothing swish of the tires on pavement. It didn't really matter why. He just knew that distance driving was one of the few times he could really sit still and think without distraction. Maybe he should have chosen the profession of a long-distance trucker instead of a private detective.

He mentally ordered and prioritized the questions he had. Who he wanted to talk to. Bowman was probably right; once Mira started to accept her son's death, she would realize that there had been signs. That Quentin hadn't been happy with himself or with his living situation. That he suffered from depression, even though he couldn't express it to her. It didn't necessarily have anything to do with having him institutionalized at Summit. Depression was rarely simple cause-and-effect. Not everybody who thought their lives sucked was suicidal, and people who appeared to have everything could be deeply depressed.

By the time he reached Summit, the rain had cleared, and the sun was peeking out from behind the clouds. Zachary hadn't set up an appointment, so he decided he should go to the front entrance instead of the private entrance he had been directed to the last time. See the front face of the institution. Ask for the people he needed to talk to before confronting Dr. Abato.

But he hadn't counted on the protesters. He didn't know if there were actually more than there had been on his previous visit, or if he just hadn't known how many people were actually there because he'd been at the private entrance. But there were a lot of them. They waved their signs at him angrily, shouting words he couldn't understand through the closed windows of the car. Zachary continued to inch forward, forcing his way into the parking lot, where he sat for a moment and considered whether to call for assistance. Abato said that security staff presence just tended to inflame the protesters. And he really didn't want to call the police when the fact was that he didn't have an appointment or anyone waiting for him and could just as easily have conducted interviews over the phone.

After sitting for a few minutes, he took a deep breath in, unlocked his door, and forced himself to pick up his bag and step out of the vehicle.

The protesters immediately homed in on him when they saw him walking from his car toward the front door. As soon as he reached the sidewalk, they were closing in, shouting at him and thrusting their signs toward him. Zachary frowned, looking at the signs and trying to take them all in. The ones about Quentin made the most sense to him. Of course people were upset that one of the children at the institution had died. They wanted someone to be held responsible, even if it was suicide or an accident. They wanted accountability. For someone to agree that it should never have happened and that they wouldn't let it happen again.

But other signs didn't make immediate sense.

Zachary shook his head at a woman who pushed her way in front of him. "What is all this?" he demanded. "I don't know who you think I am, but I don't work here."

"Do you know what goes on in there?" the woman demanded. She had ash blond hair and deep wrinkles around her mouth and throat, making it look like she'd recently lost a lot of weight and her face was collapsing in on itself. There was a harsh, M-shaped frown line between her eyebrows. She wore blue jeans and a shapeless t-shirt. Maybe the mother of one of the residents there. Or a former resident.

"Yes," Zachary said. "I was here a couple of days ago. Got a tour. Watched a therapy session. I've seen what goes on."

"Really? Did they show you the aversives? Did they let you see how they treat residents they consider stubborn or violent? The hard cases?"

Zachary let the words sink in. The woman gave him a little shove back on his shoulder. Nothing that hurt Zachary, but he was shocked that she would touch him. Organized protesters were normally trained in what qualified as a peaceful process and what they could not do. Of course, pushing around someone who was trying to get past the protest was way out of line. Something that could get her arrested and jailed for assault. If there had been any police officers around.

"Tell me about that," he suggested.

She looked surprised at his response. She looked around, then back at Zachary. Not straight on, but sideways, wary, as if she were no longer sure what to think of him. He could be a threat. He could just be teasing her, stringing her on like he was interested in what she wanted to say when really, he just wanted to get past her to the big brick building.

"What?"

"Tell me what you mean. What are aversives?"

She again looked around, then leaned in toward him, too close into his personal space. But he was surrounded by jostling protesters, so he wasn't sure why he even noticed how close she stood to him.

"An aversive is something you do to cause the subject pain whenever he performs a bad behavior."

Zachary thought back to Ray-Ray's therapy session. "Do you mean like yelling at him or forcing him to do something he doesn't want to? Physically?"

"I'm not talking about yelling. I'm talking about causing

pain." She pointed to one of the signs with a lightning-bolt symbol on it. "Like skin shocks."

"Skin shocks?" Zachary shook his head. "Really? I thought shock treatment was out in the seventies."

"Shock treatment is passing an electrical charge through the brain. ECT. Not the same thing as skin shocks."

A male protester jostled Zachary. "Like cattle prods."

Zachary looked at the lightning bolt sign and then at the woman. "They don't use cattle prods. That wouldn't be legal."

"I said 'like cattle prods,'" the man repeated. "Cattle prods. Stun guns. Skin shocks."

"I didn't see anything like that."

"Of course not," the woman scoffed. "Do you think they would let you see that on a VIP tour? They're going to try to show the institution in its best light. All the good stuff. Show you kids playing happily and appearing to have a good time in their therapy sessions. Just like the pictures and videos on their website. Do you think they would show you what it is really like?"

"No." There had been tours through Bonnie Brown and other facilities Zachary had been housed at too. He remembered the way they had been lectured on giving the VIPs a good experience so that the facility could get more money. How they had sanitized everything, making sure that the kids were all in clean, fresh clothes, and that anyone who they knew would give the tourists a bad impression was hustled off to detention or another unit. They were ordered to smile and play nicely and answer questions positively if they wanted to earn a treat and avoid retribution. The VIPs never got to see what the institution was really like in day-to-day operations. Real life was messy and raw. Kids who had been locked up because they were too difficult for foster families to deal with were not cute, polite, respectful automatons.

The protesters were quieting a little. The fact that Zachary was listening to them instead of just shoving his way through was having an effect.

"I'm Margaret Beacher," the blond woman said, thrusting her

hand toward Zachary.

He had a hard time catching her hand squarely and ended up squeezing her fingers instead of getting a good grip. She pulled away and stood there looking at him, her eyes boring into him.

"And what's your name?" she demanded, as if he'd missed an important cue.

"Zachary. My name is Zachary Goldman."

"What are you doing here? If you're not working here and you don't know enough about the program to know what an aversive is, why are you here?"

Zachary bent to put down his briefcase, which was starting to get a little heavy. "Can I get a little space? I'm feeling a bit claustrophobic."

The protesters looked at Margaret like she was the one in charge, but she didn't give them any sign. The majority stepped back, giving Zachary a bit more room. Some looked elsewhere, eyes sharp for anyone else they should talk to. Missionaries looking for a convert.

"So?" Margaret demanded. "Who are you and what are you doing here, Zachary Goldman?"

"I'm a private investigator. I'm here looking into Quentin's death." Zachary nodded toward one of the signs with Quentin's picture on it.

Margaret's eyes got big. "A private investigator?" she squawked.

"Yes. Don't go getting all excited. It's not like on TV. I'm just here to ask some questions, follow up on some reports." Zachary indicated his briefcase. "It's lots of paperwork and talking to people. Not all romantic…"

"But you're looking into Quentin's death."

"Yes."

"So you don't think it was suicide."

"I haven't come to a conclusion yet. There's no reason yet to think that it wasn't just what it looked like. But I'm trying to find out."

"His mother doesn't think it's suicide." She said it like it was something he didn't already know.

Zachary nodded. "I know. She hired me."

"Quentin Thatcher didn't have to die," Margaret said loudly, her inflection like a chant. Everyone raised their signs in agreement. "Quentin Thatcher didn't have to die!"

Zachary studied Margaret. "What do you think happened?" he asked. His brain was buzzing through the possibilities. Her chant wasn't that he was abused, neglected, or murdered. Their statement wasn't that it wasn't suicide, but that he didn't have to die.

"Autistic people all around the world are being hurt and traumatized by ABA therapy. It has to stop! They have to stop treating neurodiverse people like they are animals."

Zachary looked for somewhere they could sit down. There was a low landscaping wall between the grass and the sidewalk, and Zachary motioned to it. "Let's sit."

She joined him, sitting just an inch too close. Zachary slid down a little and took a breath.

"How are they being hurt? By skin shocks?"

"By skin shocks. Other aversives like pinching, hitting, kicking, holding, strong smells, loud noises, hot pepper sauce, whatever their tormentors can think of to punish them for behaving the wrong way. For being autistic instead of neurotypical. Do you have any idea what it feels like to be punished for who you are? For the way your brain was formed? Something you have absolutely no control over?"

Zachary watched an ant carrying a crumb along the sidewalk block in front of him. He'd spent his entire childhood being punished for something he had no control over. Not autism, but other diagnoses. For being incorrigible. A troublemaker. When all that he'd ever wanted was to be good.

"You don't believe me?" Margaret demanded, her tone aggressive.

"Yes. I believe you."

"Oh." She gave him another look and lowered her voice to a more reasonable tone. "When ABA was first devised, Lovaas recommended slapping or pinching. He said to practice on your friends, so you knew how hard to hit so that it would hurt, but not do permanent damage. Cause the autistic child pain every time they responded the wrong way, and they would learn not to do it. Reward them every time they responded the right way, and they would learn to do the right thing instead. Or, you could always torture them until they gave the right response, and then stop."

Zachary looked at her. "This is an approved therapy?"

"It's mainstream. Almost all of the autism therapies are based on it. They all make their own adjustments, of course, but even if you take the aversives out of the loop, it's still torture."

They hadn't been hitting or shocking Ray-Ray, but Zachary had still felt like they were going too far. Like they were doing something dirty and callous instead of teaching him. But Kenzie had pooh-poohed the idea. Sometimes therapy was painful. Like physiotherapy or debriding a wound. Zachary gave a little shudder just thinking of it again. Trying not to let himself get swept away by the memories. He needed to think clearly about Ray-Ray's therapy. Good or bad?

"And how did shocks come into it?" he asked Margaret, who was looking impatient for him to get it all through his head.

"Shocks were a wonderful new development. You can't standardize a pinch or a slap. I might slap one way, and you might slap another. Yours might not be hard enough to be effective, and mine might be too hard and cause damage. We can practice on each other like Lovaas says, but we'll still end up with everyone in Summit punishing differently. But with shocking, you can set all devices to one level, and everybody can administer exactly the same punishment for wrong behaviors. Hurt them enough to deter them, but not enough to harm them permanently. Unless, of course, they have a heart condition or something, and you kill them."

"Has that happened?"

"Children have died."

Zachary thought of the reported deaths at Summit and wondered whether he would be able to get any details on the deaths other than Quentin's.

"Or," Margaret says, "they might just be injured. Burns and blisters. Or with other aversives, maybe atrophied muscles from being strapped to a restraint board for weeks, months, even years." She gave a shrug as if that were nothing. "Or maybe no physical injuries. Maybe just PTSD for the rest of their lives from the hell Summit puts them through. Or whatever ABA program they are in."

"But you said that not all programs use aversives."

"Even without aversives, therapy can still cause PTSD or other anxiety or emotional problems."

Zachary scratched the back of his neck. "Do you have proof of that?"

"I *am* proof of that."

He looked at her, studying her face and her body language. "You did ABA?"

"Yes. I did."

"What for? You aren't autistic, are you?"

"Yes, I am."

"You... must be very high-functioning. I wouldn't have guessed it..."

"Do you think that's a compliment?" she snapped.

Zachary fumbled for an answer. He had clearly said the wrong thing. He'd somehow insulted her. And he didn't know what he'd done or how to undo it.

"You think I want to be like *you*?" Margaret persisted, her eyes flaming.

"Like me?" Zachary let out one bitter bark of laughter before he caught himself. "No, I don't think you would want to be like me."

Neither of them said anything for a few minutes. Margaret

looked like she had a lot more to say on the subject, but she closed her mouth and just looked at him.

"Why do you say I wouldn't want to be like you?" she asked finally, in a normal, non-confrontational tone. "What's wrong with you?"

"What *isn't* wrong with me?" Zachary rolled his eyes. "I wouldn't even know where to start."

The other protesters were milling around, holding up their signs, occasionally yelling at the passing motorists. As parents arrived for therapy, they were harassed, and in some cases simply got back into their vehicles and drove away. Others came out of the facility and made their way back to their cars, sheltering children from the yells and sneers of the crowd.

Zachary watched one such mother and child make their way in tandem toward their vehicle.

"Don't you think it's ironic that you're scaring the same children you're claiming need to be protected?"

Margaret turned slightly to look at them. "Wouldn't you steal Jewish children away from the Nazis if you could? Even if you scared them in the process?"

"I'm not sure you can make that comparison."

"They are torturing children," Margaret said with a loud voice. "They need to be stopped."

"They need to be stopped!" echoed one of the other protesters in a yell. The chant was picked up for the next few minutes.

"You don't think so?" Margaret asked. "You don't think it's wrong for them to imprison these children because they are different? To shock them, or withhold food, or restrain them for weeks on end?"

"I don't know what to think. This is all new to me."

"Well… that's honest. I guess I should be glad you're not telling me that I'm a liar. I get that a lot. Or that I'm trying to ruin the lives of all of the families of the children here. People don't like it when you threaten to take their comfort away."

"Do you mind if I get my notepad out?" Zachary gestured to

his briefcase.

"I'm not holding a gun on you. You can do whatever you like."

Zachary got out pen and paper. "What about the kids who are violent?" he asked. "It's not a matter of their families' comfort, but their safety. Quentin was here because he was violent. His mother feared for herself and her other children. What would happen to families like that if you shut down all of the ABA programs? Or even just Summit?"

"ABA isn't the only way to deal with violence. There are other methods out there. What about the thousands of autistic people who aren't at Summit? I don't see them creating havoc. Their families have found other ways to manage difficult behaviors."

"Other than medicating them?"

"Sometimes medications are appropriate. Sometimes they're not."

"What else can they do?"

Margaret looked at the brick building for a minute. "How about taking them out of therapies that traumatize them? Making accommodations? Improving communication? Whatever form of communication they prefer, instead of pushing speech. Reducing stressors instead of escalating problems?" She shook her head. "I was violent as a teenager. I didn't know how else to react to people I felt were attacking me. And trust me, there were plenty of things my parents and therapists could have done other than terrorizing and torturing me with ABA and other aggressive therapies."

But those therapies had apparently worked, since Margaret was no longer solving her problems with violence. How could anyone know what the outcome would have been if Margaret's issues had been solved through other means?

He wondered if he should go into the building, now that the conversation seemed to be winding down. He had listened to the protesters' side. He would be remiss if he didn't ask the staff at Summit for their response. He couldn't make any kind of judgment without hearing both sides of the story.

"So what's wrong with you?"

Margaret wasn't looking at Zachary, and at first, he thought she was asking someone else. But her silence and waiting attitude convinced him that she was asking him.

"I have PTSD too," he told her eventually. It was easier without her looking at him. He didn't feel so much like a bug under a magnifying glass. "I was in a fire when I was young. I haven't done a lot of psychotherapy. I was forced into it when I was younger, and I don't like other people digging around in my brain. But the guy I've started seeing says my PTSD probably originated way before the fire. With the way our—my—parents were."

"How were they?"

"They fought a lot. A lot. Constantly. Not just arguing. It was like a war zone. And I guess that means we—I—developed PTSD just like someone in a war zone."

"You have flashbacks to the fire? To them fighting?"

"Yes." Zachary turned his head to look at Margaret. She looked off into the distance. Her jaw was rigid. Teeth clenched. "And you have flashbacks to therapy?"

"Yes."

It seemed like a bizarre idea at first. But he thought about watching Ray-Ray being bullied by Sophie and Dr. Abato, and how it had stirred up so many unpleasant memories for Zachary. And he thought about how Kenzie had compared therapy to debriding. And he'd instantly flashed back to debriding. If debriding his burns—something that had to be done for him to heal properly—had caused him that much trauma, then why not the behavioral therapy that Ray-Ray and Margaret had gone through?

"Were you in a program like this, where they shocked you?" he asked Margaret.

"No. No physical aversives. But plenty that was uncomfortable and painful *in here*," she tapped her head. "Mental and emotional abuse is still abuse."

"Of course." Zachary made a few more notes for himself. "I should go in there now. I have more investigating to do."

"Yes, you do. Will you call me later? Let me know what you find out?" Margaret pulled out a business card wallet and put one into Zachary's hand.

"I really can't do that," Zachary said. "You're not my client. There is confidentiality. I can't share my findings with you just because you're interested."

She gave a grimace. When Zachary tried to hand the card back, she pushed his hand away sharply. "Keep it. Call me if you have questions." She looked over at the looming brick building. "You *will* have questions."

———

Zachary felt like he had moved into a parallel reality. Even though he had not been through the front doors of the building before, the themes and architecture were the same as they were throughout the rest of the building. The receptionist had a soupy smile pasted across her face. The potted plants and furniture were the same. But everything felt different. When he had walked into Summit before, he had been open to it being positive. To being impressed by what they were doing and to give them the benefit of the doubt. He'd done his best to compartmentalize the emotions and memories that the institution had stirred up in him and to focus on what Abato was showing him, no matter how uncomfortable it made him. But after talking to Margaret, he was no longer able to separate his own feelings about institutions from Summit. Were all institutions corrupt? Was it inevitable that there would be abusers? Bullying? Predation? There had been everywhere he had gone, and it sounded like Summit and the other facilities like it were not exempt.

So in spite of the bright colors and cartoon themes, Zachary felt a pall of darkness over the whole place. The knot that had been in his stomach on his first visit there had at least doubled in size.

"How can I help you?" the receptionist asked, the smile forced over her tired, cynical features.

"There are a few people I need to talk to," Zachary explained. "I've cleared all of this through Dr. Abato. He took me on a tour of the facility earlier in the week."

She frowned at him. "I didn't get any memos from Dr. Abato. No emails or messages that you would be making inquires, Mr. …?"

"Zachary Goldman," Zachary enunciated clearly. He looked at her expectantly, spelling it out slowly so that she got the message and wrote it down on the pad on her desk. "And I need to talk to Quentin Thatcher's psychotherapist, his residential unit supervisor, the person who discovered his body, any night guards who were on shift in his unit the night he died, and… his behavioral therapist and any aides he may have had."

He waited between each person's role, waiting for her to write them down. She looked at the list. "That's a lot of people. They won't all be on shift today, and of those who are, most of them will be busy. If you don't have an appointment, people won't have the time for you. We all keep very busy here."

"I'm sure you do," Zachary said, in as understanding a tone as he could manage, trying to give the impression of being calm and professional while the back part of his brain was flipping out. "To start with, you can get me their names. Then I can contact them and see how many can meet with me today, and how many I can schedule for another day. I'm from out of town, so I'm sure you can understand how I need to see as many as I can in one day. I can't be back and forth for ten different appointments."

She squinted at him, either trying to figure out the best way to thwart him or trying to decide if she should make an effort to help him.

"I'll see if I can get the names for you," she said finally. "It's going to take a while."

"I'll just be waiting over here." Zachary motioned to the couch in the reception area.

Zachary's list of witnesses was quickly whittled down to one. The night staff were not on. The aide who had been with Quentin most recently was booked up and he would have to set up an appointment later.

"He doesn't have a psychotherapist," the receptionist said. "He has a BCBA, but she's got back-to-back appointments all day."

Zachary frowned. "He doesn't have a psychotherapist?"

"Our program here is focused on ABA. We are proactive in avoiding problems, rather than waiting until they become issues."

"You must have someone on staff to deal with depression, learning disabilities, things like that."

"We're not treating mental illness and learning disabilities. We're treating developmental and behavioral issues."

"But other conditions can go along with autism."

She just stared at him blankly.

"So no one was treating Quentin for depression."

"No."

"Who prescribes medications if they are needed?"

"Dr. Abato or one of the other senior staff. But no medications that are behavioral crutches. We demedicalize as soon as they get here."

Zachary had been on med holidays several times in order to 'establish a baseline' with a new doctor. A hellish process of getting all of the chemicals out of his system and then trying desperately to hold it all together until they started adding prescriptions back in one at a time. It was better as an adult, when he could use just what he needed under whatever circumstances he was in and could tell a doctor to take a hike if he wanted to reduce the number of prescriptions Zachary was using. A med holiday was never a holiday for him.

He closed his eyes briefly, his heart going out to Quentin and all of the rest of the kids who were going through the same thing. Off of the medications that would help balance out their brains, instead being controlled by punishing electric shocks. What was it Margaret had just been saying?

Do you have any idea what it feels like to be punished for who you are? For the way your brain was formed? Something you have absolutely no control over?

He knew; he'd spent his whole childhood living it, but at least the punishments he had faced for his incorrigible behavior hadn't included electrical shocks. Prescriptions weren't the full solution, but the right ones made things a little easier to handle.

Zachary looked down at the list the receptionist had made.

"So who is left? There's someone I can talk to?"

"The unit supervisor for Quentin's unit. Her name is Nancy Whitmore. She can come out and see you. I'm afraid the rest… you'll have to make appointments with them." She slid the paper across the desk to him. She had filled in the names and numbers where appropriate.

"So where do I find Nancy Whitmore?"

"She will be out to get you when she's free. She said it wouldn't be too long."

Zachary wondered whether, like Dr. Abato, Nancy Whitmore was making a point to him. She had more important things to do than talk to an interfering private detective. She was a busy person. But at least she had agreed to talk to him. He was sure she could have told the receptionist the same thing the others had, that they were too busy and couldn't meet with Zachary, no matter how far he had come.

So he smiled and nodded politely, and went and sat down on the modern, flat, uncomfortable couch where he had spent the last forty-five minutes. Sooner or later, she would be out to see him, and he could get some of his questions answered.

11

Eventually, Nancy Whitmore came to fetch Zachary. She was a redhead, her hair short and frizzy, her clothing a size too large so that it was sloppy and didn't fit to her form properly.

"Zachary Goldman?"

Since he was the only one sitting there, it was a good bet. Zachary pushed himself to his feet. "Hi. I guess you're Ms. Whitmore."

"Just Nancy, love. Why don't you come with me, then? You were here just a few days ago, weren't you? With Dr. Abato."

"Yes. But I didn't manage to talk to you. I appreciate you taking the time today, with no appointment. You must be busy."

She made a sweeping-away motion with one hand. She led the way to the other side of the reception area to an unimpressive unmarked door.

"Things are pretty quiet for most of the day. Until the kids start getting finished with their sessions. Then we have a few hours of barely-controlled chaos before bed."

Zachary nodded, smiling. He appreciated her good humor. The supper hour through bedtime was always difficult in institutional settings. Tired, cooped-up, and frustrated kids in a less-controlled environment. Kids coming off their meds and rebounding. Dealing with low blood sugar, meals, and trying to keep things peaceful until night meds and lights out. "The arsenic hour," he'd heard one of them refer to it as. Except that it was more than just an hour.

"So you're the head supervisor for the unit Quentin was in."

"That's right. Here most of their waking hours. Someone takes over at night, but of course things are pretty quiet then."

"How was Quentin that last day before he died?"

She ran her fingers through her already-frizzed-up hair. "Quentin was Quentin. He wasn't one of the easiest children."

"What does that mean? In terms of his usual behavior?"

"Parents often wait until their children are completely out of control and they can no longer manage them before putting them into a program like Summit. That puts a lot of pressure on us, trying to get a child from intractable to manageable. If they get them in early on, it's much easier to train them."

"That makes sense."

"When Quentin started out at Summit, he was on strong antipsychotics and still couldn't be controlled. He was violent and there were other children in the home, which made it an emergency situation. He would be held in the municipal jail until a placement could be found for him. And the municipal jail doesn't have the training or resources to deal with a violent teen with autism."

Zachary had seen the inside of a couple himself. Sitting by himself in a barred cell, while the adults in the other cells, the real criminals, catcalled and mocked him, uttering threats and sordid remarks when the guards were out of hearing. Feeling like he'd been dumped there like a bag of trash. No one to turn to. No one who wanted to deal with one more minute of his crap.

"Mr. Goldman?"

"Zachary," he corrected automatically. "Sorry. Just thinking."

She motioned him through the big door, which turned out to be the security door for Quentin's unit.

"So he came here," Nancy said simply. "Home sweet home." She made a twirling motion to include everything in the unit.

"Can we sit down and talk somewhere? Do you have logs of what happened that day and night that we could look at?"

"We log everything." Nancy considered for an instant. "I suppose the response room would be the best. Just let me grab some books."

Zachary waited while she got together what she thought she would need. The unit was quiet, just a few supervisors around, no residents in sight. They were in therapy for long hours every day. They probably wouldn't be found in the unit during the day unless they were sick.

"Had Quentin been sick recently?"

"Sick? No, who told you that?"

"Just wondering. Sometimes an illness can lead to depression…"

"No. He hadn't been sick."

Zachary sat down and glanced over the books that Nancy had collected. "So what do we have?"

"This is Quentin's personal file." She nudged a black binder toward him. "That should contain everything you need. His therapy logs, any observations made during the morning and evening, outside of his therapy. Any… negative behaviors and consequences. Anything that is applicable to him should be in there."

Zachary opened it up. "By consequences, do you mean punishments? Aversives like electric shocks?"

She studied him for a minute, uncertainty written on her face. "That is part of the program here," she agreed. "That's one of the keys that helps us to reach kids like Quentin. Just saying 'no' isn't effective at all on a child like that. There are some children where that's all you need to do. But kids like Quentin need a stronger aversive."

Zachary slowly turned the pages of the binder. It appeared to all be in chronological order. Logs from various sources. Mostly from therapy and the daily log of the unit, checking off the steps to his daily routine. A few narrative lines here and there.

"Okay. And what have you got there?"

"These are the unit logs. Everything that is written in the unit logs should have been transcribed to the personal files. But if you want to double-check…"

Zachary nodded. He looked at the last couple of therapy logs. A brief entry as to what behavior was being taught, followed by long rows and columns of checkmarks and X's. Mostly X's.

"So the checkmarks mean that he showed the right behavior, and the X's mean he showed the wrong behavior," he suppositioned.

Nancy nodded. "Right."

"And when he got a checkmark, he got a reward?"

She smiled at him. "You know the way the program works. Very small rewards, so that we can stretch them out over the length of the therapy. Obviously, you can't give a child a candy for every right behavior, when you're going to have them repeated hundreds of times throughout the day."

"One lick of a lollipop."

"The favorite reward for many of our children. Children with autism can be very motivated by food. You wouldn't believe the number of lollipops and gummy bears we go through here. I go home, and I can't stand anything that smells like a gummy bear!"

"And when he got an X, he didn't get a lick or a gummy bear."

"Right again." She nodded.

"Did he get an aversive?"

"Yes. More than likely."

"So can I interpret this log to mean that every X represents an electrical shock?"

"No, no. You'd have to talk to the therapist or his aide. He might have gotten any aversive. A stern word. Planned ignoring. Taking something away from him. There was a court ruling…" she trailed off, looking hopeful that he already knew about it and would jump in with the details.

But Zachary shook his head, indicating he didn't know about it.

"There were threats that they were going to shut the program down. Some video that got out there on the internet and was being shown out of context. What did people ever do before they could upload to the internet? But our parents are very strong supporters of the program. So they argued in the court to keep the program going. Eventually, the judge agreed, but with some specific guidelines. One of them was that skin shocks were only to be used if a child was being violent or could not physically be controlled without it. So they wouldn't have used shocks for the aversive during therapy. Unless he was being violent."

"Can you tell from the log?"

She turned the binder around so she could look at it right-side-up. Her eyes went over the various headings and comments on the page.

"Well… yes, his therapist does note that he wouldn't cooperate without physical intervention. And Quentin… I know the boy. If he didn't like something, he would hit, bite, spit…"

"So they would have used shocks as the aversive."

"Yes."

"For every one of these X's."

"Maybe not all of them… but probably."

Zachary ran his eye down the column, tallying up the X's. He turned the page and kept going.

"So the day before he died, he had around sixty shocks during therapy."

Nancy swallowed. "If you say so. I wasn't there. You'll have to talk to one of the people who was."

Zachary looked down the evening and night log. It was strange not to see a section for night meds to be checked off. The logs that he'd seen kept at other institutions had always included morning and night meds.

"It looks like there was an incident before lights out." He

rested his finger under the brief words in the log. "What is 'Loss of Privilege Food'?"

"Well, as I said, a lot of the residents are very motivated by food."

"Yes."

"One of the negative reinforcers that is used is the Contingent Food Program."

"What does that mean?"

"It means that food is withheld until the desired behavior is demonstrated."

"During his therapy."

"For as long as necessary to reliably demonstrate the desired behavior."

"You starve him until he does what he's told."

"They don't starve. That's why Loss of Privilege Food is provided. At the end of the day, if their nutritional intake has not been adequate during the Contingent Food Program, they receive Loss of Privilege Food."

Zachary breathed out long and slow. He knew what was coming. Prisons sometimes provided meal replacement foods. Foods that were designed to be unpalatable, but to meet dietary requirements. They had the appropriate levels of calories and macronutrients that were needed, and they were given a vitamin supplement, but the bricks of food replacer were like eating sawdust held together with beef fat. Not pleasant. Not something the prisoners eventually acquired a taste for.

"What was the Loss of Privilege Food?"

"I told you, the food that they received at the end of the day if—"

"No, what is it made of? What form is it in?"

She sucked in her cheeks, looking at the stack of binders. There wasn't any point in avoiding the question. If Nancy refused to answer, he would get it from someone else.

"It's like a meatloaf," she explained. "Ground meat mixed with potato flakes. Spinach and liver powder for additional nutrients. It meets all of the RDAs."

"Would you eat it? Have you tasted it?"

"Uh… it's not meant to be appetizing. They're supposed to be motivated to earn their regular food."

"I don't suppose it's served with gravy and biscuits."

"No… just served cold."

Zachary's stomach turned over. "How long was Quentin on the Contingent Food Program?"

"I'm not sure. It had been a while."

Zachary flipped backward through the daily logs, looking for the notation on each day's chart. It had been more than a while. He returned to the evening before Quentin's death.

"What does this say?"

Nancy leaned closer to the page.

"Uh…" She was reluctant to read what Zachary had already clearly understood. "It says that he refused his Loss of Privilege Food."

"So he went to bed hungry? He didn't get his RDA that day?"

"We can't starve them," Nancy protested. "He could go one day refusing the Loss of Privilege Food, but after that we had to take positive action."

"And…?"

"Force feed it to ensure that he'd had adequate nutrition."

"How?"

"What do you mean?"

"I mean, was he tubed? Fed by mouth? How was he force fed?"

"Uh…" She shifted uncomfortably. "By mouth."

Zachary shook his head in disgust. They wouldn't give him regular food because he liked it and they wanted to use it as a reinforcer. But he still had to get calories and he refused the crap food they tried to give him, so they had held him down and forced it down his throat.

Nancy cleared her throat a few times. He looked at her face and saw that she was struggling with emotion, holding back tears.

"It's not right," she whispered. "I've never agreed with the Contingent Food Program. It's cruel. Food is the only pleasure some of these kids get. To use it against them is… inhumane."

And there was more on the log sheet. They both knew it.

"Were you here or had you gone home?"

"I was still here. I go home right after supper."

"So you saw them doing it. Forcing him to eat the alternative food."

"Yes." She dabbed at the corners of her eyes. "I was here… I saw. It was my job to make sure he got the food he was supposed to."

"Were you the one who did it?"

"No. I couldn't. The security staff and a couple of aides…"

"And he gagged."

"Yes. Some kids are very sensitive to certain textures. Quentin often gagged on the Loss of Privilege Food. It's sort of a lumpy paste…"

"So what happened?" Zachary was looking at the log sheet. He didn't need her to tell him what happened, because it was right there on the log sheet in front of him. But he wanted to hear it from her. To understand just how far the institution was willing to go to break the children they had charge of.

"He threw up. That made them angry. But it wasn't like he did it on purpose! He wasn't just being willful. They shocked him for throwing up. Kept shocking him for struggling. Eventually… they got it down. And it stayed down."

"And what happened after that?"

"By then, it was lights out. I stayed until they had gotten it all down him, a couple of hours past my usual shift change. And then I went home. They were getting him ready for bed."

"What had to be done to get him ready for bed?"

"Changing his clothes. They were soiled. Showering him off. Giving him night clothes and returning him to his room."

Zachary felt like he needed a shower himself. He had done nothing to Quentin; he hadn't participated in his torture. But he felt like he had, just by living his life in ignorance that such barbarism was being practiced right there in his own country. He went on eating what he wanted and sleeping when he could, oblivious to the practices that Margaret Beacher was protesting.

"I expect that after all that, his door was locked."

"No." Nancy shook her head. "Not while I was there. Quentin didn't wander at night. He preferred to stay in his room. We didn't need to lock his door."

"Dr. Abato said that if there had been an incident during the day, his door would be locked at night."

She rolled her eyes. "Dr. Abato isn't here at night and there are no policies that say Quentin's door should be locked if he refuses food. If he'd been violent with one of the staff or the other kids, that would be different. But he hadn't been. He'd just had trouble with therapy."

"He came here because he was violent, didn't he? You didn't have trouble with him with other residents? Or just not that day?"

"Kids are violent in different ways for different reasons. Quentin was pretty typical. He would get angry and violent when he was frustrated. If someone was in his space or took a toy away from him. He couldn't communicate what he wanted. But he didn't wander at night and he didn't attack people at random."

She was silent then, but the tilt of her head and the way that she was leaning toward him suggested that she wasn't finished talking, so he waited.

"If he did get upset or threatening, seeing this is usually all it took to back him off." She tapped one of the little boxes on her belt. The ones with pictures of the children.

"What's that?" Zachary asked. "I thought they were pill boxes, but if you don't give them meds…"

She pulled one of them straight and flipped it over, so that Zachary could see the red button recessed in the back. An inkling of what Nancy was telling him crept into Zachary's consciousness.

All of the guards and aides with boxes on their belts. Boxes with pictures of the residents stuck to them. Not pill boxes. Not schedules. Not keys. A single button that did only one thing.

"That's how you give them shocks?"

"Yes."

Zachary just stared at it. He had thought it was sweet, each of the staff members carrying with them the pictures of the kids they helped care for. He couldn't have been farther off base.

He went back over what Nancy had said last in his mind, rewinding the track and replaying her words. "And Quentin understood what it did. If you showed him your remote, he knew you were going to shock him."

She nodded.

"And that kept him from attacking anyone."

"If he got upset and started to show threatening behavior, seeing the remote would stop him in his tracks. Usually."

"So… him being violent like he was when he was at home… that wasn't a concern."

"Not usually. Though he'd had *some* issues lately. We were usually working on more complex issues."

"Like…" Zachary thought back to his interview with Mira, "speech."

"Speech is one of the most important social skills. If he could have become more adept at communicating with others… it would have been a huge step for him."

"Was that something he could learn to do?"

"He was definitely showing progress. He was able to engage in short conversations."

"His mother said something about them being scripted."

"That's how we start. Getting them to repeat phrases. Learning that one response generally follows another in conversation. It's very complex and takes a long time to teach, but broken down into the smallest building blocks…"

Zachary nodded slowly.

"His mother said that he'd been agitated on her last few visits. Had you noticed any difference in his behavior?"

Nancy ran her fingers through her hair again. "I would say… he'd been having some issues. Maybe hormones. Teen moodiness. More aggression with a boost in testosterone."

Zachary flipped back several pages in his notebook. "She said that when he got agitated, he picked his skin and flapped. He made noises and didn't want to sit down. And banged his head."

Nancy gave a little shrug. "Those are all pretty common behaviors for kids with autism. We try to break them of stims."

"Stims?"

"Self-stimulating behavior. Repetitive, self-soothing behaviors that children with autism often have. Lovaas dictated that all behaviors that make them appear different need to be eliminated, so that nothing will set them apart from their peers and they can become full members of society."

"But… is that really possible?"

"Some of our kids have gone on to become very successful. You really can't tell, looking at a young child, which ones will be successful and which ones will limit themselves. A child that you would have thought was low-functioning leaps over hurdles, and one that you thought was high-functioning and really didn't have that far to go just can't seem to get any movement at all. We tell parents that the younger they can get their kids into the program, the better their chances are. That's just emphasized when you get a child like Quentin, who's basically been allowed to do whatever he wants to for the first twelve years of life and is being asked to work at something for the first time."

"His mom made a mistake not getting him into a program sooner?"

"Yes. He hadn't had any discipline, any consequences. She had babied him. So the program was quite a shock for him."

Zachary grimaced at her choice of words and bit his lip to avoid saying 'literally.'

"You said that he liked to stay in his room and didn't wander at night, so his sleep was pretty good?"

"Most of our kids have some sleep issues. Especially if they've been taking sleep aids for years before they come here. We find that a strict schedule, with no variations in lights-out and wake-up time on weekends and holidays is the best remedy."

"They didn't get negative consequences—aversives—if they had sleep problems?" The institutions Zachary had lived in had been pretty strict about any nighttime activities that varied from the prescribed sleep and wake time. No getting out of bed. No wandering. No trips to the bathroom. No complaining about having nightmares. Even having nightmares was considered bad behavior. So was sleepwalking.

"We tried to keep things calm and relaxed after lights-out," Nancy hedged. "You don't want to be upsetting the residents at bedtime, when they're supposed to be settling down."

"No shocks after lights-out?" Zachary ventured.

"Well… not usually."

Zachary scratched his head and wrote a couple of lines in his notepad. It was obvious Nancy didn't want to make things sound any worse. Zachary decided to back off a little. If he wanted her to answer any more questions, he was going to have to take it easy and not back her into a corner. She was currently his only cooperative information source.

"Tell me what happens after lights-out. Bed checks? What's the night-time supervision like?"

"The security staff make sure that everyone is in their rooms and accounted for. Some of the kids pace or stim for a long time before going to sleep, so there's no rule that they have to be in bed, just in their rooms. There is someone on the unit all the time, making sure there are no problems. Security does rounds a few times each night." She pulled one of the binders out of the stack and flipped pages to find the night that Quentin had died.

Zachary studied the initialed spaces. The initials were not readable, but the same squiggly mess was on each of the lines. Two hours apart. Which meant that Quentin's death should have been noticed on three separate checks.

"And the guard who signed off on these checks is no longer with Summit?"

"Dr. Abato said he should have noticed Quentin's death some time before it was discovered. So… he was asked to resign his position."

"To take the fall. So that it would look like Summit was taking this seriously."

"He *should* have noticed something was wrong," Nancy said.

Zachary nodded. He tried to visualize everything in his mind. He had seen the bedroom. He had seen the pictures of Quentin's body in the bedroom before it was removed. He had spent many hours locked in rooms like that, peering through windows like the one in Quentin's door. The viewing angles were limited. A child lying on the floor might be difficult to see clearly.

"The person who found him in the morning. Was that… you?"

Nancy nodded. She looked tired. Like she had seen too much, and she just didn't want to see any more. Too much sadness. Too many kids in pain. Too much loss.

"Yes. I went to see why he hadn't come out for breakfast. He'd been on Contingent for so long, he was always one of the first ones out, looking for something to eat."

Zachary refrained from pointing out that they would then refuse to give him breakfast because he wasn't able to demonstrate all of the proper behaviors. He waited for Nancy to gather her thoughts and tell him what had happened.

Nancy stared off into space, looking past Zachary.

"I thought maybe he was sick. Or maybe he'd just given up after the night before. I opened his door and I saw him on the floor."

"Did you know right away…?"

"I didn't want to accept it. I imagined he was still sleeping or not feeling well, or that it was some kind of prank or joke, and someone was watching to see what my reaction would be."

Zachary had been in that type of situation before. There was always the initial moment of disbelief. The moment when his brain refused to believe what he was seeing and sought any other explanation.

"He was on the floor with his blankets around him, but he didn't look like he was asleep." Nancy swallowed, and went on, voice strained. "He had wrapped his blanket around his neck and then twisted it tighter and tighter…"

The pictures from the police hadn't shown that. The blanket had been removed from his throat in order to check his pulse or administer first aid.

"How was it positioned? Did it look like he could have done it himself? The twisted ends… were they in the front…? Not the back?"

Nancy nodded. Her hands moved of their own accord, as if she were untwisting the blanket. Fingers gentle.

"I couldn't believe it. I kept thinking that it was all a mistake. A nightmare. But there he was, stiff and cold. Like he was made of wax."

"I'm sorry. That must have been very hard on you."

She nodded, blinking tears.

"I have another question for you, and I know it's very difficult. But… did he have the ability to form the intent to commit suicide?"

"I'm not sure what you mean."

"Just… this is a child who couldn't carry on a real conversation. Who lashed out when he was upset. Who banged his head. Did he… did he have the ability to decide he wanted to kill himself and then devise a plan like this to strangle himself, and then to follow through with it? I would think… those are some sophisticated thought processes. Could he do more than just react to a stimulus? Did he have the ability to think all of that out?"

Nancy looked at him. She stroked the smooth cover of one of the binders.

"I don't think I'm qualified to judge," she said finally. "So often, I would think that a child wasn't paying any attention to me. That they hadn't even been aware of the fact that I was talking to them, much less actually paying attention and able to understand what I had said. Just to have them do something that proved me wrong. I think that difficulty with speech is the most disabling thing for our kids... No feedback into what's really going on in their brains. Quentin might have been brilliant; I have no way of knowing. He was definitely adept at resisting a stimulus. He proved *that* to us time and time again. But was it evidence of higher reasoning abilities? Or just stubbornness? Or maybe he had no idea what we wanted him to do. Maybe it was an accident. Maybe he was just soothing himself with deep pressure, and then it was too tight, and he couldn't get it off."

"Who was here that night and had access to his room? If his door wasn't locked, then that includes anyone with access to the unit."

"That would include practically everyone at Summit. We can all go from wing to wing and unit to unit with very few restrictions. I can give you a list of the people I know were here that night. But everyone who *might* have been here? Like I said. Anyone."

"Was there anyone who had a problem with Quentin? Someone he got into fights with? Or who resented him? Someone he had hurt or made to look bad in one of his violent outbursts?"

"No," Nancy shook her head. "It's not like that. We're just here to do a job. Sure, it's stressful and some of the residents can be miserable to deal with. But at the end of the day... we go home, and they stay here." She shrugged. "As far as any of the other residents doing something to hurt him... no, no one in the unit would do that. We have other kids at Summit too, kids who have mental illness or are delinquent rather than developmentally disabled and they're different... I'm sure some of them would be able to do something intentionally violent or evil. But our kids with autism, no. All of the children in this unit are the same. They are all developmentally delayed, not mentally ill or delinquent. They don't make enemies with each other. Mostly, they'd rather just be left alone."

Zachary nodded and made a couple more notes. "Did he have any particular friends?" he asked. "Do any of them develop friendships…?"

"Of course, yes. Even those who are the most socially awkward still seem to be able to transcend language and social convention and hit it off sometimes. It can be quite sweet. I know that Quentin had one little fellow who was quite attached to him. They went to therapy one after the other, so they would pass in the hallway or waiting area. Started noticing each other and waving. This little guy gave Quentin a hug one day. And another day, Quentin spontaneously tries his 'hello, how are you?' script on him. So cute."

Zachary nodded. "Who was his friend?"

"Raymond. Ray-Ray, they call him."

"I met him. So does that mean Sophie was Quentin's therapist too?"

"Yes."

Would Sophie have seemed like a big, scary woman to Quentin as much as she did to Ray-Ray? Remembering how dogged she had been about getting Ray-Ray's compliance, Zachary had to wonder how she got the compliance of the bigger, stronger, more violent boy.

But he knew how.

With sixty shocks in one session, as recorded in Quentin's log book.

12

Zachary had planned on getting a good night's sleep. It had been a long, emotionally taxing day, and it would have been best if he could have gotten in a full night's sleep for once and woken up refreshed in the morning, ready to take on the day.

But he'd emailed Margaret Beacher when he got back to Bowman's apartment, asking for some more information and she had emailed back some reference material. He didn't want to go to bed until he'd had a chance to look over what she'd sent.

He skimmed over articles by adults with autism who echoed what Margaret had said about ABA and similar therapies causing long-lasting problems such as PTSD and other issues that the ABA practitioners had never anticipated. Margaret's was not a lone voice.

One of the files she sent him was a book by Ivar Lovaas, whose name Zachary had heard several times in connection with ABA. He opened it up, expecting that it would be filled with a lot of clinical studies and dense medical language, but it was written as a guide for parents and was quite readable. Zachary started to skim over the introduction, then stopped and went back to the beginning to read it carefully. He checked the copyright page. The copyright was 1981, not the Victorian Era. He used his cursor to highlight a few of the lines in the introduction.

No one has the right to be taken care of, no matter how retarded he is. So, put your child to work; his work is to learn.

They have no right to act bizarrely.

No right? Zachary's mind immediately went to Margaret Beacher talking about being punished for who she was. According to Lovaas, she had to be trained to act like everyone else. Lovaas gave instructions to parents on managing their child's weight, clothing, hair, and appearance to make sure they couldn't be differentiated from their peers.

Zachary went on to read the next chapter, outlining the basics of the program. He read about the reward system he had already seen in action, using small treats and praise to encourage the desired behaviors. Then the references to punishments started to pop up. Zachary read on.

By becoming firm with your child, and perhaps making him a little upset or scared by yelling at him or hitting his bottom, your social rewards (saying "Good" and your kisses and hugs) become almost immediately more important and effective for him. It is as if he appreciates you more, once you have shown him that you also can be angry with him.

Zachary put his hands over the words and looked away from the page. He closed his eyes, breathing evenly.

Zachary was intimately familiar with the phenomenon Lovaas referred to.

'Traumatic bonding' resulted when the victim was alternately abused and rewarded by the perpetrator and was most effective when the perpetrator controlled the necessaries of life, such as food and freedom of movement. It was the abuse/remorse cycle that made battered wives and abused children cling to and defend their abusers. In kidnap situations it was referred to as Stockholm Syndrome. It was the method cults used to brainwash their victims and gangs used during initiation to gain the loyalty of their members.

Of course, Lovaas hadn't intended the parent to traumatize the child. He apparently didn't anticipate that his training methods would cause PTSD. Spankings were not commonly considered abuse in the eighties. But what looked 'a little upset' to an adult could actually be an expression of trauma in a child. A few pages later, in recommending that adults practice hitting friends to see how hard was hard enough, Lovaas reported, "We have heard about children who have been hit or pinched so hard that their skin is dramatically discolored. It seems quite unnecessary to use such strong physical aversives." Well, bully for him.

Zachary left the document on his screen and got up to pace across the room. Lovaas's words made him physically ill. He was nauseated. He tried to focus on the movement of his body and not slide into flashbacks. He wasn't sure how many more times he could read words like "Use as much physical force as is necessary to make him complete the task" before he succumbed.

He returned to his computer and went on to the next page, hoping it would be less offensive, and found:

You may have to exert considerable physical force to help him comply. You may at such times run the risk of bruising or physically hurting the child, or the child you are working with may be physically so big that you can't budge him. This is a serious drawback.

Zachary clicked ahead to the next chapter. It was, unfortunately, titled "Physical Punishment," so he had a pretty good idea it wasn't going to be any less upsetting. He went into the kitchen and made a pot of coffee. He would have preferred alcohol, but he couldn't combine that with his meds.

With caffeine and Xanax on board, Zachary paced for a few more minutes, then went back to the book. Lovaas made a good argument for putting a stop to life-threatening behaviors like self-injury, extreme aggression, chewing on electrical cords, and running in front of traffic. Any parent could see the importance of eliminating the activities that could get their child killed. Zachary could almost see the justification for using aversives in those cases.

But then Lovaas threw the baby out with the bathwater in advising:

For other sets of behaviors, the decision of whether or not to use physical punishment may seem less clear-cut, although these behaviors may be just as damaging to the child. For example, there is a group of behaviors, such as endless rocking, spinning, eye rolling, arm flapping, gazing, etc., that seem quite "addictive" to many children ... You may attempt to suppress such behaviors by using punishment.

Of course, he recommended using non-physical punishment before resorting to causing pain, but if nothing else worked, "painful electric shock" was offered as an option.

It was almost morning when Zachary finished working his way through the book and closed his computer. His eyes were itchy and aching. After an emotionally challenging day, he'd spent the night working through the text, fighting to stay focused and to push his way through the anger and nausea it engendered. Even with chemical aids, it was a hard-fought battle, and he fell into his blankets on the couch thoroughly exhausted.

For once, sleep came easily. His brain had been trying to shut down for hours, assaulted by the images brought on by the book and Zachary's past. When he finally let go, he spun quickly into darkness.

The images that came to his dreams this time were not of Annie at Bonnie Brown. Instead, Quentin's face stuck in his mind. And Ray-Ray's. And those of others he had seen at Summit just in passing. He saw a menacing Dr. Abato with a cattle prod. Children who were crying or afraid.

Zachary himself had been silenced. He couldn't speak to Dr. Abato. Couldn't protest the treatment of the children the institute was supposed to be helping and protecting. Abato and Sophie and the other staff he'd been introduced to talked as if he weren't there, yelled at him, pushed him from place to place and forced him to perform menial tasks; gluing pages, washing floors, putting toys into a bin, just to have them dumped out again and to repeat the job again. They gave him terse commands, like an animal. Like Lovaas instructed in his book.

Sit! Good sitting.

Quiet hands!

Touch your nose.

Touch your ear.

Give me a hug.

Any time he hesitated, someone grabbed his hands and forced him to perform the task. He felt demeaned. Humiliated. When he did well, and they tried to put a gummy bear in his mouth, he spat it out, disgusted.

And then he was watching as Quentin fought and fought against their commands. He tried to escape Sophie's strong hands as Dr. Abato stood by, brandishing the cattle prod, getting closer and threatening to shock him.

Ray-Ray was there, in the other direction, crying about something. He was alone, his face pressed against the observation window, babbling something incomprehensible to Quentin. Dr. Abato was there and grabbed Ray-Ray by the arm to pull him into the room. Quentin and Ray-Ray gravitated toward each other. Quentin held the smaller boy against himself protectively, sheltering him from Abato and Sophie. Quentin's eyes were hidden by his fringe of hair.

"Leave them alone!" Zachary tried to shout. He couldn't get the words out. Nothing would come out of his mouth. He tried to move between the boys and Abato. Dr. Abato just laughed and shoved the cattle prod toward Zachary, hitting him in the shoulder with it.

Zachary let out a shout, trying to pull away from the jolt of pain.

And he was on the couch. Or half-on, half-off the couch,

hands raised defensively against Bowman, his shoulder still buzzing with the charge he had only dreamed.

"Chill out," Bowman said. "It's okay. Relax. You were just dreaming. Hell, I thought we were under attack the way you were screaming."

Zachary tried to catch his breath.

"Are you okay?" Bowman asked.

"Yeah." Zachary blew out a stream of air and looked up at the ceiling, trying to banish the dream. "Yeah. I'm sorry. I just… I guess it was all just a dream." He shook his head and shuddered. It had felt real. He felt like he had been there. Like he had been one of them. It made perfect sense that he would identify with the residents at Summit, after all the times he had been institutional- ized, all of the times that he had been silenced and prevented from making his own choices. From being his own person.

"That must have been some nightmare."

Zachary pushed himself into a sitting position on the couch, rather than sprawling like a spider across it. He rubbed his eyes and looked around, trying to get reoriented.

It was getting light out. Bowman sighed and sat down on the couch next to Zachary. He had on pajama bottoms and a robe, not done up, so that Zachary could see his hairy belly and drooping physique. Bowman's hair was mussed and he smelled sweaty and garlicky.

"Look, Zach," he said slowly. "You know it's time for you to move on. You've got your check for the fire from the insurance company. That means you have the money to put down a deposit on a place of your own. You need a place where you have the room to move around as much as you like, your own bed, to keep whatever hours you want. You need all those things. You can't just stay here forever."

Zachary rubbed his forehead, his face hot and uncomfortable. He hadn't even been the one who had asked Bowman if he could stay there. That had been Kenzie. And it had been for 'a few days' while Zachary sorted out his problems and got back on his feet again. Zachary had long since outstayed his 'few days.' Bowman had been remarkably patient about having someone around the place. He even seemed to like it sometimes. But it had to be wearing for him to have someone underfoot all the time. For him not to be able to use the living room whenever he wanted to, or to come and go without worrying about disturbing Zachary, or to bring a lady friend home.

"Yeah, you're right," he agreed sheepishly. "I should have been out of here ages ago. I'll find something and get out of your way. I'm sorry."

"No, no need to be sorry. I'm happy to help out someone down on his luck. What were you supposed to do with no home, or car, or even a wallet? I was glad when Kenzie said you needed something. It's just time now."

No one has the right to be taken care of.

The phrase echoed in Zachary's head. He was a grown man. Not a teenager. Not like the residents at Summit. He had the ability to take care of himself, and he needed to do it instead of relying on Bowman or someone else. It didn't matter how anxious it made him to think about living on his own again. About how he had already burned two homes to the ground. That wasn't going to happen again. He had lived on his own for twenty years. It was wrong to go on taking advantage of his friend. Before he had moved in with Bowman, they had barely been nodding acquaintances. They certainly hadn't known all of the intimate details of each other's lives. Bowman had known about Bridget and the disastrous end of their relationship, but he didn't know the details, only the broad strokes.

"You don't have to be gone tomorrow," Bowman said, putting his hand on Zachary's knee. "But it's time to start finding alternative arrangements."

"Yeah. For sure. I'm sorry to have put you out for so long."

Bowman nodded. He pushed himself back up from the couch. He stood looking down at Zachary.

"You're going to be okay?"

"Yeah. I'm okay. Just a dream."

"You're still seeing that new therapist…? And going to your group…?"

"Yeah. Of course." Though Zachary had skipped both that week, deeming the homicide case to be more important than sessions where they would just tell him the same things they had been telling him the past few weeks. He knew that they were supposed to be helping him, but he couldn't help but feel like they just stirred things up that were better left alone.

"Good. Try to get back to sleep."

Bowman returned to his bedroom. Zachary wondered whether Bowman would be able to go back to sleep again. The faint light of the rising sun meant that it wasn't long before Bowman would have to be up and getting ready for his Saturday morning shift.

Zachary knew that if he tried to go back to sleep again, he would only keep on dreaming. And Bowman would not be able to get any more sleep if Zachary kept waking him up with nightmares.

Zachary opened up his computer and started searching for a new apartment.

As much as he was learning to hate Summit Living Center, Zachary knew that he had to go back again. He had spent the weekend focused on finding a new living arrangement, pretending that he didn't have anything else pressing to do. But when Monday rolled around, he knew he had to leave the house-hunting alone and head back to Summit. He hadn't learned everything he could from the witnesses. He hadn't fully investigated the circumstances surrounding Quentin's death. Before he could decide whether Quentin had killed himself or had had a little help in that direction, Zachary needed to better understand what Quentin had been going through.

"We don't have a lot of people who want to know all of the

details of Electric Shock Devices and how they fit into a therapeutic program," Dr. Abato told him, after having Zachary sit down in one of the big cushioned chairs of his spacious office. "A few reporters. Every now and then, someone else from the outside who wants to see how it works."

Zachary nodded. So far, he had been surprised that Abato was willing to talk about the shocks and hadn't told him to stay away and just drop the case. He kept waiting for Dr. Abato to say no, he couldn't see anything else. But Abato had instead said that Zachary could observe shocks being administered and be shown how ABA worked using shocks as an aversive.

"I understand that it all sounds rather barbaric," Dr. Abato said with a reassuring smile. "But it really isn't any different than what regular parents do with regular kids in need of discipline every day. A spank or a slapped hand or arm to deter a child from reaching for a hot stove or to put an end to a tantrum. We're doing the same thing, just on a larger scale. And by using the skin shocks, we can ensure that the discipline is always consistently applied and there is no risk of injury."

Zachary was reserving judgment on that one.

"I've arranged for you to observe a training session with one of our residents and his parents. Parents need to be trained in how to control their children properly so that when they are able to return home, they don't lose the progress that they have made in the program. The parents can keep applying the program consistently so that the child can continue to learn and grow and become more normal and independent."

"But you can't really make them normal," Zachary said. "I mean, there's no cure for autism, right? What you're doing here is trying to make them act more normal, to develop better skills and functioning… not to cure them."

"If we can make them indistinguishable from their peers, then what do you call that? Do you call that a cure? Autism is a developmental delay, so even if they develop to their full potential, it is going to take longer for them to get there. But having taken longer to get there, are they then cured? It's all a matter of semantics, Mr. Goldman, and I'm not sure it matters. Our goal here is to push them as far as we possibly can, to become as normal as they possibly can be."

"Okay," Zachary agreed uncomfortably, not sure what to make of Dr. Abato's answer.

"Come with me."

Dr. Abato once again escorted Zachary to his destination. But this time, their destination wasn't the reward rooms or even the therapy rooms. It wasn't the living quarters that Quentin had been housed in. Instead, Abato took him to another unit. Though it had the same layout as Quentin's unit, it was obvious as soon as they arrived that it was different. Zachary could hear yelling and banging going on behind the doors. He caught glimpses of residents who looked wild or furious. Young children, older adults, but mostly teens, and mostly boys. Zachary believed without being told that the cell doors were all locked.

Dr. Abato was watching Zachary for his reaction. "A little different, isn't it?" he asked indulgently, seeming to enjoy Zachary's discomfort. "It's one thing to philosophize about what is best for children with autism; it's quite another to see the sort of war zone they can cause."

"Yes," Zachary agreed.

They went past the individual bedrooms to a larger room that Zachary was reluctant to call a meeting room, even though that was what the plaque beside the door said. Meeting Room B.

It was a large, empty room. No table and chairs. No rug or bean bag chairs. It was completely bare. But it wasn't unoccupied. There was a boy who appeared to be fifteen or so, a stocky boy with brown hair curling down over his ears and into his eyes, a round, cheeky face that had probably made him a cute baby and little boy. But cute wasn't what he was anymore. A woman and a man were focused on him. The woman had blond and gray hair pulled back into a half bun, and the man was husky, with shaved-short hair and stubble on his face. They both looked irritated and angry. There was also a therapist standing nearby, with smooth red hair and a white smock, and a slim, blond female aide with a heavy utility belt hung with shock remotes. One of which was bound to have the stocky boy's picture on it.

Dr. Abato took Zachary to an observation window, where they sat down to watch like it was a movie being played for their own entertainment.

"This is Angel Salk," Dr. Abato told Zachary. "And his parents, of course. We won't go in, as it looks like the room is quite crowded enough already. We'll just observe for a while."

Zachary nodded, his stomach tight with anticipation.

"Angel is violent, a danger to both himself and others. We are having some success in teaching him, but his parents need to learn how to control him. They are here to see how it all works."

They seemed to have caught Angel and his parents mid-confrontation. Angel had his back up against the wall, both parents in his face. The man grabbed Angel's wrists in one hand and his shoulder in the other and shoved him violently into the wall.

"You need to listen!" he said to Angel in a furious tone.

Zachary was ready to jump right through the window to save the boy from the assault. But neither of the professionals seemed to find it the least bit disturbing.

"Mom, you need to get in there too," the therapist directed. "You need to show him that you are both united. He can't play one of you against the others like he might have done in the past."

The mother moved in closer, but was clearly reluctant to touch her son.

"Put your hand on his chin," the therapist said. "Open his mouth. Tell him he needs to use his words."

When she reached her hand out, Angel tried to pull away, thrashing his head back and forth. But the father had a tight grip on him and kept pressing him against the wall. The mother eventually managed to grasp Angel's chin, and she pulled it down, squeezing her fingers into his cheeks between his teeth to separate his jaws farther.

"Use words," she said, her voice quiet, catching in her throat.

"Louder, Mom," the therapist instructed. "He needs to hear your directions clearly, or this doesn't work."

"Use words!" the woman said in a near-shout.

Angel was wincing and trying to pull away. Then he suddenly went rigid and cried out. Both parents looked at the therapist in surprise. It was the aide who had pressed the shock button, but the therapist nodded that this was the correct action.

"Tell him again," she said. "Don't let go. Give him the same instruction again."

"Use words." The woman's voice was quieter this time, but still clear.

Angel yelled something incomprehensible around his mother's fingers.

Again, the same reaction as Angel suddenly went rigid again, his arms splayed out.

Zachary looked at Abato, who apparently saw nothing to be concerned about. Zachary studied Angel, seeing the cuffs around his arms and legs, wires leading under his clothes, and then out of his clothes and into the black backpack he had on. The same black backpack that Zachary had seen so many of the other residents wearing. He had thought they were schoolbags, but they were apparently part of the shock device.

"Tell him again," the therapist said.

"Use words," the mother said. Her voice dropped slightly. "Come on, Angel. Be a good boy. You can use your words."

"Don't coddle him. Don't use more words than are necessary for him to understand what you expect of him."

"Use words," she said again.

"No!" The sound burst from Angel's throat in protest.

"Good talking," the mother said immediately, looking over at the therapist for approval. "That's good talking, Angel." She stuffed something into his partially-open mouth.

Angel gagged and struggled, breaking free of his father. He bounced to the other side of the room, hands up defensively like an animal ready to claw someone's eyes out. He was closer to the observation window, so Zachary could see him better.

Angel's arms were pitted with scars and scabs. He had a bruise on his forehead, mostly hidden by his messy brown locks. His parents had apparently not read Lovaas's instructions on keeping their son's hair properly cut so that he wouldn't look different from his peers.

Angel went rigid again and let out an animal-like cry. He reached for one of the armbands and slid his fingers underneath the shocking device. There was another shock from the aide.

"Leave the electrodes," the aide snapped. "Don't touch the electrodes."

Angel tried again, then flailed his arms and tried to shake off the pain of the shock.

"You need to control him again," the therapist instructed. "Hold him in one place and give him the instruction again."

"But he did it," Angel's mother protested. "He spoke."

"Once. He needs to do it every time. Without fighting."

The father circled, trying to get ahold of him again. Angel evaded capture and was shocked again. His father managed to get ahold of him during the couple of seconds he was being shocked and shoved him into the wall again.

"Use words," the mother instructed, her voice high and tight, not holding on to his jaw this time.

Angel's father grabbed his jaw and squeezed until Angel was forced to open his mouth. "Use words," he growled.

Angel garbled out a sound, but if it was speech it was incomprehensible. He was shocked again. The mother started sniffling and protesting.

"You need to be strong with him," the therapist ordered. "You can't be crying and letting him control the session. You are in charge. Whatever he does to manipulate you, you have to be strong and resist it. Give him a different instruction. Tell him to give you a hug."

Angel's father let go of him so that Angel would be able to obey the instruction if he were so inclined. Angel backed away from them, scratching his arms and then his face. He started to flap his hands beside his face.

"No stimming," the aide said, immediately shocking him.

Angel went rigid, but as soon as the shock was finished, he was flapping again, faster and more frantic this time. He opened his mouth and started to make a noise, a guttural hooting.

"He's trying to communicate," Zachary said to Dr. Abato.

"He's merely voicing."

Another shock, which stopped Angel in his tracks for a moment, and then he started flapping again. Another shock within seconds of the last, and he fell to the floor, screaming in pain and scrabbling at another electrode that must have been on his torso under his shirt.

Angel's mother cried out and she took a step forward to go to him. But Mr. Salk reached out and stopped her. "He's just trying to get attention," he warned.

"He's hurt! My baby."

"He's not hurt," the therapist said. "He's just fine. He's drama- tizing to get your sympathy. You need to ignore this behavior. Insist that he get up. Tell him to give you a hug."

Angel's mother was unable to follow the instructions. His father made a noise of disgust and reached down to grab Angel by the arm. He was a big boy; he had to be at least a hundred and eighty pounds, but Mr. Salk had no trouble pulling him to his feet.

"Hug your mother," he instructed. His expression was blank. If he felt any sympathy for his son, he had shut it down and locked it away in order to continue with the training session.

Angel held his arms wide. He didn't look in his mother's direc- tion or walk over to her, but the invitation was there. His mother crooned and got closer to him. "Good boy. Good boy, Angel," she praised, putting her arms around him. His arms went tightly around her body in a squeeze that was clearly not meant to be a gentle hug of affection, and Mrs. Salk yelped in pain.

Angel's arms flew open as he was shocked, and his mother freed herself, her face pale and frightened. Angel flapped his hands. "Ma!"

"He didn't mean to," Angel's mother excused him. "He didn't mean to hurt me." She put her arms out for him again. "Gentle this time, Angel. Give me a nice hug. Gentle."

Angel continued to flap his hands, not approaching his mother, trying to watch all of the people in the room at once.

"No stimming," the therapist commanded. If anything, Angel flapped harder. He moaned, pacing the room. He jolted with another shock.

"Give me a hug," Angel's mother repeated.

"No…" The word was a long moan. Angel's head snapped back with another shock.

"He's trying to talk," Zachary said to Dr. Abato. "Isn't that what you want?"

"He is refusing to speak when he's asked to speak, and speaking when he's asked to hug," Dr. Abato said. "Does that sound like he's being obedient or manipulative?"

"I don't think he's being intentionally disobedient," Zachary protested. "He's upset. Confused."

"And you're drawing upon what expertise?" Dr. Abato asked, his lip curling slightly.

"I don't have any expertise. I'm just observing…"

"Well, we have decades of expertise and training between us. And we have dealt with Angel before. This is typical, and he's suckered better than you. He'll do whatever he can to resist doing what he's told. We need to break him of that behavior if we're going to get anywhere with him."

Zachary shook his head. "This isn't right. He's got to have some basic human rights."

Quentin had undergone sixty shocks the day he had died.

Zachary now had a much clearer picture of what that entailed. And they had withheld food. *How was what they were doing any better than the torture in a POW camp?*

"I understand this is hard to watch. You asked to see how the skin shock therapy works. I'm not sanitizing it. Angel is just the type of child that we need the shocks for. He has been in dozens of other programs that have not been able to help him and curb his violence. This is the only program that has any chance of rehabilitating his behavior, and his parents know it. Do you think they would go through this if they thought there was any other way?"

Zachary swallowed and shook his head. Obviously not. Especially not his mother. But his father too had been driven past his limits, disengaging from his own emotions in order to continue the therapy.

"Let's do some sensory work," the therapist suggested. "Angel is obviously sensory-seeking at this point. Flapping. Hugging too hard. Behaving in a way that demands we hold him still. Acting-out behaviors that he knows will get him shocks. He's actually seeking out the negative attention."

His parents both nodded as if this made sense. Zachary shook his head. The suggestion that Angel wanted to be shocked was ridiculous. It was obvious that it caused him pain and distress.

"We know Angel," Dr. Abato reminded Zachary. "You haven't seen the lengths he goes through to get attention."

"Sit with him on the floor," the therapist directed. "Make sure he's sitting properly, and we'll work on desensitization."

"Sit down," Mr. Salk ordered in a loud voice.

Angel didn't comply. He jolted with a shock and brushed at his arm as if trying to flick away a fly or stinging insect.

"Sit down."

He still ranged about the room as if he couldn't stop moving. Zachary could see him trying to watch everyone at once, an impossibility even in the small space.

"Angel, please sit down," his mother contributed, her voice pleading.

When he didn't obey, he received another shock. His father caught him, grappled with him for a minute, and tried to throw him to the floor.

"Stand clear of him," the aide instructed. Zachary switched his attention to her, and he watched her finger depress the button on Angel's remote once, then again, and again, without giving him any time to recover or comply in between. Angel howled and fell to the floor writhing and trying to pull the electrodes away from his skin. "He's got his arm band loose," the therapist told the aide. "You'd better secure it."

In spite of the fact that Angel was a large boy and known to be violent, the aide didn't appear to have any fear of approaching him. She picked up Angel's right arm, and Zachary could see that the electrode band had slipped from its previous position. There was a large red welt where it had been attached. The aide moved it to just below the welt and tightened the band again to secure it in place.

"He has a mark," Zachary told Dr. Abato. "There must be something wrong with the electrode. It's not supposed to cause any damage, is it?"

"Repeated shocks can cause some redness. It's superficial and will fade. The aide has reattached the cuff away from the irritated skin. That's appropriate."

"But what about the other electrodes? If that one has caused damage, aren't the others doing the same thing? Shouldn't they all be moved? Maybe he's had enough today."

"Just watch, Mr. Goldman. Let's give them a few more minutes."

Zachary pressed his lips together and watched the mother and father sit down on the floor with their son. The aide moved Angel into a sitting position, prompting him with 'Good sitting, Angel. Show us good sitting,' and guiding his limbs into place until he was sitting cross-legged in a triangle with his parents.

"Good job," his mother praised softly.

"Let's work on light touch. You are going to work on giving

Angel light touch and encouraging him to give you light touch in return," the therapist explained.

Both parents nodded, looking at him.

"Mom, I want you to rest your hand on Angel's arm, and to stroke it gently downward."

"He doesn't like—" she started to protest.

"I'm aware he doesn't like it. That's why we're trying to desensitize him."

Angel's mother put her hand tentatively on Angel's forearm and brushed it down the length. Angel jerked back, grimacing as if she had hurt him.

Zachary leaned forward, trying to get a better look at Angel's arm. As he had noted, the surface of Angel's arm was pitted and dimpled with scar tissue and small red scabs. It must have been painful for him.

"That's gentle touch, Angel. Can you give your mother gentle touch?" The therapist moved closer to the little group, making Angel cock his head sharply to keep an eye on her.

Angel's mother lifted his hand and placed it on her arm to encourage the desired action. Angel jerked back, his shoulders hunching protectively. He scratched his arm and started picking at one of the scabs.

"No picking. Show your mother gentle touch. Give gentle touch."

When he continued to pick the scabs, Angel received a jolt. He turned his head to watch the aide, completely aware who it was causing him pain.

Angel's mother again picked up his hand and placed it on her arm, then gently drew it down. "See, Angel? Gentle touch. Good job!"

She put her hand into her pocket and produced a small candy, but when she tried to put it in his mouth, Angel batted her hand away, sending the candy flying across the room. He went rigid with the resulting punishment shock and tried to reach the electrode positioned behind his back. Zachary frowned. *Was* Angel preferring the shocks over the positive reinforcer?

"Dad, your turn. Give Angel a gentle touch and then encourage him to reciprocate."

Mr. Salk gave Angel's arm a cursory pat.

"That's not enough," the therapist scolded. "Give his arm a slower, gentle stroke."

Angel's father scowled at her. He put his hand again on Angel's scarred, pock-marked arm and stroked down gently.

Angel again reacted as if the touch were painful, flinging his father's hand off and making a mad-bull sound of protest. His shoulders went back at a shock and he dug at his belly, trying to get at an electrode under his shirt.

"Give your father a gentle touch," the therapist ordered, her voice hard. The contrast between the words and the woman's tone was surreal.

Angel reached his hand out and placed it on his father's meaty arm.

"Good," the therapist praised. "Good gentle touch. Give him a reward, Dad."

Angel's father pulled away from his son's touch and checked his pockets. Mrs. Salk handed him a candy. He held it out toward Angel. Angel pincered it between his fingers and held it up to his nose.

"In your mouth," the therapist told him. She looked at Angel's father. "Put it straight in his mouth, don't give him the opportunity to play with it."

"Last time I did that, he bit me."

"In your mouth," she said again, as Angel touched the candy to his tongue. The therapist sent a look at the aide, who again pressed the shock button.

Angel flung the candy away. He struck out at his father, howling in pain or anger. Mr. Salk turned aside to avoid a blow to his face, getting hit in the shoulder instead. Angel writhed on the floor. Zachary again saw the aide hitting the button repeatedly, overriding the built-in two-second shock, cycling through all of the electrodes.

So much for delivering a consistent punishment every time.

"Stop them!" Zachary told Dr. Abato, grabbing him by the arm. "They can't do that! She's not following the protocol. She can't keep shocking him like that! Stop them!"

Abato looked at Zachary for a moment, his dark eyes glittering. Then he reached out and rapped his knuckles twice on the observation window.

The adults in the room all looked at each other. Angel paid no attention to the noise, moaning and making loud, incoherent noises of protest, his body doubled up on the floor. The therapist nodded at the aide, who went to the door, opened it, and looked out at the observation chairs to see what was wrong.

Her eyes widened when she saw Dr. Abato sitting there.

"This session is over," Dr. Abato said calmly. "Return Angel to his room."

"His parents came for a full day of training," she protested. "They had to drive all that way and we've just barely started…"

"Explain to them there is a problem with the equipment. We'll have to reschedule."

She stood looking at him for a long moment, then nodded and returned to the meeting room.

The therapist's face grew red as the aide explained the cancellation of the session to the Salks. The aide coaxed Angel to his feet and took him from the room. His hands were flapping as he was escorted past Zachary and Dr. Abato. The therapist apologized to Angel's parents and she stalked out into the hallway to find out what was going on. Dr. Abato rose from his seat to talk to her. Zachary was happy to get to his feet. His whole body was clenched in a tight knot. He turned his head back and forth to try to loosen up his muscles.

"It would appear there is a problem with the ESD," Abato told the angry therapist. "Miss Kelly was having to press the remote several times to get a proper shock. We may need to re-evaluate alternatives."

"He was getting a shock, that was obvious!"

Dr. Abato glanced over at Zachary. "Mr. Goldman noticed that Miss Kelly was having to press the remote several times. Whether that is an equipment malfunction or whether it is becoming less effective, I don't know. We will have to investigate further."

The therapist glared at Zachary, then apparently decided she'd better listen to Dr. Abato. She nodded. "Fine."

"Please have his parents reschedule for another day."

She nodded again and walked back into the meeting room to discuss it in a low voice with Mr. and Mrs. Salk.

"We will look into this matter," Dr. Abato told Zachary. "I appreciate your help."

"You would have let her just keep shocking him continuously."

"Sometimes the equipment malfunctions. I'm glad you noticed there was an issue. I'm sure I would have seen it before long, or Miss Kelly would have brought it to our attention, but your quick eye was a great benefit."

Zachary wondered if Dr. Abato ever quit putting on a show.

"Do you count that as one shock or several in the therapy log? Was Quentin shocked sixty times in his last therapy session? Or several hundred?"

Dr. Abato raised his hands in a calming gesture.

"Where *was* the log sheet just now?" Zachary looked back into the meeting room. There was no paperwork in evidence. Neither the therapist nor the aide had been marking the prompts and the shocks on a session log.

"Miss Stewart will be filling it out as soon as she sees the Salks off, I'm sure."

"It's supposed to be filled out in real time. Every prompt and response. Every time he is shocked. You can't just remember that and fill it in later!"

"You're right, of course. Real-time record keeping is a very important part of the program. I will talk to Miss Stewart about it."

"This is ridiculous." Zachary's anger was rising, his voice getting louder. "What you're doing here is abuse—"

"What we are doing here, Mr. Goldman, is saving children and saving their families. Do you know how many people are trying to get their children into this program? Families who are at the ends of their ropes and have nowhere else to go. No other hope. We can only fit so many Quentins and Angels into our program. There are limits as to how many people this facility that accommodate. And that means that for every child you see being helped here, there are a thousand others across the country who are just as bad off. Who need our help just as desperately."

"You can't just keep shocking them and hoping that something works. You could be causing them injury. Maybe Quentin had a weak heart and the shocks were just too much for him. You don't know, do you?"

"Quentin Thatcher had a full physical, including an EKG, just like every other child who enters our program. He didn't have any heart problems. Nor do any of the children who enter the program. You led me to understand you had seen the police report and photos. If you did, you know Quentin died of strangulation, not from skin shocks."

13

Zachary was speechless. He stood there shaking with anger, trying to put his thoughts into words that would somehow reach Dr. Abato and make him see what he was doing to children like Quentin and Angel, and even ones like Ray-Ray who were not being shocked, but who were still being traumatized by the punishment/reward cycle that Lovaas so unashamedly promoted to gain psychological control over them.

"Would you please wait here while I deal with a few points?" Dr. Abato requested.

"What are you doing? I want to hear."

"This is not part of the tour. I have administrative matters that need to be dealt with, and that is not any of your business. If you will please just wait here for me, I won't be long."

There wasn't anything Zachary could do but agree. He didn't have the right to be wandering through the institution on his own. If he tried it, he was just going to end up stopped by one of the security staff. Dr. Abato strode out of Zachary's sight.

Angel was confused by the abrupt end to his therapy session. He flapped his hands anxiously beside his face, unsure what to expect next. Being released from a therapy session early in the day was something unknown to him. Kelly led him by the hand to his room.

His skin was still buzzing. Angel scratched at it, trying to calm the itching of a hundred fire ants under his skin.

"Angel. Here. Come here," Kelly encouraged, taking him to the desk in his room. She picked up a pump-bottle of lotion. "Here, cream. Let me put some on for you."

He held both arms extended out from his body, and she pumped cream, cold to the touch, onto each one.

"You rub it in now. I know you don't want me touching you, so you do it. Rub it in, Angel. Come on."

She pretended to be rubbing lotion onto her own arms. Angel mirrored her movements, matching the timing of every movement to hers.

He couldn't rub the cream where the bands went around his arms, which was where it burned the most. He moaned as he tried to slide his fingers under the arm bands.

"Since you're done your session," Kelly was looking at the printed schedule. "That means you have computer lab."

Angel tried again to get his fingertips under the armbands, but Kelly caught his fingers and gave them a tug.

"Computers. You like the computers, don't you, Angel?"

He barely heard her. He did like computers, but he was distracted by the change in schedule and the man who had been in the hallway when he got out. He knew Dr. Abato, but not the man with him. The other man had been angry. His fists were clenched and shaking. His demeanor was a welcome change to Angel, because Angel was also angry. Usually the people who were angry were the ones with the shockers, but the man in the hallway had not had a shocker.

Angel let Kelly pull him out into the hallway. The man was still there, his eyes wide and his fists still clenched. His face turned toward Angel.

"Where is he going now?" he asked Kelly.

"Computer lab."

"Mind if I tag along?"

Kelly's body shifted and her grip on Angel's hand tightened. "Who are you, again?"

"Zachary Goldman."

Angel liked the name Goldman. He envisioned a tall statue of a man made of solid gold. That would really be something. He mouthed the name Angel Goldman to himself. The two names went together well. Kelly started to move down the hall again without telling Zachary Goldman that it was okay for him to go along, but he followed along with them anyway. As they went by the unit administration desk, Zachary Goldman spoke to a woman whose name tag said Agnes Peal. "If Dr. Abato is looking for me, I'll be in the computer lab."

Mrs. Peal made a motion with her hand like she wanted to stop him, but he didn't pay any attention. Angel kept his head turned so that he could watch Zachary Goldman out of the corner of his eye as he walked with them. Goldman didn't try to touch him or ask him questions.

Zachary could see Angel keeping an eye on him, but Angel seemed calmer than he had during the therapy session and didn't make any threatening movements.

Kelly too kept looking at Zachary, but she was more circumspect about it. Looking at him when she thought he was distracted by something else. She didn't know that Zachary had learned in places just like Summit to have eyes in the back of his head; to always be aware of everyone's movements around him. She'd have to be a lot more careful to keep him from seeing her nervousness over his going to the lab with her.

Zachary had given her his name, but not who he was or why

he was there, so she had to be wondering whether he had the right to go with her or if she should be stopping him.

"Here we go, Angel," Kelly announced, steering Angel into the computer lab. Angel looked around and headed for an empty chair. It appeared to be somewhere he knew the expected behavior and was willing to comply. He hadn't, Zachary noted, had his ESD equipment swapped out. His arm cuffs were still at different heights, exactly where they had been after Angel had pulled one of them loose and had it reattached below the inflamed skin. Dr. Abato hadn't been concerned enough about the possibility that Angel's equipment was faulty to ensure that it was fixed or replaced. Zachary was sure that, like him, Abato knew very well that Kelly hadn't been pressing the button repeatedly because she wasn't getting a good shock. She had been attempting to escalate the punishment.

It was a strange feeling, seeing the pretty young blond and knowing that she had essentially been torturing Angel. As much as Zachary knew it wasn't true, it was hard not to associate beauty with goodness. He simply didn't expect someone as pretty as she was to be someone who could intentionally hurt a young boy. Angel had been thrashing and crying on the floor and she just kept pressing that button.

Even so, Angel hadn't avoided her after leaving the meeting room. He hadn't protested about her being the one to escort him down to the computer lab or pulled away from her touch as she directed him there. It would appear that the alternating cycle of pain and rewards had securely bonded Angel to his aide, as Lovaas had predicted.

Kelly didn't follow Angel to his computer to stand behind him, as a few of the other staff members were doing. Instead, she stood a short distance away, watching not just Angel, but the other students in the lab as well. Zachary studied the boxes hanging from her belt. Angel's wasn't the only student whose remote she carried. How many of the other children in the lab did she have the ability to punish?

Most of the other students in the lab were wearing backpacks, and if Zachary looked closely, he could see the wires leading out of them that connected to the electrodes. How naive had he been to think they were simply bags of schoolbooks, not even seeing the wires?

A couple of the aides watching over the busy students were talking to each other in low voices, laughing occasionally. Zachary couldn't hear what they were saying, and moved a little closer, trying to catch the gist of it. As he got closer, he saw one of the kids near him make a deliberate motion toward him. He turned his eyes to her, careful not to move too fast and appear confrontational.

The girl angled a paper toward him, keeping her face toward her computer screen. Zachary looked down at the page.

HELP ME

It shouldn't have surprised him that some of the residents had the ability to write a communication. He had met Margaret, who appeared to him to have all of the abilities of a neurotypical woman. If there were women who could pass as non-autistic, there had to be younger people who also appeared to be neurotypical. Teenagers, children, all age groups. Nancy had said they had some residents who were not developmentally disabled, too. Kids who were mentally ill or delinquent.

Zachary looked at the back of the girl's head. She didn't look at him. But he could tell by the angle she had her head cocked at that she was still paying attention to him. She didn't have an aide hovering right behind her, so Zachary sat down in a vacant computer chair the next station down from hers and turned it toward her slightly.

"Are you okay?" he asked, barely above a whisper.

She tapped away at her keyboard. She appeared to be playing a game or manipulating a three-dimensional object for a math question. "I want to get out of here," she whispered back, not looking at him.

"I'm sorry... I can't do anything about that."

"You gotta. You gotta do something."

"I'm just a visitor. I don't have any power around here."

"Power." The girl snorted. "We're all wired for power around here."

"What's wrong? You look… like you're okay."

"Oh, yeah. I'm great."

"What's wrong?"

"You know what day it is today?"

"Uh… Monday…?"

"Yeah. And Monday is when the staff review all of the weekend security footage to see what happened over the weekend."

"I still don't see…?"

She didn't answer at first, looking intently at her computer screen as if working out a complicated puzzle. A shadow passed over Zachary, and he realized that someone had been standing close behind them.

"It's catch-up day," the girl said, barely opening her mouth. "They watch to see what everyone did over the weekend and if you did anything that should have been punished, they give it to you Monday afternoon."

"No!" Such a policy went directly against Lovaas's program, which dictated that a reward or punishment should be given within one second of a good or bad behavior. To wait several days and punish retroactively was completely wrong.

She nodded infinitesimally. "Just sittin' here… waiting… waiting to see who gets shocked and who gets away."

"That's not fair!"

He could see her smile. Unamused. In agreement with his assessment. Zachary massaged his temples, trying to figure out if there was something he could do. It seemed like a hopeless cause.

How was he supposed to do anything to change the institution's policies? Newspaper articles had been written, trials had been held, protests had been made, and inspections had been done. And no one had been able to fight the administration of Summit and the devoted parents who insisted their children needed to be there and needed ABA therapy to keep them safe.

The two aides who Zachary had been trying to hear drifted closer to him. He kept his head down, trying not to look as if he'd been talking to the girl or had any interest in the conversation.

"It works best if you catch them off guard," the older man said. "An unexpected aversive is more powerful than one that the kid is expecting and already braced for. They build up a resistance over time. That's why the doctor is trying to get these new ESDs passed. The ones we've got now," the guard tapped one of the remotes on his belt, "they're stronger than the ones we started out with. Work a lot better. But even with how strong these ones are, some kids are barely affected by them. They can sit there and just look at you while you press the button. Just daring you to do it again."

The younger of the two aides, a boyish-faced redhead, nodded earnestly.

"I guess that makes sense."

"So what works best is if you can stand across the room. Even around a corner. Where they can't see you and won't be expecting anything." The aide glanced around at the students working industriously away on the computers. All heads down. All fingers on the keyboard. A boy at the end of the room laughed and started to flap his hands excitedly. Zachary watched the aide reach for one of his remotes, take a quick glance at it to make sure it was the right one, and punch the button.

The excited little boy gave a shriek and nearly fell out of his chair. The two aides laughed. Zachary saw red. It was all he could do to clamp his fingers around the table and hold himself back from jumping up and punching the aide who had pressed the button. The other students in the room were looking around, eyes wide and anxious. An aide who was closer to the boy who had been shocked settled him back in his chair, warning him not to disturb others with his noises and flapping.

Zachary could see that Angel was no longer engaged with his computer program. He would look at the computer for a moment, and then turn around and look warily at the aides. Was he vigilant because of the other boy who had been shocked? Or like the girl, did he know that it was Monday and there might be retroactive shocks in store for him? A teenage girl seated a few chairs down from Zachary started to rock back and forth and to cry quietly. The atmosphere in the room thickened, everyone hyper-aware of her behavior. Zachary watched the older aide who had been showing the young redhead the ropes to see if he would be the one to respond, shocking her unexpectedly from a distance. But he didn't seem to be concerned about it. Maybe he knew that hers wasn't one of the remotes hanging from his belt. A female aide moved toward the girl instead and coaxed her to stand up and leave the room.

Zachary could see Angel starting to rock, could see his anxious looks around the room increasing. Would Kelly catch his anxiety escalating and remove him from the lab, as the girl's aide had? Or would she try to shock him into quiet, compliant behavior?

The girl who had written 'help me' pounded on her keys, glancing at Angel and at Zachary. "Just chill, Angel," she murmured, very quiet so that one of the aides wouldn't hear her or wouldn't know the sound had come from her. She was too far away for Angel to have heard her. She just wanted to avoid what was coming next.

And so did Zachary. He didn't know what to do. Approach Angel and tell him it was okay and to calm down? Talk to Kelly and see what she could do to settle Angel down without shocking him?

Zachary had the feeling that Kelly's go-to solution would be to shock Angel. That's what Dr. Abato kept saying worked, even if he did think that the effectiveness might be wearing off somewhat for the boy.

Angel was probably one of the kids that Abato was hoping to get his new, upgraded device approved for.

14

It doesn't work, Angel," the girl beside Zachary said, her voice a little louder than it had been. "It doesn't work. Nothing does. Even if they send you home. They still send you home with these." She tapped one of her armbands. "They train your folks to shock you, so even if you can get away from this place for a few days, even if you can get a weekend pass, you can't get away from them. You can't get away from this crew and their shocks!" The girl's voice had gradually risen and was slightly sing-songy. She was definitely starting to attract the attention of the staff, and that wasn't good for her. It was distracting some of the attention from Angel, but Zachary was afraid that she was just setting herself up for trouble.

"Shh. Better stay quiet," he urged.

"They're going to do it anyway. You can't stop it. None of us can stop it. They're going to do it anyway, no matter what!"

The older aide had noticed Zachary and was frowning at him, trying to figure out who he was and what he was doing there.

"Shh," Zachary tried again to soothe the girl and keep her from escalating further. It felt impossible. He saw himself again facing Annie, on the other side of a steel security door, unable to do anything to help her or to stop them from hurting her. "Come on. What's your name?"

"They don't care about your name. Your name doesn't matter, only whether they have your picture."

Zachary supposed that was true.

"It's Monday!" the girl said suddenly, in a loud voice. She turned her head and looked directly at the older aide. "It's Monday, so why don't you just go ahead and do it?"

The aide reached for his belt. Zachary saw what was going to happen an instant before it took place.

"No, wait, you've got—"

The man pressed the button on the box, meeting the girl's eyes. She didn't move. But a few seats down, Angel shouted and splayed out his arms. He made a gurgling, choking noise. The aide looked down at the box in his hand, realizing that he'd just hit the wrong button. He swore and moved his hand over one to grab the box with the girl's picture on it. Double-checking that he had the right one this time, he pressed the button on the second remote. The girl immediately reacted, throwing her head back and laughing. The hair rose on the back of Zachary's neck at her paradoxical reaction. The girl slammed both palms down on the table with a crack like the lash of a whip. Her eyes were bugging out and she looked like she was on a fairground ride, her whole body vibrating.

The seconds seemed like hours. All of the shocks that Zachary had seen had been the prescribed two-second shocks, other than when Kelly had been pressing Angel's button repeatedly to stack them up. Zachary turned his head to look at the aide to see if he was still holding down the button or pressing it again, but the older man's hand was no longer on the remote. But the girl still juddered and made guttural noises of protest beside Zachary, starting to slide out of her chair.

"It must be malfunctioning!" Zachary shouted. He grabbed one of the armbands and tried to pull it away from her skin and undo the Velcro closure at the same time. It was difficult to work with when the girl kept bucking and vibrating, unable to help herself. The smell of singed hair wafted up to Zachary's nose, making him nauseated, triggering flashbacks. Zachary struggled to keep from slipping back into the past. He got one armband off, but the girl still had three other electrodes that he could see, plus whatever was on her torso under her clothing. "Help me!"

The experienced aide was finally at Zachary's side, pushing him away. Rather than starting to work on the second armband, he went for the backpack, doubling one of the girl's rigid limbs up to get her out of it. He yanked the backpack away, tearing at the wires to disconnect them. The girl collapsed, sobbing.

The aide dropped the backpack to the floor.

"The battery pack's in the backpack," he informed Zachary. He wiped sweat from his forehead with the back of his arm. "No battery, no juice. She'll be okay. We'll get this unit to the shop for repairs."

Zachary was still gasping for breath. He could smell burnt flesh, could feel his own skin shriveling and searing in the fire. The girl was injured, and the aide was more worried about getting the ESD fixed than getting her help. Zachary knelt back over the girl, fumbling to remove the second armband to assess the damage.

The aide swore, staring at the blisters already forming where the electrode had been. "Just get out of the way. We'll get her to the infirmary."

He reached down, grabbing the girl's arm where it wasn't burnt, jerking her to her feet.

"Get the other electrodes off," Zachary said. "Get them off so they're not rubbing against the injuries."

"Don't worry about it," the man growled. "These kids don't feel pain like you do. Didn't you see Trina laugh when I shocked her? She wanted me to do it. She asked for it!"

"She's injured, and she does feel pain! We need to get the electrodes off and get them to bring a gurney—"

"She can walk." The aide gave the girl a pull that made her stumble. "No need for a damn stretcher. It's not that bad."

He headed for the door, with the girl in tow, moaning in pain.

Zachary Goldman was still kneeling on the floor beside Trina's backpack. He had helped Trina; maybe he would help Angel too. Angel turned his head back and forth, looking around the room. Kelly was across the lab, talking with one of the other aides, not paying Angel any attention. He got out of his seat and moved as quickly as he could toward Goldman. Goldman was a man who made things happen. He made them stop Angel's therapy session. He made them take off Trina's backpack. Angel wanted his backpack off too.

When he reached Goldman's side, the man was hunched over like he was in pain. The scent of Trina's burned hair and skin still hung in the air. Had Goldman been hurt by the electrodes when he'd tried to remove them from Trina's arms? Angel grabbed Goldman's arms and tried to ask the question, but the words wouldn't come to his mouth. They always fled when something bad happened so that even the few he could normally get out wouldn't come out. The sounds that came out instead were angry, animal-like noises, frustratingly incoherent.

Ants still crawled beneath Angel's skin. He heard Kelly, way on the other side of the room, far and faint, call out to him to stop. He struck out wildly, trying to stop her, trying to head off the shock he knew would be coming. If Goldman would just help him to take off his backpack, the shocks would stop for him too. He could go home and there would be no more shocks. He could put up with the hitting and other pain, if he just didn't have to be shocked anymore.

He yelled in frustration, holding on to Goldman and trying to show him the marks the electrodes left behind. Goldman would let him go to the doctor too, with no electrodes. They could put cream on his skin where he picked and gouged at it to stop the ants, and he could watch the TV mounted up by the ceiling.

Angel had been to the hospital many times, and he liked it when there was a TV.

Then the shocks came. It was too late for Goldman to prevent them. Fire raced through Angel's body from one location to another. Kelly was pulsing the button so that the shocks didn't go away, but multiplied like a hundred wasp stings inside his veins.

"Stop!" Goldman shouted. "Just leave him alone. I'm okay!"

The shocks stopped, the wasps gradually subsiding. Goldman was trying to pull off Angel's backpack, growling curses. Then his hands were gone. When Angel opened his eyes, squinting through the red haze to see what was going on, Goldman was being pulled away by a couple of security staff, and more stood by to take Angel back to his unit.

***

Zachary watched them take Angel away, fighting back waves of fury and frustration. Angel was not fighting the security staff who led him away, but he still voiced and groaned. Kelly trailed after them. Zachary felt impotent, on the very edge of being able to understand what Angel was trying to communicate, but unable to interact with him further.

He didn't understand what had made Angel come after him like that. Maybe he was confused after being shocked. Maybe it was because Zachary was the stranger there and Angel thought he was a threat. Maybe it was simply because he had been the center of attention and Angel had focused in on him.

Once Angel was removed from the lab, the security guards who had pulled Zachary away from Angel let him go. Zachary looked around the room at the pale, frightened faces of the other children.

After seeing three of the children shocked in quick succession, everyone seemed to just be waiting to be attacked or shocked themselves. They didn't go back to working on their computers, they just kept looking around at each other and at the aides and guards, waiting for it to happen again.

Zachary prodded the tender tissue around his eye where Angel had hit him, already swelling up.

"Are you alright, sir?" one of the security guards asked. "I'm not sure who gave you permission to be in here, but you have to be aware that some of the residents can be violent."

"Yes, I was aware of that," Zachary said. Though he had to admit, he hadn't foreseen being attacked himself. It drove home the message that Mira and Dr. Abato and others had been trying to convey to him; that living with a violent, unpredictable teen or adult was an untenable situation. Even in an institution like Summit, equipped with intensive therapy, aversives, one-on-one aides, and security staff couldn't guarantee safety.

No one had suggested Quentin might have been killed by another inmate. But if the majority of the doors in his unit were not kept locked, then any of the other residents in the unit could have sneaked into his room during the night and strangled him.

The one hole in that scenario was lack of motive. But did the residents need the same kind of motive as neurotypicals? Hadn't Angel just attacked Zachary out of the blue for no discernible reason?

Maybe one of them had a beef with Quentin, or maybe they were just acting out of impulse, confusion, or an effort to communicate something.

If the staff knew or suspected that Quentin had been killed by another resident, would they cover it up? Zachary had to think that they would. They were already under scrutiny for their use of aversives and a resident killing another would indicate that their program wasn't quite as effective at quelling violence as Dr. Abato had claimed. It wouldn't be hard to convert a third-party strangulation to a suicide. The staff had removed the blanket that had been wrapped around Quentin's neck, so there was little that could be concluded from the scene. If there had been evidence that it had been another resident, it could have been removed.

"Mr. Goldman!"

Zachary turned around to see Dr. Abato approaching. "I did ask you to stay and wait for me." Abato looked around. "What's been going on here?"

One of the guards filled him in on the attack by Angel. Dr. Abato shook his head, but his expression was smug.

"Let's get you some ice for that," he suggested, and indicated the direction he and Zachary should walk. "I'm afraid you've just had a crash course in what we deal with every day here. I did my best to warn you, to explain the type of problems we are dealing with, but that's not quite the same as when it walks up and hits you in the face." He chuckled at his own turn of phrase. "Quite literally, in some cases. Like our residents, you need to learn to follow instructions. This wouldn't have happened if you stayed put."

"It just would have happened to someone else," Zachary argued. "Angel was upset because he was shocked by mistake. And the girl who they meant to shock, her device malfunctioned, and it kept shocking her. She had electrical burns. I had to help get them off of her..."

"There will always be equipment malfunctions," Abato sighed. "As I'm sure anyone who uses computers knows well. She'll be taken care of, and she'll be just fine. If it helps, you should know that the pain sensation is quite different for people with autism than it is for you or me. You'd be amazed at some of the injuries I have seen where the resident doesn't even seem to know that they are hurt. They don't have the same connection to their body as we do. So even though this was a terrible thing to happen to her, she's probably already forgotten all about it."

"Her skin was burned and blistered!"

"As I say, the severity of the injury really doesn't seem to have an impact. Sometimes a resident goes quiet, and you really don't know what the problem is, because they don't act sick or hurt. Then you do an exam and find that they have a broken bone or ruptured appendix and never tried to tell anyone."

Zachary tried to square this with what he had seen in his few visits to Summit. The electric shocks certainly seemed to cause pain. The kids that he had seen shocked reacted immediately, crying out, going rigid, even falling to the floor. They didn't look like unfeeling zombies.

But the girl *had* initially laughed when she was shocked. Abato had suggested Angel might be seeking the shocks rather than avoiding them.

And Lovaas… what had Lovaas said? He had said something along the lines of some children being rewarded by negativity and punishment, so that the parent or therapist had to be very angry and hard on them to get the proper results, and that weeks or months of such intense therapy could be taxing on the parent. *Poor parents, having to be so hard on their kids.* Zachary shook his head, thinking about the arrogance of such a statement.

"Angel is one of those that I have concerns about," Dr. Abato said, though Zachary hadn't asked. "You saw how difficult it is to get his compliance, even with multiple shocks. We have a little engineering company that helps us to work out problems with our electronics, and they're working on a device that is more powerful that our little units. More along the lines of the stun belts they use for prisoners when they go to courts or have disciplinary problems. I am trying to get authorization to introduce them into our program for problem students like Angel. But so far," he gave a little shrug, "no luck getting the necessary approvals."

Zachary said nothing. Abato gave a shrug.

"But parents will have their way. Sooner or later, the bureaucrats in their little glass towers will be forced to see the reality of the situation. That these kids need stronger measures. That they're not the same as we are. They are physiologically different. If we're going to achieve any progress with them, we need to be able to do whatever it takes. However unpalatable that might be."

Zachary stared down at his feet as he walked down the hall with the man who had to be the biggest lunatic in the asylum. "It seems like the devices they have on now do enough damage. I can't imagine anyone approving something more powerful."

"But that's just the point, don't you see? The damage occurs when you have to keep shocking repeatedly. Like Trina's ESD malfunctioning. You don't get damage from one shock. If you can give just one shock; one shock that is enough to get their attention and stop them from harmful behavior, then you don't have to shock them again. They learn the first time. Do you know how much faster it is to train a dog with a shock collar? There's no comparison! Why would anyone train any other way? If you can give one shock and get compliance, it changes the child's life. It changes *everyone's* lives."

They arrived in a first aid room, and Abato went to a mini-fridge and retrieved an ice pack for Zachary. "There, that should help."

Zachary put it over his face. The cool pack made his throbbing face feel a hundred times better.

"You said this is one of the only facilities like this in the country," he said.

"Yes." Dr. Abato drew himself up proudly. "That's right."

"Where do all of the other kids go?"

Abato shook his head. "Excuse me… what?"

"All of the other kids with autism. Kids who are violent like Quentin or Angel. Or who are adults now, not teenagers. Where do they all go? They can't all come here."

"Well, no!" Abato laughed. "I think we'd have to expand quite a bit for that. Where do they go…? They go to institutions, ninety-nine percent of the time. Because family members don't want them in their homes. They can't live independently, and they can't live with their families. It's too dangerous. So an institution. Like Summit, but not like Summit. Because they don't have a progressive program like ours, so they can't actually break kids of violence."

Zachary nodded. Abato motioned to a couple of tubular chairs clustered around a break room table and they both sat down.

"Because they are violent, they have to be kept in isolation. There are no classes, no reward rooms, no socialization. A locked cell that they only see the outside of if they need to go see the doctor. Sometimes restraints to keep them from hurting themselves. Or, since the family tend to prefer it, put them on medications that reduce violent behaviors. Antipsychotics, anti-anxiety pills, sedatives. They drug them into a stupor, so they can't do anything. They can't form a thought. They can't carry through an action. They probably can't stand up or sit down without assistance. Kids like Quentin and Angel become zombies. Their parents don't like it. They don't like to lose their kids. So they pull them from those places and try to get them in here."

"There isn't anything in between?"

"Where is the in-between? We use ABA to train them to behave. Others use physical or chemical restraints to keep them from harming themselves or others. There is no middle ground, no other way to overcome the violent behaviors."

"It just seems like… there are so many people with autism or other disorders… they're not all in institutions."

"Ones that are that severe are. You can't keep a child like that home." Abato wiped a hand over his face, frowning. "Though, there is one other option some parents take."

Zachary didn't like the sound of that or Abato's foreboding expression. He knew that Abato, with his flair for the dramatic, was waiting for Zachary to ask what it was. He hated to give him the satisfaction, but Abato was waiting.

"What?" Zachary finally prompted.

"You hear about it in the news more and more," Abato drew out the tension. "I don't know whether it is happening more, or if we are just hearing more of it due to modern communication systems. But more and more, you hear about parents who are killing their children. Especially children disabled by autism."

Zachary had known he would regret asking.

"Maybe it is something that used to be kept under wraps," Abato said. "Socially acceptable euthanasia. A pillow over their face while they sleep. Poison. Carbon monoxide. Throwing them off of a bridge. Parents are very creative. When they get to the end of their ropes, when there are no more services, no one else to help, they are burdened with a child who will drag them down for the rest of their lives…"

"You sound like you sympathize with them," Zachary snapped. Acid burned in his chest. How could anyone think that there was any excuse?

"Of course I do. I see them every day, these parents who have been ground down and crushed by year after year of taking care of a child—or children—who are emotional sinkholes. They pour everything into them and get nothing back. Or maybe their reward is a black eye," Abato nodded at Zachary's face. "Or a broken arm. Or a ruptured kidney. Do I think it's right to kill your child? Of course not! My whole job—my whole life—is about helping these children. And their families. I will do what-ever it takes to save every child I can from being drugged into a stupor, restrained twenty-three hours a day, or killed by the people who are supposed to be protecting them."

Zachary wished he could tell himself that Abato was exagger-ating. That children like Angel and Quentin were not being consigned to either live in a hellhole or be killed by their care-givers. But he knew it was true. Every time he saw such a story in the news, his first reaction was a sense of relief that his mother had made the choice to break up the family and put the children into foster care rather than killing them. He'd read, with horrified fasci-nation, the stories of mothers who drowned their children one at a time in the bathtub. Or stabbed them in their beds. Or drove them into the lake. Everyone nodded gravely and commented about what a hard row she'd had to hoe. Too many children. Chil-dren with handicaps or special needs. Children who were violent and too big to handle any longer.

Zachary's mother had lived it. Six children too close together in age. An abusive marriage. Grinding poverty. No relatives to help. Social programs that had already been tapped out. Then the final straw… the house burning down. Being left with no home and no possessions.

She could have killed them, just like those other mothers who had chosen family annihilation. Many of them had not faced as many challenges as she had. But for some reason, she hadn't. She'd given up on them, rejected them, but she hadn't killed them.

Zachary's first reaction was always relief and a sense of gratitude that she hadn't.

But often, the feeling was followed by a sense of hopelessness. Looking back over his life and all of the trauma and suffering that had followed her choice. Had she been weak to choose to leave them to someone else to take care of instead of dispatching them like a litter of unwanted kittens? His pain and suffering could have ended three decades earlier, instead of being in the position he was in; alone, beaten down, hopeless, and once again homeless.

Dr. Abato nodded gravely. "We have to put a stop to it, Mr. Goldman. I have to save as many of these children as I can, by whatever means I can devise. To hell with rules and regulations. Somebody has to do something for them."

His eyes were dark as burning coals, a lone voice crying out in the wilderness.

15

He was headed back to his car when he saw the woman standing a few feet outside the doors, a cigarette between her fingers. Dark hair pulled into a smooth, sleek ponytail. Young and pretty with perfectly-applied makeup. A common sight. Except for the one detail that Zachary's shutter-quick eyes immediately took in. There was no smoke coming from her cigarette.

He saw the way that her head turned slightly in his direction when he exited the building. He slowed a little, waiting to see whether she was going to confront him, but she didn't. Would she follow him to his car? Had she already planted a bomb or tracking device on his car and stayed to watch the fun?

Zachary measured the distance from the woman not smoking to the protesters. Was she one of them? Camouflaged by her nicotine habit so that she could get right up to the building when security was supposed to be keeping the protesters back fifty feet, at the property line? But she didn't look over at them. Didn't flash them any sign or signal.

Zachary stopped and patted his pockets as if he were looking for smokes of his own. "Do you have another one?" he asked, giving up on finding anything. "I'm trying to give it up by not carrying them with me, but... after this place... I need a hit."

She looked nervous about Zachary talking to her, but she complied, pulling out her own pack of cigarettes and handing one to Zachary.

"You're right," she said cautiously. "It's… quite the place."

She didn't stare at his black eye or ask him what had happened, which suggested she already knew. Zachary held the cigarette she had handed him and didn't light it up or ask her for a light. They both stood there with their unlit cigarettes. Her face started to get pink. She was very attractive. Very young. It was probably her first job out of college.

"Alright!" She blew up, as if he'd been interrogating her. "You caught me. I wasn't out here to smoke, I was out here to get a chance to talk to you."

"Here I am," Zachary said, giving her a weak smile and handing the cigarette back to her. "What did you want to say?"

"Someone said that you're here to investigate Quentin Thatcher's death."

"They would be right."

"You don't believe it was suicide?"

"Suicide is still a possibility," Zachary said. "If you think he could actually form the intent to kill himself. What do you think?"

She put both of the cigarettes back into the pack, which then appeared to be full. He didn't smell stale smoke on her and wondered if she had bought the cigarettes just for the ruse.

"I don't know. I'm no expert in suicide."

"Okay. How well did you know Quentin?"

"I worked with him a few times. Just a few. I didn't know him well."

"And you don't know if he could have killed himself?"

"I suppose he could have. Accidentally or intentionally, I don't know. He was a sensory-seeker."

Zachary rubbed the back of his neck. "What does that mean?"

"A lot of children with autism are thought to feel things differently than… a neurotypical adult. They may be overly sensitive and avoid certain kinds of sensory input. Or they may be less sensitive and seeking more sensory input—banging into walls, stimming, hugging, running, swinging. Just like some normal adults like to bungee-jump and some can't step down from a chair without holding on to it. Most children are a combination of both, seeking some sensations and avoiding others."

"So Quentin was a sensory-seeker. He wanted more input."

"Right. With a blanket wrapped around his throat, twisted up tight so that it strangled him… he could have just been seeking deep pressure. He might not have known that it could harm him until it was too late, and he couldn't get it unwound again."

"It's possible. The blanket had already been removed from the body when the police got here, so there's no way to analyze the way it had been twisted. The police say he could have done it to himself."

She nodded and didn't add anything. She had frown lines between her brows. Lots of stress indicators.

"What's your name?"

"Oh. Clarissa. Clarissa Hill. I'm an aide here. I help with therapy sessions, provide one-on-one support…"

"Right. And sometimes you supported Quentin."

"Yes."

"Shocked him?"

Her lips squeezed tightly shut.

"That's how it's done here, isn't it?" Zachary asked. "I'm not going to pretend I don't know what's going on."

"Yes," she admitted. "That's how it's done here. So yes, I have shocked Quentin. And other kids that I have been in charge of. It's part of the job."

Zachary nodded. Her face was white, and she didn't know how to deal with Zachary just waiting to be told whatever it was she wanted to tell him. She had probably anticipated that he would interrogate her. Ask her a lot of questions. And she would have to hold back and give him just the few bits of information she wanted him to have. But Zachary didn't do that. He just waited. He watched a bird flying overhead, waiting for her to sort out her thoughts.

"How do you feel about your job?"

"I love it. I love helping people. Helping these kids to do things their parents were told they would never be able to do."

But...

Zachary waited for it.

Clarissa's face crumpled. "I hate it. I hate the shocks and other aversives. I hate not being able to communicate with my kids because Dr. Abato says they have to use speech and there are no communications boards or sign language, or any other kind of assisted communication allowed. I hate not being able to get down to their level and figure out what their wants and needs are. To get a real look at their personalities. I hate the damage that we are doing."

"If you're helping them to do things that their doctors said they'd never be able to do, then how are you damaging them? Isn't that good?"

"Have you heard what they have to say?" Clarissa gestured toward the protesters. "Have you heard what actual adults with autism have to say?"

Zachary nodded. "I have."

"If what we are doing is actually traumatizing them and not helping them to become better people, then what are we doing here? Why cause them pain if we're not making them any better?"

"I believe you." The guilt in her eyes seemed genuine. "I wonder, though, if there are some people who get something out of hurting them."

"Sadists?" Clarissa shifted her feet, looking toward the big double-doors of the building that they had exited. She cleared her throat. "I guess there are anywhere, aren't there? Statistically, there are bound to be a few."

Zachary wasn't looking for statistics. He had already seen for himself. He had already seen aides who enjoyed shocking students. If Clarissa had been working there for weeks or months, or even years, she would know beyond a doubt that some of the men—statistically it was more often men—who held the remotes in their hands were enjoying inflicting pain.

"Okay," Clarissa admitted. "Yeah, there are a few of those. It does go on."

"And were any of them working with Quentin?"

She opened her mouth to answer, then thought about it more deeply. "I don't know. I'm just… not sure."

"Could someone on Quentin's unit, either a staff member or another resident, have strangled him?"

"Quentin was strong. Smothering or strangling someone takes a lot of strength. They fight back hard."

That gave Zachary pause. "Yes," he agreed.

"I don't know… I guess someone else could have done it. But there's not any evidence of it, is there? And what motive would anyone have?"

"What motive do you think they could have?" Zachary bounced the question back at her.

She was silent for a moment. "Can we walk to your car or something? I didn't plan on talking here by the doors where anyone could walk by and see us together."

Zachary nodded, and they started a slow wander toward the parking lot.

"A cover-up," Clarissa started to list possible motives. "Sadism. If it was another resident, or Quentin himself, it could be accidental. Even… some twisted kind of mercy killing. To release him from his troubles."

"Did Quentin have a lot of troubles?"

"Sure. Of course. He was violent, unpredictable. He didn't get to see his family much, and when he did, he got more upset. More angry. Maybe someone… just wanted to put an end to the pain."

It was territory that Zachary hadn't explored, but it was possible.

As they made their way past the protesters, Zachary saw Margaret Beacher making her way toward them. He didn't know whether to warn Clarissa there might be trouble, or let it just play out and see what happened. He ended up saying nothing.

"Who's your *friend*, Zachary?" Margaret asked, looking Clarissa over.

Clarissa looked at Zachary anxiously.

"Clarissa is one of the aides here," he told Margaret evenly. "She helped with Quentin. So she had some things she wanted to tell me."

"Do you people know what you're doing in there?" Margaret demanded, wheeling on Clarissa.

Clarissa was not quick to answer. "Yes," she said eventually, "and I know you don't like it."

"*Don't like it.*" Margaret gave a mocking laugh. "That's what you call an understatement." She looked at the other protesters for their reactions. There were a few jeers and catcalls, but nothing too threatening. "What you do in there, your *therapy*, it ruined my life."

"What am I supposed to do? Quit? I'm helping people." Clarissa's voice was sharp, defensive.

"What you do doesn't help. It causes damage. Irreparable damage."

Clarissa took a deep breath, but ended up saying nothing. What could she say? She'd already admitted to Zachary that she knew they were causing harm.

"You should get out of there," Margaret said. "You should get out of there, and get out of ABA, and start treating autistic people with decency and respect."

Clarissa looked close to tears. "I need that job. And those kids need me. I love my kids."

"You love them? If you loved them, you wouldn't hurt them."

"But I do love them. And I want to help them. And I need to do the therapy that they're there for. If I don't do it, someone else will." She glanced at Zachary. "Maybe someone who *does* want to hurt them."

"You'll hurt them so someone else doesn't? What kind of lame excuse is that? Somebody is going to do it, so it might as well be you?"

Clarissa gave a helpless shrug. "Isn't it better if it's someone who loves them? Who wants the best for them?"

"What hurts more, being brutalized by someone who hates you, or someone who loves you?" Margaret shook her head. "Someone who *pretends* to love you."

Tears brimmed over Clarissa's eyes. "You don't know what it's like in there." Her voice was cracked and shaky. "You don't know what it's like to have to be there every day. I'm there because I want to help. I want to make a difference! I haven't slept through the night since Quentin died. A few hours here, a few hours there... but whenever I do, I dream about Quentin. The... the hopelessness in his eyes... he hated it here. He wanted to go home."

"Of course he did," Margaret agreed. "Don't you? At the end of the day, don't you just want to go home, where it's comfortable and safe?"

"After two years, I didn't even think he'd remember home. Any homesickness he had initially should have disappeared... it had been two years."

"He was autistic, not amnesiac. Why wouldn't he remember home?"

"Dr. Abato said they wouldn't. That they regarded Summit as their home. After a few weeks, they wouldn't remember anywhere else."

"Why wouldn't they?" Margaret challenged. "They were getting skin shocks, not ECT. Not lobotomies."

Clarissa swallowed hard and scrubbed at her eyes, smearing her mascara. "Do you know we're not even allowed to talk to each other?" she asked. "Under our employment agreements, we're not allowed to talk to media or anyone about the institution's protocol. And we're not even allowed to talk to each other. No personal discussions, even on breaks. No discussions of the cases or therapies except in case review meetings. The only conversations we can have are to communicate with each other during therapy or a follow-up report. Anything else is personal discussion and we're not allowed."

Zachary blinked at this. He'd never heard of such a policy before. He could understand that Summit didn't want their employees gossiping or debating the merits of skin shocks or going to the media. But to completely ban all personal discussion seemed cruel and dictatorial, seriously overreaching.

Of course, Clarissa could be telling a story. Those tears could be fake. They had come on disconcertingly fast. She could be trying to manipulate him.

"You have to talk," Margaret said. "You can't listen to them. You can't let them control you like that. How do you think the Nazis convinced people to commit the atrocities that they did? Do you think all of the soldiers and citizens who helped them were horrible people? They were doing what they were told. They were convinced that what they were doing was right and necessary. They listened to what they were told."

Clarissa looked back over her shoulder at the building. "They can still see me here," she said. "We need to get out of sight."

Margaret waved her concerns away with one hand. "As far as they're concerned, I'm blocking you and you're just trying to get past me. Terrible how the police can't do anything about the protesters setting up camp here day after day."

Clarissa sniffled and gave a weak smile. She rubbed her forehead. If she'd been sleeping that little, she probably had a hell of a headache.

"'The only thing necessary for the triumph of evil is for good men to do nothing,'" Margaret quoted. "If you stand by in silence, because they told you not to talk, and you keep shocking defenseless children and taking away their rights to make choices and be who they are because you're afraid someone else will do worse damage, then you *are* the problem. If you're not fighting against the evil people who are pushing these therapies, you are as guilty as they are."

"They aren't evil," Clarissa protested. "They want to help the children. Their parents want them to be there. They know all about the aversive therapy. They have to sign off on it. And the parents know what is best for their kids—"

"Their parents have been told it's the best thing. They've been given statistics. They've been told horror stories. They've been shown videos of children who have miraculously recovered and look normal. And they want that for their children. They've been told that whatever the cost, it's worth it to have children who are indistinguishable from their peers. Whose brains have been wiped and reprogrammed to always give the right response. All of their uniqueness and individuality stripped away. Because the only way for an autistic person to succeed is by not acting autistic."

Clarissa opened her mouth to argue the point, but she didn't have the oily smoothness of Dr. Abato. She'd been indoctrinated just like those parents had been, but the arguments didn't come naturally to her lips She looked at Zachary, as if he might jump in and tell her why it was okay.

"They're even telling you the same lies as the Nazis," Margaret said. "That autistic people are subhuman. No more than animals that can be trained with a system of pain and rewards."

"I know they're not animals."

"Do you believe that the only way to teach autistic children is with ABA?"

Clarissa's reluctance was almost comical. "I don't know," she said finally. "It's the standard for treating autism, isn't it? I suppose there might be other therapies, but I've only been trained in ABA. That's what *everyone* uses, not just Summit." She rubbed her forehead again. Zachary could see the lines of fatigue not fully disguised by her makeup. "Using ABA without aversives may not be as effective, but lots of people are doing it, so it must have some efficacy."

"What about *no* therapy?" Margaret suggested.

"No therapy?" Clarissa repeated stupidly. "How could you treat children with autism without therapy?"

"Maybe they don't need to be treated at all. Maybe just because our brains are different, that doesn't mean that we are defective. That we need to be reprogrammed somehow."

"But these children aren't like you. They can't communicate. They have no life skills, no social skills. Some like Quentin are violent."

"Why?"

"What?"

"*Why* are they violent?"

"Why?" Clarissa shook her head in confusion. "Because they get frustrated. They can't communicate. They have sensory overload. Sometimes because they are hurt or ill… I don't know."

"And which of those things do electric shocks fix?"

"It… stops them."

"So you don't care about fixing the underlying problems. Just stopping certain behaviors."

"We're trying to teach them to communicate properly. So that they can tell us what's wrong."

Zachary watched the two of them argue back and forth, fascinated to hear the two different viewpoints explored.

"What is 'communicating properly'?" Margaret asked. "You mean communicating the same way that you do."

"Well… yes. The way *everyone* does."

"Not everyone, or there wouldn't be anyone to teach. Why not try to figure out what communication method works for them? If they have trouble learning yours, why don't you learn theirs? Why is speech the ultimate solution?"

Clarissa shook her head, looking at the group of protesters. "I wish we were allowed to use ASL or PECS, but Dr. Abato is right… *You* speak. That's how you get along in the world. It's just... so much harder if you can't use speech to communicate. People aren't going to take the time to figure out what you are trying to communicate. But if we can teach them to talk like everyone else..."

"Do you see these signs?"

Clarissa looked at the various signs people were holding. There were various words and phrases about getting Summit shut down. There were pictures of Quentin. Lightning bolt symbols. And various other combinations of pictures and words.

"Yes."

"Do you understand them?"

"Yes, of course."

"But they are not speech."

"No... but in a way... I mean, they represent speech. It's just another medium."

Margaret arched her eyebrows. "Oh. I see."

Clarissa turned away from Margaret, her face red and eyes still teary. She grasped Zachary's arm. "I wanted to talk to you," she said. "I wanted to help you. I feel bad about Quentin. I want his mom to know... that we loved him here." She squeezed Zachary's arm more tightly. "Everything we did was to help him. We're devastated by what happened."

Margaret opened her mouth. Zachary shook his head at her sharply. The time for arguing methodologies was past. He needed to find out what Clarissa knew. To tease out details that she didn't realize were important.

"I know you cared about Quentin," Zachary said in a low voice, as soothing as he could manage. "What happened was tragic and unexpected, so of course you're knocked off your feet about it. Do you mind talking to me about it?"

"No, of course not." Clarissa shot another look toward Margaret. "Just... can we just talk somewhere private? Not because I know any secrets or anything important to your investigation. I just... would like to be alone for this."

"Sure. I don't know the area. We could check the GPS to see

what's close. Or is there somewhere you and your coworkers go…?"

"No. We're not allowed to… fraternize…"

"Where do you go?" Zachary asked Margaret. "You must know all of the places nearby."

"There's a diner two blocks down," Margaret pointed the direction they should go. "Blue and white striped awning. They have good grilled cheese sandwiches."

"Okay." Zachary looked at Clarissa. "You want to walk or take my car?"

"Let's walk."

He nodded. The started down the sidewalk toward the diner. The road was fairly straight, and they could see the striped awning before they got to the end of the first block.

"You haven't been sleeping?" Zachary asked.

"No. Not for long. Every night I think it will be tonight, that my body is so tired it has to give in. And I end up tossing and turning or sitting up… until my eyes finally close and I start dreaming. But I just keep dreaming about Quentin. And I wake up and I'm so sad for him. I know I shouldn't be, he's gone on to a better place, and all that. And I really do believe that. But I still feel so sad, so guilty."

"Of course. That's a totally natural reaction. I imagine the sleeplessness will wear off… like you say, your body will take over and insist that you sleep."

Though that had never been a workable strategy for Zachary. He needed something to help him sleep. He didn't like having to take meds to sleep, so he would go as long as he could without, but eventually he would break down and take something so that he could shut down his brain and get a few hours of unbroken sleep.

"I don't know," Clarissa said. "It started before Quentin died. It's been going on for some time now…"

"When did it start?"

"I'm not sure exactly… a few weeks… a month or two…

things just started falling apart in my life. I stopped being able to sleep. Started having nightmares. Couldn't focus during the day. I feel like… like something bad is going to happen. All the time. But I don't know what."

They walked for a minute in silence. Reaching the diner, they found a seat, and both ordered the grilled cheese sandwich, then looked at each other like an awkward first date.

"What were your nightmares about before Quentin died?"

"Not all that different… the kids at Summit. Sometimes Quentin, sometimes one of the others. Dreams that they were hurt or dying, and no one would help me. Or dreaming that…" She tapped on the Formica table with a long, polished fingernail, "… you're going to think it's stupid."

"No. I won't. I have some doozies myself."

"Sometimes that I am a resident there. That I am the one with autism. Or that I don't have autism or anything wrong with me, and I am still locked up there and can't get out or do anything but sit in my room or in therapy. It was really… terrifying. I know that's silly. It wasn't that there was anything bad happening to me, just that… I didn't have any control over my life. No control over anything."

"Yeah. That would be pretty frightening."

And it was the truth of the situation for every one of those kids. If they did well, they could earn their big rewards. They could go to the fancy reward rooms and play video games, or crawl in the ball pit, or pick one of the quieter rooms. And that was the highlight of their lives. The rest of the time, they had no choice over where they could be, what they could do, no choices at all.

There were residents without autism there too. Youths who were too violent, runaways, who couldn't fit in with families or whatever other living situations they had been in. Kids like Zachary had been. He couldn't imagine being stuck in a more terrifying place than Summit. Things had been bad enough at Bonnie Brown and some of the other institutions or homes he had been in. But at least at Bonnie Brown, they didn't give him electrical shocks. He'd been treated roughly. Had guards who figured it was okay to tune him up if he were misbehaving. But the thought of being wired like the residents at Summit, where anyone who had authority over him could punish him at any time, even from across the room, was daunting.

He'd seen Angel writhing on the floor. Trina, with her skin cooking under the electrodes. All of it court approved. Their parents signed off. The courts signed off. Everybody said it was perfectly okay to punish children and adults who had been judged incapable of controlling their own behavior. How was that fair?

"Mr. Goldman?"

Zachary roused himself and focused in on Clarissa, who was looking at him with questions in her eyes.

"Sorry. Did you ask me something?"

"No… just… I thought you were going to say something else, and then you kind of… drifted off."

Zachary placed both of his palms on the table, trying to feel the cool, flat surface, to ground himself in the present with the sensations around him. It was a bright, friendly place. A sort of a fifties or sixties diner theme. Comfortable home cooking. He could smell their grilled cheese sandwiches on the grill; the waitress would be bringing them to the table soon.

"Do you know if anyone else you work with is having the same kind of symptoms?" he asked. "Sleeplessness, anxiety, depression…?"

"Like I said, we aren't allowed to associate with each other. We're not supposed to talk outside of the therapy sessions, only to sort out logistics, get reports filed, that kind of thing."

Zachary waited. There were rules, and then there was what really happened when there were no snitches around to report the rule-breaking.

"I guess… yes, there are a lot of others who complain about having trouble sleeping. Or who drink too much. Or who take a lot of sick days. It's kind of a running joke, taking all of your sick days in the first three months of the year... turnover is pretty brutal, we're always having to train new staff. Dr. Abato likes to get people right out of school, when they haven't already been trained in other methods. So that therapy sessions don't get 'contaminated' with someone else's program or ideas."

"A lot of people quit? Or are fired?"

"I think more quit than are fired. Even though the rules are strict, there aren't a lot of people breaking them flagrantly enough to be fired. Everybody wants to keep their jobs. Wants to do the best they can to help these kids. They need us."

"Everybody talks about kids," Zachary observed. "But a lot of the residents are adults, aren't they? And not all just eighteen or nineteen."

"Oh, I know. But that's how we think of them. As our kids. Even if they're older than us. Because they're like children. They need us to look after them. To care for them."

"You get pretty attached to them."

"Yes. We're everything they've got. It's like a parent-child relationship. And I guess that's how we see it, even if they are older. A lot of the really old residents aren't doing any therapy. They've advanced as far as they can, and they're just... living out their lives. So I didn't really work much in those units. Now and then to cover when they were understaffed. But there's not a lot to do, other than making sure they are fed and washed."

"What do they do with their time? Do they just sit around all day?"

"It depends on their level of functioning and what their interests are. Some do puzzles or have a hobby. Something that their families keep them supplied with. As long as they don't have anything that can be used as a weapon, Summit is pretty open to whatever pastimes they choose."

"What did you think of Quentin?"

She couldn't hide the fact that she was startled by his sudden change of direction. But the waitress chose that moment to bring them their plates, so Clarissa had time to change gears and think about her answer.

"I don't know… in what way? He wasn't a happy boy. He was homesick, even after two years. Signed for his mom a lot." She tapped her cheek with her forefinger. "And you know that he came to Summit because he was violent."

"But the shocks took care of that."

She gave a little shrug. "They seemed to, mostly," she admitted. "I hate the ESDs, but they do seem to work."

"Lovaas, the guy who wrote about ABA?"

"Yeah…?"

"Did you know that he recanted later? That he said that shocks didn't work in the long term. The children became inured to them over time. And he said what they had learned in ABA didn't generalize over other environments." Zachary paused. "Is that the right word? Generalize?"

"Yes," Clarissa agreed faintly.

"Dr. Abato thinks the solution to getting used to the pain is just to increase the shocks. Increase the pain level to get control over them again."

Clarissa frowned as she took a bite of her sandwich. Zachary nibbled at his own, but had no appetite. It was perfectly done. Just crispy enough. The cheese melty, the butter salty, but he couldn't eat it.

"But he can't do that," Clarissa said. "There's already controversy over whether the phase-two ESD we are using right now is acceptable. It works for most of the kids, and the court won't rule against us using it because the parents say they have nowhere else to go. But another device? A stronger one?"

"The kind they use to control adult prisoners," Zachary informed her. "That's what he said. And I guess if they're already in use in other circumstances, maybe it won't be impossible to get it approved."

"I don't think they could ever get it approved for use with our kids."

"Do you want to leave Summit?" Zachary asked after a lengthy pause in the conversation.

"I do… and I don't… I want to help children, and it's a good job with good pay and benefits. But it's eating me up. I can't sleep. I can't think. It's not making me happy." She pushed around the remaining corner of her first half-sandwich. "It didn't make Quentin happy."

"I think you need help."

"Me? Help with what?"

"Someone to talk to about your symptoms. You should talk to a psychologist. A therapist. Someone."

"It's nothing. It's just stress. Being upset over Quentin's death."

"I don't think so. I think it's more like PTSD. And you said it started before Quentin died."

She picked up the bottle of Heinz ketchup on the table and spilled a pool onto her plate. "This better be real Heinz, and not just a Heinz bottle refilled with generic stuff." She dabbled the second triangle of her sandwich in the ketchup and took a bite. Since she didn't complain about it being generic, Zachary assumed that she found it acceptable. She pretended for a couple of minutes to be completely engrossed in the meal, then finally looked up at him again.

"PTSD?" she repeated. "How could it be? PTSD is for war veterans. People who have been through traumatic events. Not ABA therapists!" She made a wide shrug.

"I don't know. I know about PTSD… but not all of the kinds of events that can cause it. But what you're describing… it sure sounds like PTSD to me."

"I don't get flashbacks," she said, a slightly derisive note in her voice. "What would I flash back to? A therapy session? They can be pretty raw, but I don't think it counts as a war."

Or war crimes.

Zachary wasn't so sure. What he had seen that day had been pretty traumatic to him. And Clarissa was a young girl, seeing that and worse every day for months. After a few hours of seeing the shocks used, Zachary had been ready to curl up in a ball and shut the rest of the world out. He knew that Angel and Trina would both be haunting his restless dreams along with Quentin. And Zachary was tougher and more experienced than Clarissa.

"I still think you should talk to someone," he said. "Get some help. And maybe a prescription to help you sleep."

I have a question," Zachary said suddenly. He was still poking at his barely-touched sandwich, while Clarissa was nearly done with hers. The afternoon sun shone through the diner window.

"What is it?" She looked anxious about what he might ask her. And he could ask her a lot of uncomfortable things. But most of them didn't need asking, unless he was trying to make her feel worse than she already did.

"No, it's nothing to be concerned about. Just... some of the logistics of the shock devices they're using at Summit."

"Um... okay. What about them?"

"They're bulky, with the backpacks, and pretty complex with all of the wires and electrodes... how many?"

"Six."

"Six electrodes that have to be attached. The residents just let you put them on every day? Or put them on themselves? How does that work?"

"Kids that are pretty compliant, it's not a problem. Some of the more reactive patients, it can be difficult. With the worst cases... they keep them on at all times. You always have at least one electrode attached, so then you can... shock them... if they are fighting against having the others attached. Each electrode is like a cattle prod or stun gun, with the positive and negative poles close together, so each one operates independently."

"And they keep them on all the time? How? When they are sleeping?"

"Yes. When they're sleeping. I don't imagine it's too comfortable sleeping with the backpack on, but they get used to it."

Zachary couldn't imagine trying to sleep with such a device attached. From what he understood, children with autism often had sleep issues. Those would be magnified a hundred times by having to sleep with ten pounds of batteries in a backpack and six electrodes attached to their bodies.

"What about hygiene? Do they bathe? Shower?"

"Shower," Clarissa confirmed. "They have to keep one arm electrode attached and hold that arm out of the water."

Zachary closed his eyes to picture it. "How do they do that?"

"Sometimes they need help. It is pretty hard to wash with one arm out of the shower. Or for them to understand why they need to. Some of them are dyspraxic—not very well-coordinated."

"And by help, you mean… one person holding on to their arm to keep it out of the water, and maybe another one doing the washing?"

Clarissa stared off into space. Zachary watched her curiously. In spite of the fact that he'd dealt with his own PTSD for thirty years, he'd never watched someone else having a flashback. He waited for her to return to herself.

Clarissa looked back at him, blinking and looking like she was just coming out of a fog.

"What?"

"You don't have flashbacks?" Zachary asked.

"No."

"What was that? Where did you just go?"

"Nowhere. I was just thinking about something else. Daydreaming."

"Who was in the shower? Who were you remembering?"

Clarissa shook her head. "They're so defenseless. And with the electrodes… to never be free of them… it's just so sad."

"Yes." Zachary finally pushed his unfinished sandwich away from himself. "It is."

Kenzie didn't have time to get together for supper. Things had been busy at the medical examiner's office and she had other evening commitments. She didn't tell Zachary what those commitments were and, after dancing around the issue and not being able to get to a satisfactory answer, Zachary forced himself to let it go. If he acted like a jealous boyfriend, demanding to know where she was going and who she was seeing, they would never be able to move their relationship forward. He'd lose the friendship and the resource that she was to him.

But she did agree to a phone call while she was on break, eating a vending-machine dinner at her desk. So he uploaded the information he wanted her to look at and waited for her call.

When the phone rang, Zachary had been trying to calm himself with a game of solitaire, and nearly launched the phone across the room in his surprise. He tapped the green button to answer and put it to his ear.

"Kenzie? Hi."

"Hi, Zachary. I don't have much time, like I said, but I've got a few minutes for you."

"I want to go over the medical examiner's report again."

"I see that. Is something bothering you?"

"No, just… now that I've been there, and seen how they operate, I want to review it again, see if I can pick up anything else."

"Okay. What first?"

"His mother said that one of the things that he did when he was anxious was picking his skin."

Kenzie made a noise of acknowledgment. "Yes… I can see

that. Pretty obvious from the photos. We discussed it the first time."

"I know. So I didn't look at his skin very carefully to begin with. I figured all of the scabs and scars were from him picking at his skin."

"Uh-huh."

"But now I'm wondering if any of the damage was done by the electrodes."

"What electrodes?"

"From their skin shock therapy. It's one of the aversives that they use. Their preferred one, so that they can give the same punishment consistently every time."

"Uh… okay. And you think they might have caused some damage to the dermis?"

"I saw a girl today who was burned by a malfunctioning unit. Blisters. Second degree electrical burns. So I wanted to know if any of Quentin's injuries might have been burns, or started as burns and he picked them as they scabbed. Would you be able to tell that?"

"From these photos? Probably not. Where would the electrodes have been located?"

Zachary described the locations of the arm and leg electrodes. "And apparently two on the torso, but I'm not sure of the positioning. I couldn't see those ones."

Kenzie hummed as she looked through the pictures on her screen. They hadn't done any really close shots of the skin on his arms and legs, where he had picked at his skin. But they were good quality digital photos and could maybe be enlarged enough that Kenzie could see the details she needed.

"I really couldn't say one way or the other," Kenzie said. "The best spots to look at are his torso, where he couldn't pick his skin as easily through his clothes. Mostly, he picked at his arms and a little on his legs. There are a couple of places on his stomach and back where I could be looking at burns from the electrodes. But it's pretty hard to tell from the photos."

"So, maybe."

"Sorry I couldn't be more of a help. What else?"

"The cause of death was strangulation."

"Right."

"What could they tell from the bruises on his throat? On TV, they can always tell what caused the bruises. Chain links in a ligature, hand size in a manual strangulation, they can always tell."

Kenzie snorted. "I gather you've already guessed that isn't always the case."

"I was hoping that a closer examination of the bruises might give us some more information."

There was silence while Kenzie examined the report. "There are probably more photos available than are in the medical examiner's report, but from these, and the narrative description, no. Can't tell much. It was not a narrow ligature like a belt or a chain. Something wider that left an indistinct bruise."

"But no pattern or impression that might be helpful?"

"No."

"The institution said that he had the ends of his blanket wrapped around his neck and twisted tight."

"That's consistent."

"But could it have been something else? Maybe a chokehold?"

"Yes, an arm across his throat, especially if it was someone wearing sleeves, wouldn't leave a mark that was significantly different than a blanket. Unless the person giving the chokehold had cufflinks or something else distinctive that left a mark."

Zachary pictured the aides and security guards at the institution. Even Dr. Abato didn't wear cufflinks. The white lab coat of a doctor with no embellishments on the sleeves, over a dress shirt. He hadn't noticed the shirt sleeves extending out of the jacket.

"No, not a lot of cufflinks around at Summit. So, nothing useful? You don't see anything the medical examiner might have missed?"

"The report seems to be complete. I'm sorry, I'm not seeing anything else."

"Nothing that you question even a little? Look twice at?"

"The cause of death is obvious. I can't speak for the police investigation, how thorough they were, but no, there's nothing in here that suggests it might have been a third party. No stray fibers, finger marks on his neck, anything like that."

"He'd never attempted suicide before."

"The suicide rate among people with autism is pretty high. It may have been his first attempt, or it may not have been. It might not have been noticed before, if he'd tried the same method and failed. He might just never have tightened it that much before."

Zachary closed his eyes. He tried to avoid the image of Quentin twisting the ends of the blanket tighter and tighter. He could hardly breathe thinking about it. He would never have thought of that method himself. Had someone else suggested it to Quentin? Had someone killed him? Or was he just seeking the comfort of deep pressure and went too far? Maybe Mira would be happier with that suggestion. That it wasn't intentional, and it wasn't murder, it was just an accident. Quentin hadn't understood what he was doing.

"You still there, Zach?"

"Yeah. I'm here."

"You okay?"

He let the question sit for a few minutes, thinking about it. The case was disturbing on many levels. More triggering for him than Declan's case had been. He wanted to help the other kids at Summit, but what could he do? The public already knew what was going on there. They knew the broad strokes, even if they didn't know the details like Zachary did. And they still wanted Summit to remain in operation. Was the public's fear of people who were different that pathological? They kept saying it was because the residents of Summit were violent, but Zachary found them to be eerily like him, or like he was when he was younger. He had not been violent, but they had locked him up repeatedly because he didn't fit anywhere else.

"Zachary? I asked if you're okay."

"Yeah. I guess. It's been a long day, Kenz. And this case is pretty disturbing. I know you don't have time to talk about it right now, but the things I saw over there today… I think you would change your mind about the kind of place Summit is."

"They're very highly acclaimed," Kenzie said. "I know their methods are controversial, but the parents swear by them."

"Yeah," Zachary agreed. "I know. But I think if you saw what I did, you'd think differently. We'll have to talk about it another time."

"Sure. Will you be okay…? Are you alone?"

Zachary rubbed the bridge of his nose and looked around. Sitting in the living room of Bowman's apartment, he hadn't even looked to see if Bowman was home.

"I think so." He got up and went into the kitchen, where Bowman's shift calendar was posted on the fridge like a kid's drawing. "Yeah. Bowman should be back in another hour. I'll be fine."

<hr>

Waiting for Bowman to get home, Zachary pulled out Margaret Beacher's business card to look up her number, which he hadn't yet put in his phone as he should have. He tapped it in and listened for it to ring. She answered it after just a couple of rings, which probably meant the first ring on her end.

"Hello?"

"Margaret? It's Zachary Goldman."

"Yeah, I know," she agreed. "What do you want?" She didn't say it in a challenging way, but it still disconcerted Zachary a little for her to completely bypass the usual niceties. He was used to having to go through all of the usual 'how are yous.'

"I have some questions for you," he said. "But… they're not about shocks or Summit specifically."

"Okay. Go ahead."

"When you talk about yourself or the residents at Summit,

you say 'autistic person.' I thought… the politically correct thing these days was person with autism."

Margaret laughed. "You spend the afternoon talking with the cute aide from Summit, and that's what you call me about? Person-first language?"

"Well…" Zachary was grateful that she couldn't see him blushing. "I just… well, I noticed that at Summit they say it one way, but you say it the other. I didn't know if it was like… black guys calling themselves the n-word, or what."

She chuckled again. "Political correctness says that you can't put autism first, because I am a person first and autistic second. Autism is not my identity, just something I am afflicted with. I hate to tell you, but… it is absolutely who I am. It is a *pervasive* developmental delay. That means it affects every aspect of my life. Political correctness says that you can't put a negative qualifier at the front of a person's identity. You are allowed to say a brilliant woman, rather than a woman who is brilliant. But you aren't supposed to say autistic woman, because autism is negative. It's like disabled or mentally handicapped. You're not supposed to admit that it is what you identify me by. That it's the first thing you see."

"But you want it to be first, because…"

"Because it *is* my identity, like I said. That's my community, my tribe. It's the language I speak. It's how I approach life. It's how I succeed or fail. It may make people uncomfortable, but that's just too bad."

"So is it only okay for someone who has—for someone who is autistic—to say it that way, or do you want everyone to use it?"

"You can do what you feel like. But I'm quite happy to be called autistic. That's what I am."

"Okay. Got it."

"And while you're at it, you can lose the 'non-verbal' designation as well. A lot of our community prefers 'nonspeaking' over 'non-verbal,' but what difference does it really make how we communicate?"

Zachary considered. "Summit makes a big deal about making their kids speak. I don't really know about other communication methods. Do they work?"

"Have you ever written a note? Typed an email? Nodded your head?"

Zachary again felt a flush of embarrassment. "Of course."

"Then you've used alternative methods of communication. Did it work?"

"Yeah."

"Yeah. Sometimes it works better than others. And sometimes nonspeaking communication works better than speaking. Just be open to other methods of communication and don't assume that speaking is the only option."

"Yeah. Makes sense."

"How did your visit with that aide go?"

"I wish I could say she gave me information that would crack the case… but she didn't really have anything new. It was really just more of the same."

Margaret made a noise in her throat. "Why was she so eager to talk to you, then? She was acting like she held the key."

"I think… she just wanted to talk to someone about what it was like to work there."

"You feel sorry for her?" It was more of a statement than a question.

Zachary considered it. "I do, and I don't," he admitted. "I can see that it's not an easy place to work and I wouldn't wish PTSD on anyone. But… she chooses to stay there. She knows what she is doing is harmful to others, but she stays there. Maybe she's not trained to do anything else, but…" He trailed off, uncertain.

"I wouldn't believe anything she says," Margaret said. "I was tortured by people like her for years. She may put on a nice front for visitors, but behind the scenes, when it is just her and a child, she's not that same person."

"Yeah." Zachary's own experience with institutions and care-givers confirmed this, and maybe that's why he was reluctant to feel too sorry for Clarissa despite her apparent issues.

He'd seen too many women and men who were all sweet smiles for the public, social workers, and school teachers, but behind the scenes, it was a whole different story.

When Bowman walked in the door, he froze. He sniffed the air. He looked around and saw the pizza box on the table.

"Any left?"

"It just got here."

"Nice!" Bowman opened the box to see that it was untouched. Zachary walked in from the living room, and they both got out plates and dished up a slice each. "What's the occasion?"

"Well, I figured you'd be tired at the end of your shift…"

Bowman raised an eyebrow at Zachary. As it was the first time that Zachary had ever surprised him with pizza, Zachary supposed he had the right to be skeptical.

"I wanted to pick your brain," Zachary admitted.

Bowman nodded. "Here, or living room?" As the one guy at the station house who knew how to bribe anyone, he had no problem with Zachary buying his time.

Sitting at the kitchen table seemed too formal, too much like a meeting with an agenda. So Zachary motioned to the living room. "We can relax better in here."

Bowman threw another piece of pizza on top of the first, grabbed a beer from the fridge, and followed Zachary into the living room. They ate for a few minutes without saying anything. Mario with gusto, Zachary just picking at his toppings.

"I know Summit Living Center is out of your jurisdiction," Zachary said.

Bowman nodded, chewing a big bite of the pizza. "Way out of it," he agreed.

"But close enough that you might hear some rumors about what goes on there?"

Bowman considered this, looking serious. "I might have heard a few things over the years," he admitted.

"Do the police have a lot of involvement at Summit? They deal with violent residents, so I would assume that sometimes…?"

"No, not that I've heard. I don't think they call the police to deal with problems with their kids. Not like some of the schools and institutions."

Zachary pulled a section of crust off of his pizza slice and worried it. "Some of the places I was at, they would call the police if someone assaulted the staff."

"Yep. Pretty common. But Summit keeps things quiet. They have some kind of therapy to deal with violent students, so they just deal with it themselves. Internally."

"So the police never get called in to arrest someone for being violent."

"No, not that I heard of. And there'd probably be a lot of questions if they ever did, because the police there would know what kind of people they have at that institution. That they probably aren't competent. Don't have the judgment. It's like when we get called to a school to arrest a six-year-old. If you're smart, you ask a lot of questions before you put the cuffs on a little kid. You know it's going to get reviewed. It's going to get to the papers—the internet. So you make damn sure there's cause for an arrest."

"Yeah. I remember when they arrested a girl with autism at one of the places I was at." Zachary paused to swallow and take a deep breath, keeping himself as calm as possible. "The police were pretty ticked off when they brought her back, because no one had told them about her… disability."

"I would have given them crap if it was me, you can bet on that. They should have known better."

Zachary nodded. He took a bite of the pizza, focusing hard on the sweetness and spiciness in an effort not to let himself slide back into the memories of Annie.

"What about other stuff? They've been investigated before, right? And then they had to be called in with Quentin's death. Have you heard anything else? What they've had to go there for? How they felt about it?"

"I can try to hook you up with someone local… I don't know very much. They get calls sometimes. There was one in the news a few months ago, you've probably already seen it online, where a mother was trying to take her child out, said that they wouldn't release him. She said that he'd been abused. The police went in with her, and there was no trouble getting him out. She just had to sign the right papers. When they investigated, the boy—or was it a girl? —was covered with bruises. But the staff said it was all self-inflicted. You know how some of these kids hit themselves or bang their heads when they're upset about something."

Zachary had read something about the incident. The news articles had kept the story very small, had sided with the institution. Made it sound like the mother was crazy or attention-seeking. But having seen Summit, Zachary was a little more inclined to side with the mother and to believe that there had been something going on there. Even if the child was self-harming, chances were, he would have been shocked for it. And maybe the mother had decided she didn't like the shock therapy as much as the other parents did.

"I get the feeling that the director over there is something of an egomaniac," Bowman said. "He likes the publicity that the place gets, even if it's controversial. They've been investigated enough times that nobody really wants to go take another look."

"Yeah." Zachary picked a piece of pepperoni off of his pizza. "He makes a big show out of how open they are. How transparent. But the therapies they use… I just don't know how the authorities can let them keep it up."

"As long as they've got the parents and the courts behind them, they can do pretty much anything they want."

"Do you know the officers who handled the investigation? Of Quentin's death?"

"Haven't heard through the grapevine. Who was it?"

Zachary put his plate aside, happy to be rid of it, and opened his laptop. "Trainer and Benz."

"No, don't know them personally. You concerned that the investigation was mishandled?"

Zachary drummed his fingers over the keys. "I don't know what to think. I think that if the police were told that it was a suicide, that's what they would investigate. And if there wasn't anything that jumped out and said, 'not a suicide,' they would just put it to bed."

Bowman nodded. "Yes. Sounds about right. If you can't disprove it… why put the family or the institution through all of the anxiety of a murder investigation? You don't investigate a suicide the same way as a murder. It would cause too much extra work."

"And so far, I haven't found anything that says, 'not a suicide.'"

"Do you think it wasn't? What does your gut tell you?"

"My gut tells me… I'm not finished yet."

Zachary felt depressed putting the thought into words. He did not want to go back to Summit again. He'd had enough of the place. Much more, and he'd be a basket case himself. "There are still… unexplored corners."

"Well, be careful. If it is a cover-up, you don't want to go turning over too many stones and making yourself a target. The reason police officers have partners is so that someone can watch their backs. You don't have anyone watching yours."

Zachary nodded. "Thanks. I'll be careful."

It wasn't *really* late when there was a knock on the door, but late enough that Zachary wondered who would be knocking on Bowman's door at that hour. Bowman lived a pretty quiet life and didn't get a lot of visitors, scheduled or not.

Bowman was in a food coma, slumped on the couch after

having eaten nearly the entire pizza. He roused a little at the knocking, but didn't get up to answer it, so Zachary did.

He didn't check through the peephole before opening the door, which was a stupid thing to do. He knew better than that. Bowman was a cop and Zachary was a private detective. Both of them could have unsavory visitors. He should have looked through the peephole and kept the chain on until he was sure who it was and that Bowman wanted to let them in. But he too was tired, his brain spent three times over.

Bridget was at the door.

For a moment, Zachary just stood there, stunned by her loveliness. By her unexpected appearance on his doorstep. His shocked brain ran through several different reasons she might be there. Did she want to get back together with him? Was she in trouble? Did she think that he had done something wrong?

He immediately searched his memory for anything he might have done to tick her off in the past few days. The compulsion to chase after her was still so strong, even with medication, group therapy, and his psychologist, that some days he felt like a junkie in withdrawal. In actual physical pain over her absence. He wanted to follow her, to watch her, to know where she was every minute of the day. So far, he'd been able to resist stalking her any further. It helped to have a case that occupied his attention as much as the Quentin Thatcher case did. It kept his brain from falling back into the same ruts again. Helped him to think of things other than Bridget late at night when the loneliness was the worst.

"Aren't you going to invite me in?" Bridget demanded.

She didn't look happy. Zachary again racked his mind for the reason she had come. What she was upset about. An old argument? A break-up with her new boyfriend?

"Zachary."

"Yes, yes," Zachary stepped back from the door, opening it the rest of the way and motioning her in. "Come in. I'm sorry, I'm just surprised to see you, that's all."

Bridget marched in as if she owned the place. She clutched her purse under her arm and looked around, her eyes sharp.

She looked into the living room and spotted Bowman on the couch, snoring. "Well, I guess we can talk out here." She motioned to the table.

Zachary pulled out a chair as she did and sat down.

He had missed her. It was nice to get together with Kenzie, but he didn't know where that relationship was going, if anywhere. He'd made some pretty serious mistakes. He and Bridget had been together for a couple of years, madly in love at the start, and he still hadn't recovered from the events that had blown them apart. Bridget had gone on, was in remission from cancer, and was in another committed relationship, leaving Zachary far behind. She was the one who had gone through cancer, but he was the one who couldn't recover.

"I just wanted to see how you were doing," Bridget said.

Flat, expressionless. Zachary couldn't read her. She put her purse on the table and crossed her legs, waiting for him to tell her how he was. Zachary looked around the kitchen for some inspiration, but it didn't come.

"I'm okay," he said tentatively. "Why?"

Her eyes scanned his face. "You're not looking very well. Are you sleeping?"

"The best I can."

"Maybe you should get something stronger. Or a sleep study. Sleep is very important for good health."

Zachary nodded, avoiding her gaze.

"Kenzie said you are having some trouble with a case you are on," Bridget said finally, with a sigh.

"Kenzie called you?"

"She was concerned about you. Said that she couldn't make it over to check on you, and did I think you would be alright. She didn't ask me to come over, but I offered."

Zachary had no idea how to feel about that. Angry? Violated? Infantilized? Comforted?

"So, how about a drink and you tell me about it?" Bridget suggested.

He searched her face for some indication of her interest level. Or for any affection or tender feelings toward him. Why would she come all the way over just on Kenzie's suggestion? She must have some kind of feelings toward him. The last few times they had seen each other, she had been angry, bursting-at-the-seams furious. Kenzie had said that just proved that Bridget still had feelings toward Zachary. But when she was worried about Zachary, who did Kenzie call? Bridget. Did that mean that Kenzie didn't consider Bridget a threat to their relationship? Or that there was no relationship, no possibility of a relationship past the level of friendship?

He got up and went to the fridge. "Uh… there's not much selection. Beer? Water? Maybe coffee?"

"Too late for coffee, I'll never sleep. And you'd better not either."

"Coffee doesn't keep me up. It helps to calm me down."

"Tea?"

Zachary checked a few cupboards, already knowing the answer. "No. Sorry."

"Well, I guess we'll go with water, then."

Zachary couldn't help but notice she had dictated what his drink should be as well as hers. His natural reaction was to go for the beer just to be oppositional, but that would cause problems when combined with his meds, and he was going to need to take something to sleep. And while coffee really didn't keep him up, he was afraid that just the suggestion might be enough to keep him from falling asleep.

So he ran them each a glass of cold water, with a squirt of lemon juice from a plastic lemon lurking in the back of the fridge, and sat back down with her. Bridget sipped the water delicately.

He studied her as she drank. She was as lovely as she had ever been. Better color since she was off of all the cancer treatments. A little bit more flesh on her face, rounding out her features and making it so that her eyes didn't look quite so large. Her hair was very short, but it was undoubtedly her own rather than a wig, and he knew that she must be over the moon that it hadn't changed color or refused to grow back.

"So, tell me about it," Bridget prompted.

Zachary could dance around the issue and say that he didn't know which case Kenzie was talking about. After all, he was always working several cases at a time. The bread and butter came from insurance claims and adultery, not homicides. Not suicides.

"Did she tell you anything about it?"

"No. She was in a hurry."

"It's a possible suicide… a young boy in an institution. Autistic." Zachary took a big gulp of his water and almost coughed. He'd put way too much lemon juice in it.

"That sounds pretty grim. Who wanted it investigated, his family?"

"Yes. Single mom, two other boys at home. Feels guilty that she put him there. Guilty for being so relieved to get him off of her hands."

"You don't think she had anything to do with it?"

"No. It was overnight, she wouldn't have been there."

"Oh, good. I don't like it when it's the parents. That's always so sad."

Zachary recalled Dr. Abato talking about parents at the end of their ropes, murdering their own children. "Yeah. It is. But that doesn't seem to be possible in this case. Either he did kill himself —on purpose or by accident—or someone there at the institution killed him."

"Why?"

"I don't know. I'm trying to figure it out. The place is… like a funhouse. Things aren't what they seem. Therapies that should be helpful, and instead are harmful. Things that you can't imagine being allowed in modern times, and people are insisting that they are good. Holding them up as saving their children and their families. Staff getting PTSD from the things they are being forced to do to the residents."

Bridget frowned and shook her head. "That doesn't sound likely. What are they doing that is so bad?"

"Giving them electrical shocks," Zachary snapped, and Bridget's eyes widened. "That or hitting or pinching them. Restraining them. Forcing them to perform actions over and over and over again. Essentially torturing them until they comply."

Bridget's head tilted, and Zachary saw her attitude change. Disbelief. Not shocked at what he had said, but doubting that it was true.

"This is happening!" he insisted. "I'm not exaggerating it. Or imagining things. There have been court cases. Do an internet search on the institution. You'll see. It isn't a secret."

"If there have been court cases, then I *know* you're overreacting. No judge is going to let them take actions that are going to be harmful to the children."

"Because the parents and therapists say it is helping. And that they're willing to do anything to help their children to become normal. To have some hope of a happy life. Because if they can't help them to recover, the alternatives are pretty dire."

"You've always had such a tender heart," Bridget said, her tone disdainful. "You always feel so bad for people. Even when they've put themselves in the middle of trouble. You need to toughen up. Or don't take these cases. You can't let them affect you like this."

"If I don't investigate it, who is going to? These kids need me. Quentin needs me, and the other kids that are being abused at Summit. Who else is going to help them?"

"You're not Superman. You can't just fly in there and save the world. You're inflating what your job there is. You're supposed to be investigating one child's death. To see whether it was suicide. You are not there to overthrow the social structure and save everyone else. That is not going to happen. If you think that's what you're going to do... then I think you'd better get in to see your psychiatrist right away. Because it might be the symptom of a manic phase."

Zachary couldn't find the words to argue with her. He took another sip of his too-sour water to try to cover his lack of verbal ability. And in the back of his mind, the doubt that she'd planted started to grow. It was true that an inflated sense of self-importance, of grandiose thinking, was a symptom of bipolar depression. Zachary's depression had always remained unipolar; the only manic episodes he'd ever had were triggered by medications.

Was he inflating his role at Summit? Thinking that he was there to do more than just investigate how Quentin died? He knew that he wanted to save the other children who were in danger, but did he think he could?

He tried to focus on the present and evaluate his own thoughts dispassionately. The trouble with disordered thinking was that the brain didn't know its own thoughts were disordered.

"I don't think I can change everything or change everyone," he said slowly. "I'd like to be able to help them. I'd like to be able to change the kind of therapy they do there, their whole approach to helping people with autism and behavioral problems..." He shook his head. "But I know I can't do that. I just want... to save a few of them. To start something. I don't know. I want to make a change, but it's not going to be something that changes the whole institution. I can maybe change things for one or two people. Maybe."

Bridget's shoulders dipped. "That's good. I want you to get help if you're having trouble recognizing reality."

"I'm not. It's just a very emotional case."

"And you think these *therapists* are getting PTSD from these therapies, not the patients?"

"Oh, the residents are too. I've talked to people who went through these kinds of therapies when they were children, heard how it still affects their lives. But yes, I think the staff members are getting PTSD too. The atmosphere there, the strict control over them, taking too many sick days, not being able to sleep, flashbacks to what they've been doing at the institution… it's PTSD. I recognize it."

"I don't think you can get PTSD from something that you do to someone else," Bridget said. "That just doesn't make any sense."

"Why not? Don't you think you would be traumatized if you were forced to torture someone?"

"No, I don't think that's possible. I think that if someone chooses to do it, it's because it isn't affecting them. Maybe they're psychopaths. But being traumatized by some therapy that is making people squeamish…? It doesn't follow."

Zachary let out his breath. He glanced toward the living room, trying to decide whether to get up and get his computer. He didn't want to wake Bowman up. Bowman had enough sleep interruptions due to Zachary's nightmares and sleep issues.

"I looked it up," he said. "There's a kind of PTSD called PITS. Participation-Induced Traumatic Stress. It is a real thing. Soldiers who have to kill at close range. Executioners. Even animal shelter workers who have to euthanize animals."

Bridget still looked skeptical, but seemed ready to believe that there might possibly be such a thing. Or at least until she had proof one way or the other.

"This really seems like… you've dug yourself into a hole. You were only there to look at one death, and now it's all of the inmates. All of the staff. You're losing focus."

"Maybe."

She waited.

"I'm going to be okay, Bridget. I know Kenzie was worried, and that this all sounds a little bit much… but I'm not here alone. And I'll… I'll dig myself out."

"You're taking your meds?"

"Yes."

He didn't tell her *mostly* or *when he felt like he needed them.* Because he knew that just wouldn't be good enough for black-and-white Bridget. He was taking his medication when he needed it, so the answer was yes.

"And you're not having suicidal thoughts?"

Zachary thought back over the last few days and shook his head. "No. Just… the regular stuff. I'm not suicidal."

"And you're not going to get yourself in trouble?"

"I'll be careful. I'm not going to do anything stupid."

"Okay." Bridget nodded. "I should head for home. And you know… you can call me, if you need something."

It was a very different position from when he was in the hospital and she was raging over still being listed as his emergency contact. He still hadn't changed it, either. If something happened, then Bridget was the one they should call to find out his history and to give the doctors direction. He wasn't putting that on Kenzie, and who else did he have?

Bowman snorted and stirred in the living room. They both turned their heads and looked toward the room to see if he was going to wake up. Zachary heard scratching, and then Bowman pushing himself up from the couch.

"Zachary?"

"In the kitchen."

Bowman cleared his throat, scratched some more, and made his way into the kitchen. When he saw Bridget, his posture became straighter and he grinned widely.

"Bridget! It's been forever since I saw you. How are you?"

"I'm good, Mario. How have you been?"

"Oh, wow. You look fantastic, woman. I thought someone said something about you being sick."

Bridget patted at her short hair self-consciously, her cheeks going a flattering pink. "Oh, really, Mario!"

"No, it's true. Isn't it Zachary? No wonder you didn't tell me she was coming over, you dog. You wanted her all to yourself."

Zachary fought his own flush. "I didn't know she was coming," he squeaked.

"Oh, sure you didn't," Bowman teased.

"I was just getting ready to go," Bridget said, standing up and giving him her fingertips to shake. "I hope Zachary hasn't been too much trouble for you?"

As if he were a child, or a dog Bowman was boarding for her. Zachary knew she was fishing, checking one more time to make sure she didn't need to be concerned about his welfare.

"Aside from the fact that he never sleeps?" Bowman responded. "No, he's a good houseguest. Even bought me pizza today. But he's looking for some place new, aren't you, Zach?"

Zachary nodded. "Yeah. I've called a few places, still need to look at them. Once this case settles down a bit…"

Bridget nodded slowly. "That's great," she said in a tone that was just a little too bright for the circumstances. "I'm glad you're getting on your feet again."

Would she prefer that he stayed at Bowman's indefinitely just so that he had someone to look after him? Did she think that he couldn't manage on his own, in his own place? It hadn't worked out very well after the divorce, but Zachary had lived on his own before and had been okay. He could do it again. As long as he was careful with his health, he would be just fine.

He walked her the short distance to the door. Bridget leaned in close like she was going to kiss Zachary on the cheek. Instead, she whispered in his ear, her warm breath on his skin.

"Maybe you should drop this case. It doesn't sound like you've found anything to indicate it's not suicide, so maybe you should just let it go. Then it can't keep you up nights."

He gave her a peck on the cheek, hugged her with their bodies apart and his hands on her shoulders, and saw her out the door.

17

Zachary's dinner with Mr. Peterson had been arranged a couple weeks earlier, before Zachary had taken the Quentin Thatcher case. It meant a drive in the opposite direction from Summit, so Zachary knew he would have to take a day off from his investigation at the institution. Maybe just let everything settle and percolate for a day, and go into it with a fresh viewpoint on Wednesday.

So he worked on other cases during the morning, cleared up paperwork and checked the logs of a couple of cars he had been tracking to look for patterns of behavior. He made a few phone calls. Did some virtual stalking on social networks. A lot of detecting was tedious research and paperwork, but it had to be done.

Mid-afternoon he was happy to lay his paperwork aside and get into the car. As he drove toward Mr. Peterson's home, leaving Summit farther and farther behind, with the brilliant greens of spring all around him, Zachary felt a weight being lifted from his shoulders.

Mr. Peterson—Lorne—was one of Zachary's former foster parents. The only one that he had kept in touch with over the years. While he'd only lived with the Petersons for a few weeks, it was Mr. Peterson who had given him his first camera, who had helped him to develop his film over the years, and who had suggested Zachary had the skills to be a private detective if he wanted to put his photography skills to some practical use.

Being a foster child, with no supports after he turned eighteen and very few after he was sixteen, Zachary had to find a job as quickly as he could, and certainly didn't have the kind of money that would be needed to become an artist showing his work in galleries. But private eye work was something he could do. He was good at candid shots, at melting into the background, and observing others. He picked up quickly on body language and little things that were out of place. He was good at anticipating what was going to happen before it did. Hypervigilance was a helpful trait for a detective.

Mr. Peterson had moved into a nice little bungalow a few years earlier. Similar to what he had lived in when Zachary had lived with him and his wife. It signaled an end to the series of seedy apartments Mr. Peterson had lived in since his divorce and the beginning of a new era for him and Pat. They had been a couple for twenty years. More than that. Society had finally reached the point where their relationship could be openly acknowledged.

There were pink tulips in the neat front garden. Mr. Peterson opened the door as soon as Zachary pulled in front. His face was wreathed in smiles. He looked older than when Zachary had seen him last. The little hair that he had left was whiter than Zachary remembered. He might have put on a few pounds. How long had it been since Zachary had seen him last?

"Zachary, so good to see you!" Mr. Peterson shook his hand warmly and slapped him on the back in a half-hug. "How are you doing? Come in!"

Zachary was hustled into the house. Pat was in the kitchen, but came out wiping his hands on a towel to greet Zachary.

"Hey, Zach. How was the drive?"

"Good. No traffic. And it feels good to get away. I didn't know how badly I needed this."

Pat smiled. He was still in good shape, but he wasn't a young man any more. His age fell between Zachary's and Mr. Peterson's, but he wore the years well, becoming more mature and distinguished.

"Well, you two sit down and start on getting caught up. I'll have dinner on the table in a few minutes."

Zachary sat down. There weren't very many places where he felt like he belonged in the world. Mr. Peterson's was one of the few. Maybe the only one, until Zachary found a new place for himself and settled in.

Mr. Peterson's eyes traveled over him. Lines on his forehead deepened and the little fan of wrinkles around his eyes disappeared. "Are you okay, Zachary? How is the house-hunting going?"

"I'm actually looking now," Zachary said. "I've got calls in to a few places, so it shouldn't be too long before I find something. Then I guess I'll need furniture and household stuff before I can move in. Just the basics. A couple more weeks, maybe."

"Good. It can't be easy just sleeping on couches."

"Well, I've done it enough before." Zachary shrugged. "But I'm wearing out my welcome. I was only supposed to be there a couple of days."

"You can't be expected to get back on your feet in a couple of days. It takes time to get your identification reissued and get your insurance check. Suddenly being without *anything* is more than just a setback."

Zachary shrugged again and didn't know what to say to that.

"So, what are you working on?"

"I have a new case. A boy who might have committed suicide. His mother hired me to look into it."

"Suicide." The lines on Mr. Peterson's forehead became more pronounced. "Do you really think that's a good idea? Doesn't that… I don't know… trigger feelings for you?"

"The possibility that it might be suicide hasn't really bothered me. I can think about it without having suicidal thoughts… but other things about it have been…" Zachary didn't want to say anything that would worry Mr. Peterson. He already had Kenzie and Bridget fussing over him. "Some of the other aspects have been… bothering me a little."

Mr. Peterson nodded. His eyes got a little wider. "What other aspects?"

"He was in an institution. He was autistic and couldn't live with his family anymore." Zachary tried to swallow the sudden lump in his throat. He wasn't talking about himself; it was Quentin. Zachary's institutional life was long in the past.

"Ah. So that hits a little too close to home?"

Zachary made a little motion with his hands, trying to downplay it. But the words stuck so badly in his throat that Mr. Peterson had to know it was a problem.

"It isn't much like any of the places that I lived. Except maybe the living units, which are pretty much the same as any detention cell." He saw again the room where Quentin had died. Remembered Annie; Zachary trapped on the other side of the security door, unable to do anything for her. Screaming for help.

Mr. Peterson sat beside Zachary on the couch and put a comforting hand on his back. It was warm and firm and grounding. "What happened?" he asked quietly. "I know Bonnie Brown wasn't the greatest place to be, but it was your safe place when you couldn't be with a family."

"Yeah," Zachary agreed. "I chose to go back there. Christmases. When things got really bad. There were times I just couldn't function in a foster family."

"So, what happened? What are you thinking about?"

Zachary swallowed, trying to clear the lump in his throat so he could speak clearly. "I never talked to anyone about it."

"Someone was hurting you? That place was full of traumatized kids. Kids who had been abused and could become perpetrators."

"It's not that…" Zachary didn't deny the fact that there had been predators there. As there surely would be at any similar institution. "It's… when I was there, a girl died, in the room beside mine."

Mr. Peterson shifted, studying Zachary seriously. "You never told me anything about that before."

"I never told anybody."

"What happened?"

Zachary stared at the framed pictures on the mantle across the room. Some of them were photographs he had taken. Portraits of Mr. Peterson and Pat together. A small one of himself as a young man, standing on the street, sideways to the camera, bashful about having his photo taken.

"She was autistic."

"How did she die? Was it suicide?"

"She stopped breathing. In the night. When they went to wake her up in the morning, she was dead."

"So it wasn't suicide or a suspicious death. Just one of those things."

"Yeah." Zachary breathed, staring at the picture of himself. "Maybe."

"Do you think something else happened to her?"

When he thought about it, Zachary's guts cramped up. He remembered the security guards, the police, Annie screaming. Too many images at once, overpowering.

"You're not there, Zachary."

You're not there.

Zachary breathed in a deep lungful of air. He could smell Pat's cooking. He was in Mr. Peterson's living room, not Bonnie Brown. Though Mr. Peterson had calmed him with a hand on his back before, he wasn't touching Zachary anymore, cautious of triggering a worse reaction.

"She had been violent the day before." Zachary forced the words out, hoping they would help him to sort and stabilize the images. "Assaulted a guard. They called the police, had her arrested. She was still upset when they got there. Fought the police. She got like that. Everyone there knew she had meltdowns. Tantrums, they called them. Like she was a toddler."

He breathed a little more easily. Blinked and tried to remain present. Annie was in the past. Zachary wasn't a child anymore. No longer eleven and helpless. It had happened decades earlier.

"You think this tantrum had something to do with her death?"

"I don't know. Maybe. Maybe something happened to her while she was fighting with the police."

"What?"

"I don't know." Zachary shook his head. "I don't remember."

Neither of them said anything. The silence drew out.

"I don't remember," Zachary repeated.

"Okay."

"Everybody ready to eat?"

Zachary looked up and saw Pat standing in the doorway, his stance indicating that he had been there for some time, waiting for the right moment to speak.

"Yeah," Zachary agreed, getting up from the couch. "It smells really good."

Mr. Peterson didn't spring up as quickly as he would have a few years previous. It took a moment of creaking and rebalancing, but then he was smiling and striding toward the table, as if denying the fact that his body was aging.

"Just give me a second to wash up," Zachary told them. He headed to the bathroom, waiting for a few moments in the still, quiet closeness of the space for his body to calm down, for the cramps to ease. He splashed cold water on his face and then toweled it off.

He returned to the dining room table to find Mr. Peterson and Pat talking companionably, not acting like he had put them out or made them wait for a long time. Zachary took a surreptitious glance at his phone before sliding it back away, trying to gauge the passage of time and anchor himself. When he was on his meds, time was more of a constant; it didn't grow and shrink so dramatically.

He forced a smile and seated himself. "Thanks for inviting me," he said. "It's good for me to get away for a bit. Get away from work."

"And then I go and bring up your case," Mr. Peterson said. "Sorry."

"No, it's okay. I didn't mean that."

They passed the dishes around and dished up. Zachary tried to hide the fact that he wasn't taking very much, spreading the food out and commenting on how good it looked. Pat knew by this time that Zachary didn't have much of an appetite when on his ADHD meds, so Zachary really didn't need to cover the fact up, but he still worried about Pat being offended.

"How's the photography going?" Pat inquired, attempting to pick the topic that was least likely to trigger a reaction from Zachary. "What are you working on these days?"

"Nothing right now. Lost all of my equipment in the fire."

"Oh… I didn't even think. I'm sorry."

Zachary shrugged. "The insurance company will cover replacing a lot of it. Can't replace the photographs and negatives, though. I didn't keep duplicates anywhere else, or digital records in the cloud. Now… I know better."

"That's a devastating blow," Mr. Peterson said, real pain in his voice. He was a photographer too. He could understand how hard it would have been to lose all of his artwork. "I'll make you copies of everything I have. And I've got a couple of cameras I don't use. Let's go through equipment after dinner and I'll give you some stuff to take back with you."

"You don't need to do that," Zachary protested. But his spirits lifted at the thought of getting his hands on one of Mr. Peterson's treasured cameras. He'd bought the digital camera he needed for his surveillance work, but he still preferred real film for his art. He smiled his appreciation and had a couple of bites of his dinner.

When Zachary got back from Mr. Peterson's and checked on the voicemails that had been piling up while he'd had his phone turned off, he listened a couple of times to one from a soft-spoken woman.

Mr. Goldman, my name is Ava Kennedy. I'm the mother of a girl at Summit Living Center. I wondered if you could talk to us sometime in the next few days. I'd really appreciate it.

She gave her number, stayed on the line breathing for a moment, and then clicked off. Zachary wrote down her information. Was it possible that she or her daughter knew something about Quentin's death? Some piece of information that was missing from his investigation? It was late in the day to be calling anyone back, so he put it aside to deal with in the morning.

He was feeling nice and calm and relaxed after his visit to Mr. Peterson's, so after checking over his camera stops one more time and making sure his film was loaded and properly advanced, he took some sleeping pills and stretched out on the couch. He lay on his stomach with one arm hanging over the edge of the couch, resting his hand on the camera, the cool metal reassuring. Then he closed his eyes to go to sleep.

18

Ava Kennedy was a striking black woman, perhaps a few years older than Zachary. While her face was unlined, she looked tired and worn. She shook Zachary's hand briefly, her slim hand small in his.

"This is Tirza," Ava said, indicating the teen girl sitting on the bed, staring steadfastly away from them. She was a gorgeous girl with many of her mother's features and a vague, innocent air. Her hair was done in neat corn-rows.

Ava sat down on the bed beside her daughter.

"Hi, Tirza," Zachary greeted.

Tirza whispered something, turning briefly toward her mother, then away again, tugging on her earlobe.

"It's okay, Tirza," Ava said. "This is Mr. Goldman; he's here to help."

Zachary wasn't sure how he was supposed to be helping Tirza. Ava had been cryptic on the phone, saying that she would fill him in when he got there. He wasn't sure what Ava thought her daughter had to do with Quentin's death, if there was any connection at all. Maybe she wanted to hire Zachary for another case and it was nothing to do with Quentin.

He noted that Tirza did not have on a black backpack and

electrodes. That made her one of the minority of students who was being treated without skin shocks.

"What is it you wanted to talk to me about today? Do you have concerns about something here at Summit?"

"I… don't know," Ava said unhelpfully. "I'm hoping you can help to sort that out. I didn't know where to go, and then someone said that you were a private investigator. I thought maybe there was something you could do to help."

"So this isn't anything to do with Quentin Thatcher's death?"

"I don't think so."

"Okay… well, I'm not sure if I'm prepared to take on another case right now, especially one that might have something to do with Summit. My plate is pretty full…"

"Would you listen to our story and then decide? If you say you can't help, I'll understand."

Zachary looked into her earnest, pleading eyes. He nodded.

"Alright. Go ahead."

"Tirza is autistic, like Quentin. She was part of an after-school program here. Living at home, going to the public school in a mainstream program with accommodations for her needs. Working on social skills and whatever else needed a little work here."

Zachary nodded encouragingly. He tried to make eye contact with Tirza, but she looked steadfastly away, acting as if she were unaware of Zachary's presence or what he was doing there.

"About a week before Quentin died, Tirza disappeared. Between when her aide at the school made sure she was ready to go and when the car that was supposed to pick her up and bring her to Summit arrived." Ava shook her head, expressing her confusion over this. "She had the same routine every day. She'd never had any trouble getting from her locker to the car. But half an hour later, I got a call from the car service saying that she had not shown up. Asking if she was sick. I dropped everything and went over to the school, but she wasn't there. I called the police."

Ava looked at her daughter with concern. Zachary could see no sign that the story was distressing for Tirza.

"They treated it like a *runaway* case." Ava's tone was outraged. "I explained to them that she was autistic. That she wasn't a rebellious teen who might have just gone off shopping with a friend or meeting a boyfriend. She wouldn't have gone anywhere other than the car, unless someone took her away. She went to the car every day."

"You managed to find her again, obviously."

"I wouldn't leave them alone. I wouldn't let them just brush it off as a runaway case. Forced them to issue an Amber Alert. Went to the media and made sure it was well-publicized that she was the victim of a kidnapping, not a runaway. Started an investigation into whether there had been any strangers hanging around the school, or whether anyone had been paying an unusual amount of attention to her."

"Doing all of the right things."

"Apparently. Forty-eight hours from when she disappeared from the school, she was found wandering beside the highway."

Zachary looked at Tirza again. She would be an attractive target. A beautiful young woman not equipped to defend herself.

"How was it handled?"

"They questioned her as a runaway. They called me to come pick her up. Case closed."

"They closed the case? What did she say to them?"

"She said she had gone with Damien."

"Who is Damien?"

"I have no idea. They decided Damien was her boyfriend and that she had just decided to spend a couple of days with him, unconcerned about the people who might be worried about her."

"Has Tirza told you anything about what happened?" Zachary looked at Tirza, unsure whether he should be addressing her directly. He had never liked it when social workers or foster parents talked about him as if he weren't standing right there.

Ava nodded. "She gave me a very detailed account about going with Damien and being… passed around to a number of different men. She told me what happened to her. She's not just making up a story."

Zachary swore. "Oh, Tirza. I'm so sorry."

Her eyes flitted over to him and then she put her face against her mother's shoulder, pressing into her.

"What did you do? Did you go back to the police with this?"

"Yes… but I don't know how seriously they are taking it. They are still pretty insistent that this is just rebellious teenage behavior. They said they will investigate, but I don't hear anything back from them. I don't know if they're doing anything."

"What about her therapist? Isn't there someone she can talk to here who will back her up, say that she's not lying?"

"They say she is just repeating what she heard somewhere else. That she's not… high functioning enough to be able to put an experience like that into words."

"No," Tirza protested, banging her fist against Ava's body. "No, no, no!"

"I know, Tirza. I know you're telling me the truth," Ava assured her.

Tirza quieted.

"Are you… is she still taking the after-school program here?" It was obvious to Zachary that they had to be there for another reason. It was morning, so Tirza should have been at school, not due for her after-school program until her day was done.

"She hasn't been able to go back to school. Or to function at home. I don't know what to do with her. She's regressed. Before this happened… she was pretty independent. She was going to school, could do things at home without me supervising her constantly, she had friends and was a happy girl. But now…" Ava put an arm around Tirza and cuddled her close. "When I take her to school, she cries and won't stay there. She doesn't want to talk. She's depressed and self-harming. I can't watch her all of the time to make sure she doesn't hurt herself. Or do what Quentin did…" Ava trailed off, looking at Tirza, obviously not wanting to put ideas into Tirza's brain. She sighed, eyes shiny with tears. "So I've had to put her into residential here. Even though I really don't want to."

"That must be very hard."

"Everything that we worked so hard for is gone, because this man, this Damien, stole her away from us. How could anyone be so depraved? To take such an innocent life and do what he did."

"You're lucky you got her back at all. They could have—" Zachary checked his tongue before blurting in front of Tirza, "—hurt her instead of letting her go. They must not have thought that she could identify them."

"She could describe their clothes and what they did to her. But I don't know if she could ever testify in court and be considered a competent witness. So they were probably right. They don't have to worry about what she could say about them."

"No, Mom." Tirza first tapped Ava on the leg, and then made a chopping motion. "No more. No." Her words cut off and she looked at Zachary pleadingly for a moment before hiding her face against her mother again.

Zachary looked at Ava to get her interpretation of Tirza's words and gestures. But Ava shook her head, not quite sure.

"No one is going to hurt you anymore," she told Tirza. "You're safe here. The bad men can't get to you here."

"No." The chopping motion again, as if she were karate-chopping Ava's thigh. But while she did continue the motion until her hand reached Ava's leg, it was obviously not a violent motion. Not intended to hurt. She jerked her hand in Zachary's direction.

"What, Tirza? Use more words," Ava prompted.

Tirza pulled her face back from Ava. She brought the arm that had been behind Ava's back in front of her body. She made the chopping gesture again, into her flat hand, and motioned at Zachary.

"Stop," Ava said. "Stop… Mr. Goldman?"

"Zachary," he corrected automatically.

"What do you want to stop, Tirza?" Ava asked. "Mr. Goldman —Zachary—is here to help. You want him to stop something?"

"No. *Him*." Tirza motioned to Zachary again, and again made the sign for 'stop.' "Him, him, him, him." Each time she said 'him,' she moved her hand over slightly, as if there were a row of men standing beside or behind Zachary.

And for the two days she had been gone, there had been a row of men, Zachary realized. It made his heart ache to think of what she had been through for those forty-eight hours. How terrified she must have been, not understanding what was going on. Or understanding and not able to stop it.

"Baby." Ava kissed the top of Tirza's head. "It's over. It is stopped, sweetie. They aren't going to hurt you any more."

Tirza looked toward her room's open door. She again buried her face in Ava's shoulder.

"No. No more."

"That's right. No more. No more hurting Tirza. Tirza is safe."

She rubbed Tirza's back and hugged her. Zachary watched a man walk down the hallway, past Tirza's room. He saw Tirza look up briefly at the sound of footsteps, and then she hid her face again quickly.

"Tirza," Zachary addressed her in his gentlest voice. "Tirza, no one here is hurting you, are they?"

Tirza moaned and again made the 'stop' gesture with one hand.

"Is somebody here hurting you? Touching you?"

She murmured and cried into her mother's shoulder.

"Does she understand what I'm saying?" Zachary asked. "Has she told you anything to indicate that she might be... being victimized here? It happens in a lot of institutions. I'm sure they have to pass police checks to work here, but..."

"I just don't know," Ava admitted. "She keeps telling me to stop it. No more. I think it's just anxiety or flashbacks, I don't think she's still being hurt. I don't think that anyone here would... Everybody has to be vetted. I don't think..."

But she couldn't know. None of them could know for sure whether Tirza was still being hurt, except Tirza herself. And she was not giving them the information they needed.

"I think it's just anxiety," Ava repeated, trying to sound more certain.

A woman walked up to the door. She was wearing a lab coat, like most of the therapists. An affectation, since none of them were doctors who were doing anything messy and needed to have their clothing protected. It was just a uniform to identify them as doctors or professionals. Was the lab jacket supposed to make it look like they had had more training than they did? Zachary remembered Clarissa telling him they liked to recruit aides and therapists right out of school, so their methodology wouldn't be contaminated by other practices.

The woman gave the room a big smile. "We have company today, do we, Tirza? That's nice, isn't it?" She focused her gaze on Ava. "Mom, it's time for Tirza to go to therapy. Would you tell her good-bye, and I'll get her on her way?"

Ava pulled gently back from Tirza, trying to extricate herself from the girl's grip. "School time, Tirza. Time to go."

Tirza didn't argue or fight, but she made it obvious from the way she sat slumped on the bed that she didn't want to go.

"Get up," her mother coaxed, pulling on her hands. "Get up off of the bed and on your feet. Therapy time. You need to get your skills back. Work hard again."

Tirza slumped down farther, uncooperative. The therapist put her hands on her hips. "This wouldn't be a problem if you'd let her wear an ESD."

"She's already traumatized enough. She doesn't need to be abused further by being given electrical shocks."

Bravo for her. Finally, someone standing up for her child's rights.

"Okay, then you need to move out of the way and I will get her going. Tirza, come!" The therapist's voice snapped. Tirza darted a glance at her. "Out," the woman repeated to Ava, and looked at Zachary. "And you too. I can get her to move."

Ava sighed. She stroked Tirza's hair. "You need to listen, baby." Then she moved out of the room. Zachary followed her reluctantly.

The therapist wasn't gentle or patient. She gave Tirza commands in a loud, unyielding tone, and when Tirza didn't immediately obey, she pushed, pulled, and prodded her to get her to move. Eventually, Tirza was on her feet and being escorted out the door. She wasn't crying or protesting her treatment. The therapist nodded at Ava, ignored Zachary, and marched Tirza off down the hall.

Ava motioned to Zachary, and they both went back into Tirza's room to talk for another minute.

"So, this doesn't have anything to do with Quentin's death," Zachary said.

"No… It's just… the police said that kids are often victimized by people like this that they meet online or in chat apps. They agree to meet someone without the parents' knowledge, not realizing that they are opening themselves up to a predator."

Zachary nodded. "Yes. I've seen it before."

"But Tirza didn't have a phone. She didn't have internet access. She didn't use a computer, except for a self-contained communications device, not hooked into any network. Nobody contacted her while she was at home. It was either someone at the school, or someone here."

"She couldn't tell you which?"

"She calls them both 'school.' I can't work out how this guy met her. The school and Summit both say there's no way. He doesn't work there. And there haven't been any strangers hanging around. They would have found him on the cameras."

"It's more likely to be someone from the school, since that's where they took her."

"Yes."

"And you said she cries when you take her back there. Not when you bring her here."

"Because that's where she was taken from. She doesn't want them to take her away again. But..." Ava motioned to their surroundings. "You saw she still asks me to stop them when she is here."

Zachary nodded.

Ava gave a wide shrug. "I can't say it's someone from the school. And I can't say it's someone from here. I have to just trust them at both places and let her keep going back somewhere she might have been stalked or victimized before. It's not much of a choice."

"No. So, you're looking for someone to investigate and find out who took her? It would not be easy, and my plate is already full with Quentin Thatcher's death."

"I just... I thought that since you're looking at things with fresh eyes here, getting to know how the place works... you could just tell me if you saw something. If you thought there is something to be concerned about. A security risk, or a person you get a bad feeling from. Just... anything you happen to come across."

"I don't think I'm going to be able to help you."

Ava's face fell. But she didn't argue or reproach him.

"I'll tell you if I hear or see anything," Zachary promised. "But don't get your hopes up. Because I don't think... I don't think I'm going to come across a pedophile while trying to get to the truth in Quentin's case."

"Okay. I understand that. And... thank you."

Zachary nodded. "Do you think I could watch her therapy session for a few minutes?"

"I'm sure we could get permission."

Ava led the way to the nursing station at the middle of the unit and smiled at the woman seated at the computer.

"Mr. Goldman would like to watch my daughter's therapy session. Would that be alright?"

The nurse or supervisor shrugged. "I don't see why not, if you give your permission. Do you know the way?"

Ava shook her head. "I have to go. If someone could take him there…?" At Zachary's look of surprise, she explained. "It's best if I leave while Tirza's occupied with something else. She's very clingy and if I try to separate from her, she cries and makes a fuss. It's better if I'm just not here when she gets back. And I need to run some errands and take care of the rest of my household."

Zachary accepted this. The supervisor waved down a security guard and indicated Zachary. "Can you escort him down to the therapy wing? Tirza Kennedy's session?"

The guard agreed. He escorted Zachary through the hallways, which were becoming a little more familiar and not so much of a rabbit's warren.

"Here she is." The guard stopped at one of the observation windows, and Zachary saw Tirza sitting across the table from the therapist who had bullied her out of her room.

"Thanks." Zachary sat down on one of the chairs. The guard nodded. "Flag someone down when you're done," he instructed. "Don't go wandering around."

Zachary agreed. He watched Tirza through the window. The therapist seemed to be working with her on speech. Prompting words and phrases which Tirza dutifully repeated, staring off distractedly into space. Her mother said that she could describe the men and what they had done. But Zachary hadn't heard her say more than a handful of words voluntarily. And those sporadically, haphazardly, without grammar.

"Eye contact," the therapist prompted, putting her hands on Tirza's cheeks to turn her head until Tirza was looking at her directly. Tirza's hands came up to cover her face.

"No, quiet hands. Keep your hands folded on the table." The therapist grasped Tirza's hands and put them back down on the table, joined together. Tirza kept her hands there, was praised, and the therapist went back to getting Tirza to repeat words back to her.

She used a communications device at the school. If they brought it to her at Summit, would she be able to tell them more about the men she was afraid of? Whether she feared someone who was actually there, or just the idea of men who might hurt her and flashbacks to the men who had hurt her. Zachary couldn't understand why Summit wouldn't allow the use of communications methods other than speech, as Margaret had suggested.

Zachary's mind drifted to Ray-Ray Maslen. He wondered how the little boy was doing. He had known Quentin. Had gotten used to seeing him after their sessions. Did he miss Quentin now that he was gone? Or did Ray-Ray not even remember that he had existed?

Zachary watched Tirza. She obeyed her therapist's commands. Each phrase repeated back perfectly. She was prompted for a few scripts like Quentin had been learning, where she was expected to give the correct reply to prompt words or phrases such as 'how are you?' or 'good-bye.'

Zachary thought about Ray-Ray's session. 'Touch your nose,' 'touch your ear,' 'give me a hug.' He had read through Lovaas's reasons for teaching commands like those in his book. By teaching simple commands and imitation, the therapist then had the tools to move into more complex behaviors and interactions that the child needed to learn. Interactions like hugs and kisses were taught because they were required in everyday life. Giving grandparents a hug when they arrived. Kissing Daddy good-bye on his way to work. Desensitizing the child so that he wouldn't have a meltdown if auntie or cousin wanted a hug when it was time to go.

Tirza continued to obey each prompt.

And Zachary saw both Ray-Ray's and Tirza's sessions meld before his eyes.

Hug me, Tirza. Good girl.

Give me a kiss and you can have a candy.

Touch your lips, Tirza. Touch your stomach. Touch me here. That's right. Good girl.

In his manual, under rewards for good behavior, Lovaas had listed "kissing, hugging, tickling, stroking, fondling."

Take a child who had been trained to follow every command an adult gave them. A child who had been trained to obey immediately, without question, and to expect treats, praise, and physical touch or games in return. Who had learned to expect pain and punishment for any wrong response. That child became the perfect victim. A child with no boundaries, no defenses, and no instinct to fight back.

A beautiful, innocent girl like Tirza would do whatever she was told.

19

Tirza was parroting the lines that the therapist was feeding her, but her mind was far away. In her brain, she was somewhere safe and protected. Not where she had to answer questions and do as she was told. She was curled up somewhere deep inside her brain where no one could reach her. Still trying to process everything that had happened to her.

The new man seemed nice. The Gold Man. But Damien had seemed nice too. Damien had praised her and told her that she was a good girl. Tirza had been happy to please. But then Damien took her away, said that she was supposed to go along. Her mother had said so. And she was always supposed to do what her mother said.

Tirza didn't know what to do. She had tried to answer the questions of the policemen, but they had thought she was a bad girl, a girl who had run off and done bad things to make her mother cry. She tried to use her words, like she'd been taught, but the police officers didn't like what she said and kept feeding her new lines.

At home and able to use her computer again, she'd tried to explain it to her mother. Her mother didn't think she was a bad girl. Her mother didn't believe that she would run away and go do bad things. But typing the things that had happened to her made it too real and too frightening. It was like bleeding into the computer and not being able to stop the flow or the pain inside her. Like being forced to open her eyes when the light burned them. It made her even more afraid. What if Damien or the men came back? What if they took her away again?

A slap on Tirza's hand brought her attention back to the game. She couldn't let her thoughts be distracted to the point that she stopped vomiting back the words to the therapist, or she would be punished. She was tired of being punished. The men had hurt her. Even when she tried to do everything they told her to, they still hurt her.

Her mother had said she shouldn't let men touch her body. She should protect herself. Fight back. But whenever Tirza fought back against the grown-ups, she was punished and told she was a bad girl. Her body wasn't hers. She wasn't allowed to say no or to decide where to go or what to do. If she resisted, they just took hold of her and forced her to perform.

It wasn't her body. It was theirs. Theirs to control and do what they want to.

Maybe the Gold Man could help, like her mother had said. He would stop them from hurting her more.

Damien would come back for her.

Damien could come to her room. Could take her out.

And she had to do what Damien said.

Zachary couldn't look at Tirza's shadowed, hollow eyes any longer. He got up from his observation chair and wandered to the other therapy rooms in the cluster. He didn't like that he was becoming accustomed to watching the therapy. It wasn't so shocking, it didn't disturb him as much, even with his dawning realization that by doing what they were, they were making autistic children into the perfect victims. How could so many professionals be wrong? Zachary couldn't claim, as a layman and someone who had not seen more than a handful of autistic children, that he somehow knew and understood more than they did. That would be the height of arrogance.

He stopped, for a moment fighting vertigo. Once again, he saw little Ray-Ray Maslen on the other side of the glass in therapy with Sophie. It gave him a sense of *deja vu*, especially after he had just been thinking about them. Could the therapy help Ray-Ray to grow up to be a strong, independent man? Able to make his own way in the world, like any 'normal' man? Could they make him indistinguishable from someone who did not have autism? Make him function just like one of them?

Ray-Ray was sitting at the table, looking engaged, eager to

please his therapist. He beamed when he got an answer right and frowned or cried when he responded in the wrong way and was corrected.

Sophie was making him repeat words when she pointed to the pictures on a board she held in front of him. When Ray-Ray got nervous or excited, he started to flap his hands, and Sophie physically repositioned them, admonishing 'quiet hands' every few answers.

Ray-Ray twisted in his seat, pivoting his little bottom one way and then the other, attempting to keep his upper body calm and still while burning off nervous energy below the level of the table.

"Quiet hands." Sophie again restrained Ray-Ray's flapping and put his hands on the table in front of him. "Quiet hands, Ray-Ray."

He kept them still with obvious effort.

Zachary studied Ray-Ray's hand positions. One hand was cradled in the other, where Sophie had put them. Not clasped or side-by-side, but one supporting the other. Both were curved slightly, but Zachary could see the vague semblance of the sign Tirza had been making. There was no chopping gesture, he just held them in position as he had been told to, but Zachary could still see the subtle sign Ray-Ray was making.

Stop.

Sophie ran him through the exercises relentlessly. As Zachary had been told, Ray-Ray and the other children were in many hours of therapy every day. It was a full-time job for them. Sophie made her demands and Ray-Ray did the best he could to give her the proper responses, to smile, to frown, to repeat words and gestures that were mostly meaningless to him. He could do nothing to protest this treatment. It was where the professionals wanted him to be. Where his mother wanted him to be.

All he could do was hold that one sign in his hands, his therapist oblivious to the silent plea.

Stop.

Zachary asked whether he could speak to Tirza when she got back from her therapy session. The woman at the nursing station in her unit considered the request.

"You can't talk to her in her room without supervision. You can talk to her in one of the meeting rooms, where you can be observed and surveillance cameras record everything."

"Sure, that would be fine," Zachary agreed. He would even accede to direct supervision. If Tirza were his daughter, he wouldn't have wanted any men talking to her alone.

Tirza was obviously anxious when they put her in the meeting room where Zachary waited for her. She looked around, ducking her head in and out of the open door, rocking and fluttering her fingers in front of her eyes.

"Can you tell me what's wrong, Tirza?" Zachary asked. "What are you afraid of?"

Tirza looked out the door again. Despite the fact that he was a stranger to her, a man she hadn't worked with before, presumably like the men she had been victimized by, she didn't seem worried by him, but by the people who were outside the meeting room in her unit. People she should have been familiar and comfortable with.

Tirza paced around the small meeting room. Zachary could relate to her need to keep moving.

"Quentin," Tirza said abruptly.

Zachary looked at her. "Quentin? Did you know Quentin, Tirza?"

They were housed in the same unit. The residents didn't seem to socialize with each other much—it wasn't in their nature, according to Dr. Abato—but that didn't mean that Quentin and Tirza didn't know each other. If Quentin was friends with Ray-Ray because they had therapy sessions one after the other, he might certainly have known Tirza as well.

Tirza made the hooked-together fingers that Zachary recognized as the sign for friend.

"Quentin was your friend?"

Tirza made some huffing noises, nodding her head. She ran light fingers over her cornrows. Zachary did his best to read her body language, every movement that might have meaning.

"Do you know what happened to Quentin?"

Tirza voiced several loud cries. She put her fingers up to her eyes, her mouth open and her features pointing down in an anguished frown. Tears gathered in the corners of her eyes, and she made the *friend* sign again, fingers tightly locked to each other.

"I'm sorry your friend died," Zachary said. "You must be really sad about that, and then everything that has happened to you… that's pretty scary."

Scary was a word that he would use in talking to a six-year-old. Zachary mentally scolded himself for talking to her like a child instead of a young woman who was nearly an adult.

"Do you know why Quentin died, Tirza?"

She moaned and approached Zachary. She took him by the arm and tugged, obviously expecting him to go with her. Zachary followed, though he was not sure about going anywhere with Tirza. She was vulnerable, and he didn't want anyone thinking that he was taking advantage.

Tirza led him past the nursing station, where the woman who had put him into the meeting room watched them stroll down the hallway together, her eyebrow raised. It was, Zachary hoped, obvious to any onlooker that it was Tirza leading him, and not the other way around.

Tirza led him to one of the individual cells. Zachary didn't think it was her room. That had been at the other end of the loop. The one that Tirza had taken him to was empty. No personal effects. Not that any of the rooms had had very much in them by way of personal touches.

But Zachary had an idea that it was Quentin's room. He had

approached it from the other direction when he had been there with Dr. Abato. Tirza looked around the room, flapping her hands.

"This was Quentin's room, wasn't it?"

She made a sound Zachary took as acknowledgment.

"Do you know how Quentin died?"

She moaned and flapped. Zachary was frustrated by not being able to communicate with her. So close to having some answers, and so far away. Would she be able to tell him if her mother were there to help interpret her sounds and gestures? Would she be able to give a detailed account if she were allowed her computer at Summit, as she had given her mother following her kidnapping? Had they intentionally deprived her of her voice? Dr. Abato said it was to force residents to use verbal communication, but what if it were the opposite? To deny them any communication at all? By keeping them from using their preferred methods of communication, they kept residents from talking about what went on at Summit. From describing what was happening to them during therapy or after lights out.

But there were still students who had good speech at Summit. Students like Trina, the girl with the malfunctioning ESD. She had been able to tell him about the procedures at Summit, about what she feared. It didn't make any difference; still, nobody listened to her or to Zachary about it. Was there a tipping point? A point at which if there were enough voices, the public and the courts would start to listen? Did Summit keep it below that tipping point by silencing as many voices as they could?

"Quentin was your friend," Zachary said, starting again at the beginning, hoping he could gain some momentum.

Tirza touched Zachary's arm.

"And he died in this room. After Damien took you away from the school."

She flapped hard and stood on tip-toe.

"Did Damien hurt Quentin?"

She looked at him sideways, one hand again resting on his

arm. Was that *yes*? Did she even understand he was trying to ask her a question?

"Is Damien here, Tirza?"

Tirza looked at the open doorway.

Was the man who had taken her away out there? Was it someone employed by Summit? Maybe a therapist that worked at both the school and Summit? Or who had followed Tirza to school? Had he gone there to snatch her, since there were too many cameras or witnesses at Summit?

He decided to approach it from the opposite direction. "Was Quentin sad? Did he kill himself?"

Tirza started to scratch herself. Not just the light scratching of itchy or dry skin, but digging her nails in as she raked them down her arms, as if she intended to peel layers of skin right off. Zachary reacted instinctively, grabbing her hands and trying to hold them still.

"No, no Tirza. Don't do that. It's okay. It's alright. Please, calm down."

She struggled to free herself. Zachary was not a big man. Stunted by early malnutrition and meds, never eating enough to put himself into a healthy weight category. He was taller than she was, but only just, and her struggles were frantic and powerful. He'd been warned that the autistic residents could be strong and not deterred by pain in the same way as he was. Tirza was like a writhing snake in his grasp. He was afraid of hurting her, but she didn't protect herself or hold back from hurting him. Zachary let go, worried that trying to control her would only escalate her behavior. He went to the doorway to call for help.

"Can I get someone here? Please?"

One of the supervisors glided down the hall toward him, unhurried. She wasn't an old woman, but older than all of the fresh-faced aides and therapists, her face lined with experience. She took in the situation in a glance.

"And this one without an ESD," she muttered.

"Can you do something?"

"Tirza!" The woman moved into the room, crowded with three people in it. "Tirza, you stop!" She clapped her hands, the noise surprisingly loud in the small room, echoing off the walls. She grabbed Tirza's hands and pulled them away from each other. "Stop!" She let go of one and slapped Tirza on the thigh, not as loud as the clap, but still hard enough to make Zachary wince. "Stop. Show me your hands. Show me quiet hands!"

Tirza was bullied into folding her hands together, compliant, her self-injurious scratching stilled. Impressive, but it also made Zachary squirm.

"What is she doing in here?" the woman asked. "This isn't her room. And who are you?"

"Zachary Goldman. I'm investigating Quentin Thatcher's death."

"Oh, yes. So I've heard." Her lips pressed together. "So you know this was Quentin's room. Tirza doesn't belong in here."

"Tirza said she and Quentin were friends."

"Yes, I imagine she did."

"Did they spend a lot of time together? Did they talk to each other?"

"They were closer to each other the last few weeks. Quentin acting possessive about her. Hormones; they can cause strange behavior in these kids."

"They weren't… uh, boyfriend/girlfriend…?"

"Certainly not. He might have been sweet on her, but there was no hanky-panky going on here."

Zachary laughed, embarrassed. Hanky-panky? At least she had answered his question.

"But Tirza… I thought she wasn't in residential until after her kidnapping. How did they know each other?"

"She went home most nights. But she has a room here, because sometimes her mom couldn't pick her up right after therapy, or she wasn't able to watch her in the evening and needed Tirza to be somewhere supervised for the night. She paid full residential rates, even though Tirza was not here most nights."

Zachary nodded. "Ah. I see. So she saw Quentin when they were both done with therapy, if she came back here to wait for her mother or stayed overnight."

"Yes." The woman cast a glance at Tirza, standing between them, looking down at Zachary's feet. Her hands were still in the proper position. But she had bloody scratches down her arms. "I'd better have someone clean her up. You'll be going, then?"

The woman who had helped get Tirza under control took her out to the nursing station to get someone to escort her to the medical offices. Zachary saw Clarissa, the aide who had helped Quentin out, talking to another staffer, getting some child's schedule amended. She saw Zachary and Tirza come out of Quentin's room. At first, she frowned, looking confused. She saw Tirza's injured arms and her face softened into an expression of compassion.

Clarissa finished getting the schedule sorted out and then approached Zachary. She introduced herself as if they had never met before, a charade that Zachary assumed was intended for the woman helping Tirza.

"Is there anything I can help with?" she offered, looking back and forth between them.

"Well, if you don't have anywhere you need to be in the next few minutes, you could take Tirza to medical."

Clarissa looked at Tirza's face, but didn't get any eye contact. "Sure, of course," she agreed pleasantly. "I can help Tirza."

She put her hand under Tirza's elbow to escort her down the hall. Tirza moaned and pulled away from her, taking Zachary's arm in both of her hands.

"Oh, looks like Tirza has a little crush on you," Clarissa laughed. "Why don't you come along so that she'll cooperate? It's so much more complicated dealing with the residents without ESDs."

Zachary suspected that Clarissa wanted to talk to him without the risk of the other staff overhearing, so he agreed readily. Not that he would have refused anyway; he would much rather walk to the medical wing with Tirza than have to watch her being *encouraged* to comply.

"Sure. Lead the way. Come on Tirza, I'll walk with you. You probably know the way all by yourself, don't you?"

Clarissa took a couple of steps. Zachary gave Tirza a little tug on the arm. Tirza resisted at first, but she didn't fight him like she had when he'd tried to stop her from scratching herself. It was just an initial balk, then she matched pace with him.

"Find out anything new?" Clarissa asked in a lowered voice.

"I don't know… not really. A lot of dead ends, mostly. I found out that Tirza and Quentin were friends. But Tirza can't tell me anything about his death."

"No. She wouldn't have been here when it happened. I don't know if she has any idea what happened to him. Just that he stopped coming one day."

Zachary looked at Tirza's face, blank, apparently oblivious to their conversation. But he'd learned from the others that he couldn't assume that the appearance of not attending meant anything. She could be listening to every word.

"I think she knows more than that. She took me to his room. She got upset when I was talking about him… I think she wants to tell me something, but I don't know what it is." He shrugged. "Maybe just that she misses him."

"Probably. I don't think there's anything else she would be able to tell you. It's too bad she's regressed so much after the… runaway incident. She really was doing remarkably well. She could carry on a conversation… a little awkward, maybe, some starts and stops, but she was far more verbal than she is now."

"Runaway?" Zachary repeated. "Do you think she ran away, rather than being kidnapped?"

Clarissa gave a short laugh and shook her head. "I know her mom would like to believe that she was kidnapped by some mysterious person. But that's just wishful thinking. She doesn't want to admit that Tirza ran away, then got in deeper than she anticipated. Got scared and discovered that she didn't have the skills to make it on her own after all. She was back within forty-eight hours. I don't think any kidnapper would have just let her go. With the danger that she could identify them…?" She flashed him a smile.

"Maybe he didn't think she could. Maybe he figured she wasn't any danger to him."

"Kidnappers don't just let kids go."

"They do if there is too much heat. If they think there are too many people looking for them. If they let her go, everything quiets down and goes back to normal. If they… do something more permanent, people are outraged. They don't give up on finding out what happened to her."

Clarissa shook her head doubtfully. "There may be a few cases where that has happened… but I doubt if it happens very often."

"Maybe she escaped from wherever they were holding her."

"Or maybe she wasn't being held anywhere, by anyone, and just wandered aimlessly until someone found her and called the police. Don't read too much into it. The mother… believes what she wants to believe. She gives the police a big song and dance with all of these details she says she got from Tirza. But look at her," Clarissa made a little motion to the girl. "Have you been able to get more than a word or two out of her? She didn't tell her mother all of those details. Her mother is making it up, trying to convince herself that Tirza wasn't a runaway."

Tirza's grip was tightening on Zachary's arm. He looked at her but couldn't see any change in her expression. He patted her hand briefly, hoping to comfort her.

"Here we are," Clarissa said with a smile.

They walked into the medical wing and a doctor or nurse in a lab coat approached. An older man, considerably taller than Zachary, with a good build.

"Tirza has some scratches that require treatment," Clarissa told him.

He looked at Clarissa's arms and nodded. "We'll get those cleaned up. Come over here and sit down, Tirza."

Tirza didn't respond immediately, but Zachary guided her over to a chair and she sat down. Zachary looked around as the doctor treated Tirza, taking the opportunity to see part of the institution that he hadn't had access to previously. He couldn't see a lot; most of the medical wing appeared to be a network of examination or treatment rooms behind the doctor.

"Were you here Monday when a girl was brought in for burns from a malfunctioning ESD?" Zachary asked.

"Trina?" asked the doctor. "Yes, I was here."

"Does that happen very often?"

"There are occasional malfunctions. But no, I wouldn't say often."

"What about other burns from the ESDs being used too much."

The doctor looked up at Zachary and raised his brows. "No, of course not."

"No burns, no marks from the shocks?"

"Skin shocks are entirely safe."

Zachary switched direction. "Were you on duty when Quentin's body was discovered? Were you called to attend at the scene?"

The doctor looked back down at Tirza's scratches, cleaning them with antiseptic wipes. Tirza didn't flinch at the sting. She just sat there, staring up and to the right.

The doctor sighed. "I was on duty when Quentin's body was discovered, but I stayed here while Dr. Weiler went to attend to the scene."

"What did he tell you about it?"

"If you're the private detective I keep hearing about, then you've already seen the police and medical examiner's report. You know more than we do. All Dr. Weiler did was go have a look, confirm that there was nothing that could be done for Quentin, and call the police."

"Was the blanket wrapped around his neck when Dr. Weiler got there? Or did he remove it?"

"He wouldn't have removed it. He wouldn't compromise the scene like that. The unit supervisor had already removed the blanket and altered the scene."

Zachary considered this. "Removed the blanket *and* altered the scene?"

"Altered the scene by removing the blanket," the doctor rephrased. "I'm sure she didn't mean any harm. People without medical training often react the wrong way in an emergency. Or in a thing like this, where it isn't an emergency." He shrugged. "I guess she didn't know any better."

Zachary paced, trying to get all the facts straight in his head. He felt like he was right on the edge of a breakthrough, if he could just line everything up the right way.

Suicide? Accident? Murder? Was it even possible to know the answer? Despite all of the money that was lavishly spent at Summit on reward rooms and developing technology, there were no surveillance cameras in the residents' rooms, or even in the corridors outside the rooms. Only at security points; at entrances, major corridor intersections, and meeting and therapy rooms. They had the night-time security logs, but Zachary already knew they hadn't noticed Quentin's death until the morning, so he didn't put much stock in their being accurate. Quentin's door had not been locked, so there was no record of who had come and gone from his room.

Was there any connection between Tirza's kidnapping and

Quentin's death? Was it just a coincidence? Was Quentin's agitation before his death just due to hormones? Maybe to his relationship with Tirza? Did he understand what had happened to her?

What was Zachary missing? Despite what he'd been told, he had a hard time believing that the skin shocks hadn't taken a physical toll on Quentin. All of those shocks couldn't be good for him. Or had he been choked out during a struggle with a security guard or someone else who came into his room and they had covered it up with the twisted blanket? Could Quentin really have successfully killed himself, either on purpose or by accident, with the blanket?

Zachary couldn't count how many times he had slept in a cell like that. While he had known it was possible to hang himself using his blanket or pants, if he could figure out a way to rig them up, it had never occurred to him to use them as a ligature. How had Quentin thought of it? Of course, it was disingenuous to assume that because Quentin was autistic, he couldn't have thought of something that Zachary hadn't. Zachary didn't know how Quentin's brain worked.

"Zachary?"

Zachary stopped pacing and blinked at Bowman. Just getting home from his shift. "Uh… yeah?"

"What's going on?"

"Just thinking. Working on a case."

"Out here?"

Zachary became slowly aware of his surroundings. Not in Bowman's apartment. He'd never even made it in the door of the apartment building, but was pacing up and down the long sidewalk outside the building.

"Oh. Yeah. Thought I'd get a bit of fresh air. Save your carpet the wear and tear."

Bowman gave him a long look. "You're okay? Nothing to worry about?"

"Sure. I'm fine. Just give me a few more minutes and I'll be up…"

"No rush, take your time. I just wanted to make sure…"

Zachary shrugged, trying to look as calm and relaxed as possible. Hopefully, he hadn't been talking aloud to himself while he paced. Doing that in his own apartment was one thing. Doing it while pacing the street could be interpreted the wrong way.

Bowman headed into the building, acting as if it were perfectly normal for Zachary to be pacing outside. But Zachary had a bad feeling he'd crossed the line. Even so, he wasn't quite ready to go up to the apartment. He felt like he was so close to sorting everything out; if he could just stay in the groove for a few more minutes, he was bound to come to some conclusion.

Five minutes later, his train of thought was broken again by his phone ringing. He looked down at it. Kenzie. *At least Bowman hadn't called Bridget.* Zachary answered the phone and held it up to his ear.

"I'm fine," he assured Kenzie. "I'm just walking outside. Clearing my head."

"I was just wondering…"

"Don't try to pretend Bowman didn't call you. He's not that subtle."

"Well… okay, then. Yes, he called me. Thought you were behaving a little… strangely."

The sooner Zachary could get out of there and find a place of his own, the better. He didn't need babysitting.

"Kenzie, since I've got you on the phone; you're sure that Quentin died of strangulation? He couldn't have died of something else and it was just covered up, made to look like strangulation?"

"Well, no. It's pretty clearly a case of strangulation. Bruises on his throat. Petechia. Swelling in his face. Cyanosis."

"It couldn't be anything else?"

"No. Like what?"

"Electrical shock."

"I thought we'd been through this already. The shocks that the institution uses are not enough to kill a person. And even if they

were, there are no signs of death by electrocution. Only of strangulation."

"Yes, but couldn't—"

"Zachary." That ever-so-sane voice that women used to bring
Zachary down to earth. Teachers, foster mothers, girlfriends; they
all seemed to have it. One of those things they knew
instinctively.

"No," Zachary anticipated.

"No," she agreed.

"Okay. Fine."

"Anything else?"

"He was dead for hours before he was found."

"Yes."

"He hadn't been moved?"

"No."

"He didn't have any signs of violence on him? Like he'd been
in a fight or altercation."

"No. Scabs and scars from self-harm. Nothing that looked like
it was from a fight."

"Had he ever tried to commit suicide before? Scars on his
wrists or any other sign?"

Kenzie was slower to answer. "No."

"Would you consider that to be unusual? If he caused his own
death, it would be normal for there to have been previous
attempts, wouldn't it? People work up to it. It takes a few tries to
get it right."

"Not all the time. It would be normal to find signs of previous
attempts. But not necessary for a finding of suicide."

"Okay."

"You should go up to your apartment," Kenzie advised. "Have
some supper. Relax and go to bed."

"Yeah. I will."

"Mario's worried. And he's not the type to panic over nothing.
If he's concerned, you need to think about why."

"I'm fine," Zachary insisted.

"Good. Then take care of yourself. Are you about ready to close this case?"

"I'd really like to tie it to institutional abuses. Even if he did commit suicide, it was because of his treatment there."

"But you don't have any way to do that."

"I'd really like to say otherwise. But… no."

"Not every one of your big cases is going to turn out to be homicide. Sometimes an accident is just an accident and a suicide is just a suicide."

Zachary spent Thursday on other things. Catching up on some of his other cases. Filing paperwork. Visiting the apartments that were still on offer to see if he could settle on a place. It was a beautiful day for being out and about, but none of the apartments suited him. Every time he looked at one, he thought of Bridget, what she would think about it, and how things had been different when they had lived together.

Was it crazy that he missed being bossed around by her? That he missed her rants over floor coverings, paint colors, and blinds versus curtains? It had all meant that he was part of a couple. Bending to her will or making a compromise meant that he was with someone. That he was functioning as part of a unit instead of being alone. Just like he had wanted ever since he was ten and lost his family forever.

He had no idea what Kenzie's views were on floor coverings. Was she a hardwood floor girl, or did she like something soft underfoot? What were her favorite colors? Did she hate orange as much as Bridget?

It was strange to miss something so mundane.

He collected the mail at his mailbox, something that he knew he had to keep up with better than he did. But who sent anything important by mail anymore? Anything important would come to him by email, too urgent to trust to the post office.

There were a couple of car trackers he needed to retrieve. They were not hugely expensive, but it still made sense to get them back when he could. Besides the fact that he didn't want to leave evidence of his activities. Leave a tracker on a car too long, and he risked someone finding it when doing an oil change or other car maintenance. And that wouldn't turn out well if they figured out where it had come from.

Thursday afternoon Zachary started writing his report on Quentin's death. He still wasn't sure what he was going to write, but he started organizing the points and laying everything out, hoping it would coalesce into something more substantial by the time he was done. His conclusion—that Summit was guilty of child abuse, maybe even human rights violations—couldn't actually be tied into the point that Mira had hired him to determine: Whether Quentin's death had really been suicide.

If he were clever, he could tie all of the possibilities back to the abuses by Summit. Quentin committed suicide because he was being abused by his therapists. He had had no hope that he would ever be able to escape the abuse. Or, Quentin was killed by one of the Summit staff members. Maybe during therapy, because he was growing more violent and was not responding to the shocks. Maybe while being restrained in a choke-hold by one of the security staff in anger, or in self-defense when Quentin attacked a staff member. Maybe because there was something darker going on at Summit, and Quentin had been in the way. Or maybe it had been accidental. Negligent security staff hadn't noticed or cared that he was on the floor all night. Weakened by starvation and multiple shocks, he had been trying to self-comfort and had gotten his blanket twisted and knotted up too tightly and quietly passed away into the night.

There were ways to blame Summit no matter what the manner of death. But that didn't matter if he didn't know which one it really was. He needed hard evidence.

Then Thursday night, late in the evening, Clarissa called.

"I wanted to know if you had figured anything out," she said, her voice low, as if someone might overhear her. "Did you figure out what really happened to Quentin?"

"I'm working on my report right now," Zachary said, though he had laid it aside some hours ago. "It's pretty damning against Summit Learning Center. The information that you've given me, together with the information I've gathered from other sources… it's pretty obvious that they're playing fast and loose with the rules. If the police and the parents knew what was really going on out there at Summit… I don't think you'd have a program anymore."

"Really?" She breathed in his ear for a moment. She sounded nervous. Zachary wondered why she had called. Did she have more to tell him? Something she had forgotten or held back before? A connection she had just made? "Mr. Goldman…"

"Zachary."

"Zachary. Can I see you again?"

"Sure, of course," Zachary agreed. "Where did you want to meet?"

"I had… I wondered if you wanted to see how the ESDs work."

"I've already seen how they work."

"Not all three versions. And I thought maybe… you'd like to try it out yourself. See what it really feels like. Instead of just watching or reading what everyone says about them…"

Zachary considered. He had ventured to ask Abato before. But Abato had brushed off his request with some comment about how they had to follow regulations and only deploy them as the court had instructed. They couldn't 'play around' with them, using them in an unauthorized manner. There were strict protocols to be followed.

"You think I could?" he ventured.

"Yeah. I could get you in there. If you meet me at Summit after six tomorrow night, I can use my pass to get us into the engineering lab and you can try them out."

"What do you mean, all three versions?"

"The initial units that were used, the ones approved for use by the FDA. Then the amped-up units Dr. Abato had engineered that are in use now. Like Quentin had. And then… these new ones he's working on. The ones that he wants to switch to."

Zachary's mouth was dry. He took a swig of the lukewarm water sitting on the side table.

"The stun belts? You could access those too?"

"Sure. You won't want to try one of those, but I can at least show them to you."

"Yes. Yes, definitely." If he could see one of the stun belts, to confirm that Abato really was serious about using them for the more violent patients; that would certainly put the story over the top. No one could doubt that Abato was unbalanced to want to use those on children. No one would approve of the use of such a device in a facility like Summit.

Maybe Abato had already been experimenting with the stun belts. Who was to say that he hadn't tried them out a time or two? On a child like Quentin who was no longer responding well to the phase-two device, who was getting more violent again after an initial period of success. A device like that could have unexpected consequences. Maybe Clarissa could help him tie it to Quentin's death.

"Okay. You can meet me here at six, then? I'll let you in a side door, so no one asks any questions about what you're doing there after hours."

Zachary agreed, and she gave him the details.

Zachary was pumped up about being allowed to see all of the equipment in the engineering lab, including the phase-three devices Abato was hoping to introduce into the program.

Clarissa came to the side door she had directed Zachary to, not in her lab coat and professional clothing, but some kind of casual Friday or after-hours look. She had on a ball cap with a green crest, with her hair in a ponytail hanging out the back. She had on a neat t-shirt and exercise pants made from some sort of high-tech fabric. They made her look slimmer than the boxy lab coat had, the material clinging to her shapely, well-muscled legs.

"Come on," Clarissa invited. She looked around, making sure no one was watching. The protesters apparently went home at the end of the work day and all of the students who went home had been picked up by their parents. The streets and sidewalks around the building were eerily quiet.

Zachary followed her into the building and stuck close to her side, noting the surveillance cameras in the various corridors they walked through. Clarissa obviously hadn't been thinking much about security when she had invited him to look at the equipment. She might be able to get into the lab with her security pass, but that was going to leave a record, and so did every camera they passed on the way there. It would be easy for anyone who looked at the tapes to follow them through the building.

But hopefully, that wouldn't matter. By the time anyone looked for him on the tapes, Zachary would already have broadcast to the world what he found there, and it would be too late for anyone to do anything about it.

Clarissa reached for the security door that led to the engineering lab, and Zachary held his breath, half-worried that it wouldn't open for her, despite her certainty. But the knob moved easily in her grip and she swung the door open.

They both stood there for a moment, making sure there was no movement inside. The lights were still on, but the room echoed with their footsteps. No one else was there. Clarissa nodded in satisfaction and let the door shut behind her. It hissed shut and clicked as the lock engaged. Clarissa moved around the lab with familiarity. Zachary was mildly surprised that she would know her way around there. As an aide, he wouldn't have expected her to be familiar with the engineering work.

"They're over here," Clarissa said in a hushed voice. She made sure that Zachary was following her. As she picked out pieces of equipment from a labeled shelf, Zachary got out his phone and started a video session. She stopped and stared at him. "What are you doing?"

"I want to get this on record. Proof of exactly what they're doing here."

He was afraid she was going to argue. She had that look on her face. Finally, she shook her head and smiled slightly. "Sure, whatever you want," she agreed.

"If you want me to be able to get things changed around here, get the aversives removed from the program, if not shutting them down completely, then I need proof."

"I hadn't really thought about it. I guess that makes sense."

She continued to get the equipment assembled, pulling a battery backpack off the shelf. "Why don't you get that filming and set it on the counter? Then it won't shake or fall down or anything and your hands will be free while you test out the ESDs."

"Makes sense," Zachary agreed. He set it up to record and propped it up on the counter. He looked at the screen, and then walked over to the spot it was pointing at. "Okay. How's this?"

"Perfect," she approved. She showed him the electrodes in her hand. "This is the phase-one unit. You ready to give it a try?"

Zachary tried to suppress a shudder. Was he really going to let her attach that to his body and press the button? He gave what he hoped was a confident smile. "I'm game. Let's do it."

She strapped electrodes to his arms and calves, positioned on bare skin. Then she had Zachary lift his shirt and attached electrodes to his back and stomach. She helped him to put the backpack on, lengthening the straps so that it would fit. Zachary tried not to think about the diminutive frame that it must have been fitted to previously.

"Are you ready?" Clarissa gave him a big smile, enjoying his discomfort.

Zachary blew out a breath. "I guess I'd better be," he said. "Are you going to give me a countdown, or—"

Before he could finish, he was seized with a jolt to his back that made him shout and splay his arms out in surprise.

It was a two-second jolt, just like all the units were programmed with, but two seconds was enough.

"Hey!" He coughed, trying to catch his breath.

"What do you think?" Clarissa asked, laughing.

"I can see why giving an unexpected shock is so effective," Zachary said, trying to keep his voice steady and not give away how much it had hurt.

Dr. Abato and articles Zachary had turned up on the internet had said that it felt like a bee sting. Zachary, never a big outdoorsman, had never actually been stung by a bee. But he couldn't imagine a bee sting would be quite that painful. His skin was still tingling. It had been more like a hundred bee stings, all at once. He had expected, when he was trying to imagine what it was going to be like, that he'd be able to resist the pain. He might flinch, but he'd be able to keep his body still. He wouldn't shout or cry. It would be like an accidental shock when touching both contacts on a battery or doing some home wiring. But the split-second before he dropped a screwdriver was nothing like the full two-second shock.

"Have you ever felt that?" Zachary asked Clarissa.

"Yeah. I tested it out on myself. I wanted to know exactly what I was doing to the kids that I was treating. That it wasn't going to cause them any permanent damage. Nice and quick, and then the pain is gone. But it's a good jolt, isn't it?"

Zachary breathed in and out. It didn't hurt anymore, but he could still feel the effects. Racing heart. Stunned senses. Feeling like the air around him was buzzing. It wasn't an experience that he would want to repeat. He could understand aversion therapy and how it worked. He wouldn't want to do something that would cause that shock a second time. He might forget just how bad it was in a day or two, but an occasional jolt would be enough to keep Zachary on task and toeing the line.

Clarissa moved closer to him and started to remove the electrodes. "Are you okay?" she asked, her voice still shaky with muffled laughter.

Zachary offered his arms and legs to her in turn. "Sure. I'm fine. No permanent damage, isn't that what everyone says? It was just one shock."

"They get accustomed to it over time."

"That's what I hear." Zachary tried not to let Clarissa see how his legs were shaking. He wondered in passing whether she had accidentally given him a phase-two device rather than a phase-one. Could she tell them apart? Had one been put on the wrong shelf?

Clarissa put the equipment away, and then picked up the next one.

"How much stronger is the phase-two than the phase-one?" Zachary asked, leaning on the counter behind him for support.

"Three times," Clarissa said brightly.

Three times.

Zachary again stood still as Clarissa again rigged up electrodes. She positioned them slightly differently so that they weren't right over the same patches of skin as the first time. He wondered if she did it that way on purpose. How many times would it take before the shocks started to leave marks on his skin?

"This is going to be bad, isn't it?" Zachary asked, trying to prepare himself for the next shock.

She didn't answer, making some minor adjustments. She straightened up and grabbed the remote. Zachary's stomach clenched. He could understand why even just seeing the remote could be a deterrent. He'd only been shocked once and just the thought of her pressing that button made his heart start to race, sending another surge of adrenaline through his body.

Clarissa gave a little salute with the remote and pressed the button. Zachary let out an involuntary yell. If the phase-one had felt like a hundred bee stings, the phase-two was like a thousand. Clarissa said it was three times as strong, but there really wasn't a comparison. He found himself thinking of the first shock as if it had been a slap on the wrist. The phase-two made his head spin. If he hadn't already been leaning on the counter, he would have toppled over. As it was, he arched into the countertop, bruising his back.

It took Zachary a few minutes to catch his breath and find his voice again. "Holy crap. That's the shock you've been giving these kids? That's what Quentin had sixty times in a row the therapy session before he died? If anyone even kept a correct count and the log wasn't a complete fiction?" He took a few more deep breaths. "They're getting accustomed to this level?"

Clarissa nodded. "Hard to believe, isn't it?"

"Wow. I don't believe that they don't feel pain. But I can understand why Abato might think so. I can't imagine getting used to that."

Without warning, Clarissa pushed the button again, activating the electrode on his right calf. Completely unprepared, Zachary flailed, tried to catch himself on the counter, and landed in a heap on the floor. He stayed there after the shock stopped, muscles quivering.

"Okay," he said weakly. "So that's how it feels to get shocked a second time. I think I'm done. Help me to get these off." He reached for the Velcro strap of one of the armbands.

A third shock made Zachary slam the back of his head into the floor. Tile over concrete was not a friendly floor-covering. Zachary groaned. For a few minutes, he just lay there, his whole body like jelly.

"Normally, we'd insist that you get back up," Clarissa said in a friendly tone. "No lying around in therapy. We'd get you back on your feet or in your chair, sitting properly, and then continue with the lesson."

"That's cruel," Zachary said. He tried to figure out what he was still doing on the floor, his thoughts as scrambled as eggs.

"You know…" Clarissa's tone was conversational. "I didn't think you were going to be a problem at first. You'd come in, take a look around, see what the police saw, and come to the same conclusion as they did. That Quentin Thatcher committed suicide. Why not, trapped in a place like this? Dr. Abato is so proud of his reward rooms, loves showing off the videos of the kids who progress so well with ABA, all of those happy faces on the website and posters and all of the other promotional material. He just loves showing everyone what a wonderful place Summit is. But would you really want to live here?"

"No."

"No, of course not. The parents say this is what's best for their kids. Really, they're just glad their kids are off of their hands. They are somewhere they are safe and everybody else is safe from them. It isn't an institution, it's their home. And the children are all happy here, aren't they?"

"They're not all happy," Zachary disagreed, trying to get his arms under him to push himself up into a sitting position.

He couldn't see Clarissa very well from his position on the floor, so he didn't see her reaching for the button, but he knew when she had pressed it again, because the bees stung and he went crashing back the floor. He tried to make sense of why she was shocking him. She had offered to help him. She wanted to show him what it felt like to be one of the residents at Summit. Was that it?

"No, they're not happy," Clarissa said. "You can get them to smile. You can get them to laugh and to pretend to be normal, but they're still not really happy. They eventually come to accept this as their home. They stop asking to go home with their parents, and they say they're happy here. But it's not true!" She said it explosively. "They're just saying what they're told to say. What we train them to say."

"Uh-huh." Zachary shifted his arms to prop himself up, then thought better of it. The last time he had tried that, she had shocked him. *See how quickly he could be trained?* "What about Quentin? Was he happy?"

"Of course not. Quentin had given up on being able to go home to his mom and brothers. He had settled into the schedule here and did pretty well with the therapy and routines. But then Tirza happened."

"What? What does that mean?"

"Tirza was staying in Quentin's unit now and then when her mom needed a babysitter. Quentin's hormones must have started kicking in, because he was noticing her. Starting to get friendly with her." Clarissa moved closer to Zachary and nudged him with her toe. "Can you get up?"

Zachary wasn't sure. He shifted and tried to roll over and then push himself up. As soon as he'd levered himself up a few inches, another shock hit him. He collapsed to the floor, landing on his face this time.

"What...? Why...?" he couldn't finish the thoughts, let alone the sentences.

Clarissa bent down and started to remove the electrodes. Zachary was so relieved he couldn't hold back a flood of tears. No more shocks. He could go home and sleep. Write his report. Whatever it was he had planned to do.

He stared at Clarissa's face as she worked over him. She was pretty. She smiled at him frequently, but her smile was like a shark's. Predatory. Like she had enjoyed hurting him.

As she removed the electrodes, his eyes moved from her face to her hat. A baseball cap with a green crest on it. He had noticed it before, when she had first let him into the building. He tried to focus his eyes on the words. It felt like his eyeballs were twitching back and forth, bouncing around in his head. He forced them to focus in on the words, but they didn't make any sense. Even when he could make out the shapes of the letters, the words themselves didn't make any kind of sense. Then he realized that he was looking at a school crest. He didn't understand the words because they were the school's motto in Latin.

But he could make out the words around the crest, with the name of the school on them.

St. Damien High School.

23

D amien."

She raised her eyebrows questioningly. Then she glanced upward, toward the bill of the hat, as if she could see the crest on the front.

"My school," she said.

Zachary lay there, wondering what to do next. What was she planning? Just to let him go home? None of it made any sense. If *she* was Damien, why had she asked him there? It hadn't been to give him more ammunition against Summit. She didn't want them closed down. Not if she was running some kind of sex trafficking operation.

His thoughts buzzed around in his head, trying to settle on one thing, one explanation that tied it all together. He should get up. But the aversion training was working. He didn't want to try getting up again. Not while there was still a single electrode left on him. And Clarissa didn't remove the last one, nestled against his back.

Instead, she brought over a black girdle.

"Elegant, wouldn't you say?" Clarissa asked. "So much simpler than the phase-one and -two devices. No messy cords, no back-pack. Everything is self-contained and just goes under the shirt.

Out of sight, out of mind. People don't get so worked up about what they can't see. Of course, this one gives you more than skin shocks. It passes the electricity through your body."

She pulled up Zachary's shirt and started to wrap it around his torso. Zachary fought back. His motions were sloppy, and his arms felt like spaghetti, but he didn't want the phase-three device on him. He couldn't let her put it into place. Clarissa just reached down and pressed the remote, activating the one electrode still on his skin. Zachary tried to protest, but it just came out as a *Zzzz* sound and he bit the tip of his tongue. While his ears were still ringing, Clarissa wrapped the girdle around him and did it up at the back, where Zachary could feel the hard boxy shape of the built-in battery pack. Once it was in place, Clarissa slid her fingers up under it and removed the last electrode of the phase-two device. She rolled him onto his back.

"Comfy?"

"Don't," Zachary protested.

"You be a good boy and I won't have to."

He waited for her to hit the button anyway. She didn't.

"Why?" Zachary asked, his voice weak.

How was he going to get out of there? He was at her mercy in a locked room and no one knew where he was. He tried to calm his frazzled nerves to come up with a strategy.

TV detectives never got in that kind of trouble. Or if they did, they had some kind of brilliant escape plan. Using the device against her or building one of his own like MacGyver. Talking her down. A backup team in the next room, just waiting for the point at which they could arrest her for everything she had done.

Which was what? Kidnapping Tirza? Killing Quentin? Zachary didn't even have any proof she was involved in Tirza's kidnapping. Just a ball cap with the word Damien on it. Suggestive, but not proof of anything. It might just as easily have been what had given runaway Tirza the inspiration for a fictional kidnapper's name.

"Why what?" Clarissa asked.

"Why are you doing this?" Zachary croaked out.

"Hmm. Good question. Because I want to hurt you? Because you are getting in my way? Because I've been wanting to see how the phase-three works?"

Zachary lifted his hand to rub his forehead and she stiffened, hand on the remote. Zachary decided he didn't need to rub the sore, tense spot on his head, and rested his hand back down.

"But… your PTSD… You don't like shocking…"

"Well, I might have fudged a little on my symptoms. For dramatic effect. You can just look the symptoms up online, you know."

Her face was close to his, close enough to see the puffy bags under her eyes and the fine lines of fatigue around them.

"But you… look tired."

"Yeah," Clarissa agreed. "I tend to stay up too late at night, watching recordings of the therapy sessions." She sighed. "The videos don't give me quite the same thrill as actually shocking them in real life." She glanced over her shoulder at Zachary's phone, the red dot indicating that it was still recording. "Nice of you to provide me with a nice high-def video of *your* therapy session. The pictures from the surveillance cameras can be pretty grainy." With a nod, she indicated one of the cameras mounted in the corner near the ceiling.

"Aren't you afraid of them seeing you here?"

"No. Nobody checks the video until the next day, or if an alarm goes. Night security just keeps an eye on the entrances and does a walk-around a few times a night. By the time they look at it, I'll have it taken care of."

Zachary was baffled. "How?"

"One of the first things they taught me when I started working here was how to edit digital video. Cut out what we don't want a record of. Repeat frames if we need to fill the timeline. Surveillance video is so simple; empty hallways and empty rooms to replace whatever you cut out."

"But… how can you access it?"

"It's all in who you know. Make friends with someone who knows the password. They never change it. Too lazy. So even if your friend has to leave…" She shrugged. "No problem."

She hadn't just acted on impulse when she'd invited him. She knew exactly what she was doing. She'd done it before. Zachary closed his eyes, trying to focus his thoughts. The effects of the shocks were wearing off, but he didn't want her to know that. He stayed still and didn't try to get up. He talked slowly, as if he were still stunned. His brain wasn't quite up to speed, but he was starting to work through the scenarios.

"You kidnapped Tirza. You're Damien."

"Damien doesn't exist. Just like the police said. There's no one by that name working here or at the school. There were no strangers lurking around. Just students and teachers, just like normal."

Clarissa might have done some outreach therapy program at the school. Or she might have pretended she was a student. She was small and slim enough that no one would take a second look at her. Not without a reason. It was the perfect camouflage. One student among hundreds.

"Why didn't Tirza say who you were? Why didn't she name you? Say that you worked here?"

Clarissa laughed lightly. "What do you know about prosopagnosia?"

"What?"

"Many people with autism have some level of prosopagnosia. Face blindness. Tirza might be able to describe my hair and what I'm wearing. Some of my features. But she can't recognize me out of context."

"Context?"

"If I'm supposed to be her aide in the therapy room, she knows who I am. If I show up at the school without my lab jacket in a baseball cap? She doesn't know me from Adam." Clarissa chuckled at this. "Literally."

"Didn't she say… Damien was a man? A man took her?"

"Maybe she did. Or maybe they misunderstood or just assumed. She *did* meet a lot of men." Clarissa smothered a laugh. Was she even aware how depraved she sounded? "Differentiating gender and using the right pronouns is difficult for Tirza. She's used to being corrected. If she said 'she' when talking about Damien and her mother or an advocate corrected her to say 'he,' Tirza would think nothing of it."

"You knew she... couldn't identify you."

"That was never a concern. A hat and a gruff voice, and I was somebody totally different to her. A stranger."

Zachary tried surreptitiously to undo the stun belt behind his back. The more she revealed to him, the more certain he was that she never intended for him to get out of there. She hadn't just brought him there to try out the ESDs. To entertain herself with shocking him a few times. Zachary wasn't Tirza. He could identify Clarissa. The more she explained, the more certain he was that she never intended for him to get out of the engineering lab alive.

"What about... Quentin...?"

"What about him? He's dead. He's not going to identify anyone."

"Is that why...?"

"Is that why I killed him? What do you think this is? Confession time?" There was an irritated edge to her voice. She was happy to talk about shocking, or about victimizing Tirza. But Quentin was another story. "Quentin's death had nothing to do with Tirza's... disappearance."

Her eyes went to the side, avoiding his. Zachary wondered why she was bothering to lie about it. She had essentially admitted to kidnapping and trafficking Tirza. To tampering with video recordings. That she was addicted to causing others pain. Why was she stopping short of admitting what had happened to Quentin?

Obviously, it wasn't just an accident.

Zachary took advantage of Clarissa's gaze being away from him to try to unbuckle the stun belt. His fingers still felt like they were buzzing. They were clumsy and weak. Nothing felt right.

How many thousands of times had he unbuckled a belt in his life? Why couldn't he remember how to get the tongue out of the hole just because it was behind his back? He couldn't remember which way to pull the strap to free the tongue enough to push it back out through the hole. In his head, he cursed in frustration. Why couldn't he undo a simple buckle?

Then the blast hit. Zachary's body arched on the floor. Pain tore through his body, deep down inside. He was on fire. Every muscle in his body tensed. He saw nothing but red. And it went on for an eternity.

The stun belt was exponentially more painful than the phase-two device.

When it ended, his voice stopped screaming and dissolved into slobbering wet sobs. Clarissa stood over him, her eyes wide. Zachary tried to make sure he was breathing, not sure he remembered how. The mechanics of it all seemed too complex. Clarissa's nose wrinkled, and she waved her hand in front of her face.

"At least we can make sure our residents using a phase-three are diapered," she mocked.

Zachary was too overwhelmed to even care.

Clarissa looked around, as if she were waiting for someone. An accomplice? Of course there was an accomplice. Someone who had given her the security password. Someone who had helped with kidnapping Tirza; maybe acting as getaway driver, maybe just sampling the goods. But she had suggested that the security guard who had helped her was no longer there. Had she given him access to the building? Or had security been too lazy to change the outside door codes either? She was expecting the ex-guard to come and help Clarissa dispose of Zachary's body.

"Where is he?" Zachary asked, when he could get enough breath to get the words out.

"He's…" Clarissa's head jerked up as she stopped herself. She looked at him, eyes narrowed. "You really are devious, you know that? You have a way of worming yourself in…"

A compliment to the man on the floor, lying in a puddle of his own fluids. So clever, Zachary. So very clever.

She continued to stare at him, her expression gradually changing to a smile again.

"What does it matter?" she asked. "Who cares what you know now? It's too late. You were too slow in putting together the pieces of the puzzle."

"You were very good," Zachary whispered. "Good at covering up."

She preened at that. She was proud of herself. Of being able to operate right under the noses of the administrators at Summit Living Center. Routinely changing videos to cut out anything she didn't want them to see. Getting around any security measures. Trafficking Tirza almost right in front of them, everyone completely blind to her deception. Except for the security guard. Was anyone else in on it? The unit supervisor who had shed tears for Quentin? Ego-driven Dr. Abato? Who else had known?

Clarissa played with the remote for the stun belt. Unlike the sharp-edged boxes that housed the buttons for the phase-two devices, the remote was small and sleek like the one Zachary had on his keychain to unlock his new car. He watched her with wide, worried eyes, afraid she was going to slip and hit the button again. Or do it on purpose. Zachary's own breathing rasped in his ears. Was it supposed to sound like that? Had she damaged his lungs or his heart with the stun belt? Zachary wasn't a big guy. The belt was designed to restrain two or three hundred pound muscle-bound men. Not someone like him. It was like putting too thin a slice of bread in the toaster. It was going to cook him. Burn him to a crisp.

"Quentin was *his* fault," Clarissa sneered. "No one was supposed to be… damaged. No scars or evidence of what was going on."

Zachary swallowed. His mouth was dry as cotton. He nodded, encouraging Clarissa to go on. "Just… business," he suggested.

"Well, not just business." She chuckled. "I mean… to start

with, it was just for fun. But we thought… why not expand? Why not make a bit of money out of it?"

She disgusted him.

Clarissa saw him shudder, but just smiled, probably attributing it to the aftereffects of the shock.

"It wasn't just Tirza… and Quentin… was it?"

"Of course not! Tirza wasn't even here most of the time. That's why we had to… get access to her using a different method. She's such a pretty little thing. And very cooperative. There was demand, so we had to find a way to supply her. Usually it was one of the others."

"How?"

"Watch the security checks and shift changes and find the right times to remove them. Security doesn't go into the rooms, so a shape in the bed is all they need to see." She shrugged. "Out for a few hours in the night. Back in bed by morning. No one knew the difference."

"*They* knew."

Clarissa considered this for a long moment. "I don't know if they did," she said, lips pursed. "They're so removed, so disconnected. Did it really make any difference?"

Clearly, she had no intention of stopping, even with her partner no longer working there and the slight wrinkle of disposing of Zachary. Zachary had to find a way to put a stop to it. To save himself and to stop her from continuing to victimize the residents of Summit.

"Then what happened… to Quentin?"

He hesitated to try to take off the shock belt again. But how else was he going to be able to get up off of the floor? Every time she shocked him, he got weaker. Slower. Less able to get himself out of the situation. It was like the shock was killing off brain cells, making him stupider and stupider with every shock.

Clarissa scowled. "Why do you have to keep going back to that? He's better off, you know. He wasn't happy. He wasn't ever going to get out of here. He was getting too used to the aversives, and once Dr. Abato started using the phase-threes…" She ran her fingertip over the red button. Zachary tensed.

"He's never going to get permission to use them," he countered.

"He will. He's very good at getting what he wants. And even if it doesn't get approved… I don't think that will stop him for long."

Zachary felt a chill. Probably just the aftereffects of the shocks. Or lying there wet on the cold floor. Would Dr. Abato really just go ahead and use the stun belts on children like Angel?

"It's not safe… They're not like the phase-twos."

"No?" She waved the remote teasingly in front of him. "You're saying you wouldn't want me to shock you again?"

"They'll cause… permanent damage."

She returned to the previous topic. "What happened to Quentin was a mistake."

"What happened?"

"Stupid Steiner meant to shock Abilene. She was being too noisy, resisting. So he shocked her. But he hit the wrong button. Hit it a few times before he figured out why it wasn't working. The idiot."

Steiner. Zachary filed away the name for when he got out of there, so he could tell the police. Tell them the whole story.

If he got out.

That wasn't looking too promising.

"So after we got her out of there, Steiner checked Quentin's room to make sure he was okay. Saw that he was lying on the floor."

Zachary cleared his throat. "Dead…?"

"No…" Clarissa stared off into space. "On the floor. The blanket wrapped and twisted around his neck. He was tangled up, choking. He had wrapped it around his neck and he got stuck when he was shocked."

Zachary nodded, waiting breathlessly for the details. Or

maybe he was breathless from the shocks or from imagining Quentin lying there in his cell, trying to breathe.

"I told him to get the blanket off of Quentin. Do CPR. Get the portable defib…"

"Nothing worked…? Why didn't you call medical? Pretend you were there for something legitimate and get him help?"

Clarissa shook her head. Her expression was dark. She was no longer giggly and laughing about the whole business. How fun it was to shock, molest, or sell defenseless children. The lines around her eyes became more prominent.

"Stupid *pig*," she said angrily. "He didn't even try to help Quentin. He said Quentin was just a troublemaker. Better if he was replaced by someone else." Clarissa turned burning eyes on Zachary. "He twisted the blanket tighter!"

Zachary felt his mouth drop open. "What?"

"Steiner killed him!"

"No."

"Gave it another twist and crouched there over Quentin watching him choke to death! Men!" Clarissa railed. "They never know what's good for them. Always have to push it too far. Everything was fine until then. But he had to get the police there investigating. And then you. The police came and were gone in a couple of hours, but you…! You have to talk to everybody. Look at *everything*. Ask about things that have nothing to do with his death. You couldn't stop at investigating Quentin's death, you have to dig into every nook and cranny, all of Abato's dirty little secrets."

And *her* dirty little secrets. She was ranting on about the injustice of Zachary's investigation instead of Quentin's death. How he had inconvenienced her.

If she had just left him alone, Zachary would have closed his investigation. She could have had her institution back, to play whatever games she devised. But she was too impatient and had to take things into her own hands.

"You need to learn to just mind your own business," Clarissa said, pointing the remote at him accusingly. "Why don't you get a life?"

"Why don't you?" Zachary snapped back, stung.

Impulsivity was one of the hallmarks of Zachary's behavior, a psychologist had once told Zachary's foster mother. The trouble was, there were no drugs that would reliably reduce or eliminate impulsivity. Zachary knew. He'd tried them all. His impulsivity would be the death of him one day. And it looked like that day had come.

Clarissa seemed to suddenly remember what the remote was for. She looked straight at Zachary, her eyes deep pits of blackness, and she pressed the button.

24

Zachary couldn't think and yet he knew he was dying. He couldn't reason or evaluate his body objectively, he just knew that the stun belt wasn't meant to be used multiple times like the ESDs, and the fire racing through his nerves toward his heart was going to kill him when it got there.

He'd read about the stun belt. He knew objectively that the shock lasted eight seconds and delivered 50,000 volts of electricity. But that didn't equate to the agony that stretched out interminably.

And then there was a light.

Zachary blinked.

He couldn't see anything, but there was a light.

And if there was a light, that meant he was alive. Didn't it?

Zachary tried to swim toward consciousness. The pain wasn't the same anymore. It wasn't burning its way through him. There was a dull ache deep down inside his bones and tissues. But that meant he wasn't dying anymore, and if he wasn't dying, he needed to wake up and figure out how to get out of the engineering lab.

He blinked again. There was a light. It was closer than it had been. Not close enough to reach, but getting closer.

It was a long time before he was able to really see anything. A light on the ceiling. Closer than he expected. And the floor was not as hard and cold as it had been. He tried to figure out where Clarissa was. She had to be close by and he had to figure out how to get out of there before she could shock him again. Maybe she had gone to the bathroom. Or to let the ex-guard in. Wherever she was, it gave him a few minutes to figure out how to get free.

He reached behind his back, trying to find the closure on the stun belt. He couldn't feel it. He grew more desperate, his fingertips burning as he searched for it.

Zachary heard approaching footsteps, heels on tile, and panicked. He had to get out. He couldn't get the stun belt off, so he would have to run. His legs were still weak and shaky. He tried to roll over and push himself up.

"Zachary. Hey. Stay put. Don't move."

He fought through a few moments of terror before processing that it wasn't Clarissa's voice. It was someone else. A woman's voice, but not Clarissa. A voice he knew.

Her voice hovered over him, her hand rested gently on his chest.

Kenzie.

What was Kenzie doing in the engineering lab at Summit?

"Hey. How are you feeling?" Kenzie asked.

"What… why're you here…?"

"I'm here to see you. To make sure you're okay."

Zachary frowned, trying to sort it out. He blinked and scanned the part of the room within his vision. It didn't look like the engineering lab.

"Where…?"

"You're in the hospital."

Zachary closed his eyes and opened them again. Tried to make sense of the inputs. She was right. It was a hospital room. The bustle of voices and footsteps. The paging system. The smell. He'd been in enough hospital rooms he should have recognized it.

He wasn't sure why he didn't figure that out right away. Was his brain permanently scrambled?

"What happened? How?"

"You should just relax. Take your time. The doctor said that you need time to recover."

"No, tell me how."

Kenzie boosted herself up to sit on the edge of his bed, her leg warm against his.

"I'll tell you about it if you'll be quiet and stay still."

"Yes. Okay."

"You should have told someone where you were going. If you're going to investigate cases alone, you have to at least let people know where you're going to be."

Zachary nodded a little. "Suppose," he agreed. "But what happened? How did I get out?"

"You set up your phone to record your meeting with Clarissa."

"Yeah."

"Not just to record it," Kenzie said. "To live broadcast it."

"Right. I thought… it would be the fastest way to get the word out… to show people what was happening at Summit."

"I got an alert that you were broadcasting. I didn't check it right away… I feel bad about that; I should have."

"Why?"

"If I'd checked your stream right away, I could have helped you faster… you wouldn't have had to go through all of that."

Zachary closed his eyes. "Did I get all of it? Everything she said?"

"Yes. All of the sickening details."

He breathed out. "Everything. About shocking kids for her own gratification. Kidnapping Tirza. Killing Quentin."

"Yes. Only she didn't kill Quentin. But she did help cover it up, so they can charge her as an accomplice."

"Good."

"It was horrible," Kenzie said. "It was awful to see her torturing you like that. Not to be able to get there to stop it. I called Mario, got him to open up your computer and have a look. He knew where you were and got in contact with the local police. Every second that ticked by… trying to convince them about what was going on, that you were at Summit, waiting for them to get there and get into that engineering lab… it was awful. It didn't take long objectively—seventeen minutes from the time we called them—but every second was an eternity."

"Wasn't so great for me either," Zachary admitted. He gave her a rueful smile.

"I guess not."

"I didn't know if anyone was watching. If anyone would see what was happening before it was too late. It's not like I have a lot of followers. I could have just been broadcasting to empty air or people might think it was some kind of joke."

"You have a few more followers now," Kenzie said. She tucked her hair behind her ear and laughed. "It sort of went viral. A bit late, but it's been shared all over the world now."

"Yeah?" Zachary was both embarrassed and pleased. He'd never had anything go viral before. He was proficient with social networking, but he'd never hit on the secret formula to actually have a post spread like that. He felt for Kenzie's hand and she grasped his in hers. Everything hurt, but he was happy to feel her touch. "If the police had gotten there sooner… they might have been too early. Before she'd had a chance to tell the whole story. At least this way… we have the answers."

"I suppose. But maybe the police could have gotten it out of her, instead of her continuing to use the stun belt. You're lucky to have survived. You're lucky they got there in time to treat you."

"Lucky me," Zachary murmured.

Kenzie snorted.

Zachary took a deeper breath than he had attempted before, trying to analyze his body, to see how badly he was injured.

"Is it bad?" he asked. "Or… is it okay now… is that it? I mean… what about permanent damage?"

"Those belts are not meant to be used more than once. They're much higher voltage than the ESDs at Summit. If they were used as an aversive like the other units, kids would be dying. Dr. Abato wanted to re-engineer them, to come up with something that was somewhere in between. Stronger than the phase-twos, but not as strong as the stun belts."

"So what does that mean? Is there permanent damage…?"

Kenzie hesitated. He squeezed her hand a bit tighter, trying not to wince.

"Only time will tell," she said finally. "Right now, it looks like you could make a full recovery… but your body will need time to heal, and we won't know for a while if there is any permanent damage."

"Like what?"

"She kept shocking you. They're only supposed to be used once. The belts are positioned to send a shock through the kidneys, not just deliver a skin shock. Your kidneys are working, but not at full capacity. The doctor isn't sure whether there will be scar tissue, or whether it will all heal up. It's like a burn, only internal."

Zachary had dealt with enough burns before. He gritted his teeth, focusing on the feeling of Kenzie's hand in his, trying to avoid slipping into the past. "Okay. What else?"

"Well, of course, with electrical shocks, there are concerns about whether there is any damage to your heart. And to your body's own electrical impulse system. Nerves. Movement. Brain."

"I can talk. So that's good."

"Yes. It seems like everything is operating normally, but they'll be wanting to do a lot of tests over the next few days."

Zachary let go of Kenzie's hand and brought his fingers up to his eyes to examine them. They were tender and reddened.

"They're burned."

Kenzie nodded. "The electricity will leave your body however it can. Feet and fingertips… anything in contact with ground… kind of like if you were struck by lightning."

Zachary closed his eyes and for a while was just drifting, dozing a little. Kenzie shifted.

"Don't go," Zachary told her. "Stay here."

"I'm staying. I just thought maybe I'd move to the chair."

"No, stay here. Where I can see you."

She gave him a tolerant smile. "Fine. For a few more minutes."

"Are they closing Summit down?"

"Closing them down?" Kenzie gave him a puzzled frown.

"Now that people have seen what's going on there."

Kenzie shook her head. "People already knew what was going on there. The aversives, I mean. Quentin's death and Tirza's kidnapping, that's different, but that wasn't operating under Summit's auspices. It was a couple of bad apples. And they've been arrested."

"They got… the man? The guard?"

"Steiner. Yeah. They got to him before he'd heard about your broadcast, luckily. Caught him off guard, so to speak. They're both being charged, and they'll go away for a long time. You ensured that by recording Clarissa's confession. But as far as Summit's operations go… nothing is changing."

"But the kids! They can't use the stun belts on children—"

"And they won't. They never were in use. They were only being used as a prototype, to try to develop Summit's phase-three device."

"But they can't just keep ramping up the power. Lovaas said that they would just keep getting acclimatized to the next level of pain, and then they'd have to increase it again. It doesn't end. Not until it's so high that children are being permanently injured or killed."

"They'll never get a higher-voltage device approved. The FDA is already threatening to ban the use of the phase-two device. It's okay; you don't have to worry about them using something that is going to cause permanent harm."

"Tell that to Margaret."

Kenzie raised an eyebrow. "Margaret?"

"All of the autistic adults who have PTSD or other problems because of therapies like ABA. And Tirza and others who are abused because they've been trained so well to do whatever they're told."

"I don't think you can put the blame on ABA. Those things are going to happen no matter what therapy you use. Or even if you didn't do anything at all." She put her hand over his again. "I think that you're seeing what you are… well, because of your own experiences. You've had some experiences with institutional abuse and therapies that you don't feel helped you. So you're naturally more sensitive about it… more sympathetic to others who have gone through it too."

Zachary's vision wavered. He tried not to get stuck in the past. He was in the hospital with Kenzie sitting beside him. Probably thinking what a putz he was for putting himself in harm's way. For being so weak. Women like Kenzie liked a strong man. She wanted someone she could have a good time with. Not someone who was always wrapped up in saving the world and failing miserably. Kenzie wasn't like Bridget, looking for someone to fix. He liked Kenzie for being a strong, independent woman. But could he ever be the kind of man she was looking for?

"You can't put the blame for all of the things people with autism go through on the therapies they've done. Think of how much worse off they'd be if they hadn't had therapy."

"But we should listen to the people who know. The people who have been through it."

"They're really not the best qualified to judge," Kenzie said gently. "They're… well, looking at it through the lens of their own experience. Distorted. I think the ones who are the best qualified to judge are the professionals. And the parents, who have seen how far therapy has brought them. These people can't remember what they were like before therapy, when they were little children. They can't judge where they would be if they hadn't ever had it."

"So the autistic adults are all wrong? What about the ones who have autistic children of their own, who see how much less stressed their children are when they're not being forced into therapy?"

"Of course they're less stressed if they're not being taken out of their comfort zones. But that means they're not being forced to progress, either. It's like we talked about before… sometimes therapy is painful. But that doesn't mean it's bad or unnecessary. Places like Summit offer an important service. Just think of where those people would be without it."

Zachary closed his eyes. He thought about Quentin and the life he'd lived in the two years before he died. Away from his home, his family, and his friends. Shocked into compliance. Zachary could understand why the therapy had worked to begin with. The shocks Zachary had received had kept him on the floor, even when he knew his life depended on getting up and escaping Clarissa. He tried to imagine how 'agitated' Quentin had been those last few weeks, when sixty or more shocks in a therapy session had not been enough to control his behavior.

And Tirza. Not controlled by shocks, but still conditioned to accept whatever abuse Clarissa and her clients inflicted on her.

Angel, his own parents being trained to hurt him, with nowhere safe to escape to.

Trina laughing and writhing on the floor, her skin burning under the electrodes.

And little Ray-Ray, his quiet hands forming a silent plea.

Stop.

Just think of where they would be without Summit Living Center.

EPILOGUE

Zachary saw a movement out of the corner of his eye and turned his head toward the door of the hospital room, startled. He pushed himself up slightly from his slumped position.

"Mr. Peterson!"

"Lorne," Mr. Peterson corrected with a laugh. "I've told you, you're old enough to call me Lorne, Zachary."

"I know… Lorne…" Even having known him for so many years, Zachary was still uncomfortable calling his old foster father by his first name.

Mr. Peterson pulled the visitor's chair closer to Zachary's bed and sat down. He looked Zachary over. "So… how are you, Zachary?"

"I'm fine. Doctors said I probably won't have any permanent damage. Just… one of those things." He shrugged. "You didn't need to come… I'll be out in a few days…"

In fact, the doctor had said that physically, he was well enough to go home any time.

"I just wanted to make sure… I got the feeling when we talked on the phone that things weren't going well."

Zachary let his breath out slowly, staring off into the distance. He knew he didn't have to put on a front for Mr. Peterson. He had seen Zachary through dark times before. "No," Zachary admitted. "This whole thing is getting me down… I thought… when people saw what was going on, there would be an uproar… they'd insist on shutting Summit down. But even after seeing it… they still don't care."

"That must be discouraging. If they were forced to close or change, you could at least feel like it had been worth the pain."

"Don't people care about anything? It's okay if people are being tortured, as long as it's not them? Guys like Dr. Abato say it's okay, autistic people don't feel pain the same way as we do. Like they're a different species. It's not right to treat *anyone* like that." Zachary's voice cracked.

"No." Mr. Peterson shook his head. "When I saw that video… I couldn't even watch it all, Zachary. I had to turn it off. That woman nearly killed you. I can't imagine allowing someone like that around children and other vulnerable people."

"But they said she's just one bad person. It doesn't mean anything. It doesn't make the institution bad."

"There's some truth to that. One bad person doesn't make the institution bad. But the fact that they didn't supervise her closely enough to see what was happening under their own noses… the fact that they put a weapon in her hand and pointed it at a vulnerable population… that they routinely edited videos of therapy sessions… and that their supervision was so lax that residents could be trafficked right under their noses…"

"Then why doesn't anyone care about that?"

"People don't want to have to get out of their comfort zones. To have to make changes. They'll watch the video and be all shocked about it… but that's as far as it goes. Then it's on to watching cats and cucumbers."

Zachary rubbed the space between his eyebrows. He was exhausted. Which made no sense at all, because he was spending most of the day sleeping. After weeks and months of insomnia, he suddenly couldn't stay awake. Though he knew it wasn't just sleepiness.

"What have they got you on?" Mr. Peterson asked, as if reading his mind. "An SSRI? Mood stabilizer?"

"SSRI… but then they gotta take me off of stimulants, so they're experimenting with other combos… waiting to see if they will work…"

"And it may take a few weeks before they know."

"Yeah."

Mr. Peterson was quiet for a few minutes.

"I was wondering something," he said finally.

"Yeah? What?"

"I was wondering about the girl you told us about when you came to visit."

"Annie?" Zachary had meant to pretend not to know what Mr. Peterson was talking about. But her name just popped out of his mouth before he could stop it.

"Annie. That was it. The little girl that died, right?"

"Uh… something like that. Or maybe it was Amy." His cheek muscle ticked, giving away the lie. Mr. Peterson was not fooled.

"Annie," he repeated. "Did you ever talk to anyone about her?"

"What do you mean? I talked to you."

"I mean did you ever talk it over with a therapist? The police? Or maybe get in touch with her family?"

"No. I talked to the therapist at Bonnie Brown… but I didn't tell them anything. Just… pretended I didn't know anything… that… it didn't matter."

"If this business at Summit was bothering you… bringing up memories of what happened to Annie, then maybe you should do something about that."

Zachary gave a short laugh and shook his head. "It's too late. It was almost thirty years ago."

"If it's still affecting you, maybe you need to talk to someone about it."

"No," Zachary said flatly. "There isn't anything to say. I didn't know her. She was just the girl who died in the cell next to me."

"It still upset you. Why don't you talk to her parents? Tell them what happened that night?"

"I don't remember what happened."

"Your body does. It's bothering you. It might have been thirty years ago, but your body still cares that you haven't dealt with it. And her parents, they won't have forgotten her. It would mean something to them to hear that someone still remembers her and cares what happened that night."

"I don't know how to reach them. I don't even know… where they live. Their names. They probably moved away."

"Maybe you could hire a private investigator to find out," Mr. Peterson said wryly.

Zachary rolled his eyes and shook his head. "They won't want to hear from me," he insisted.

But a couple of weeks later, Zachary and Mr. Peterson pulled up in front of the Sellers' house. A dark brick bungalow with neat gardens in the front filled with various kinds of greenery, but no splash of color from spring flowers.

"Is this the right thing?" Zachary asked Mr. Peterson. Not for the first time. "I mean… they put their daughter to rest years ago. Here I am, stirring up memories for no reason. What good is it going to do for them to hear this?"

Mr. Peterson considered the question seriously, even though he'd already answered it, in one form or another, half a dozen times. "If it was my child… I'd want to know. Even if it was years later."

Annie's father answered the door. He had been a tall man. He was still taller than Zachary in spite of how stooped he had become. Zachary was glad he had asked Mr. Peterson to go with him. Lorne seemed to know what to do; he connected with someone in his own generation. Introductions were made, and Mr. Sellers invited them in. They went to the living room, where they met Mrs. Sellers, a tiny woman, and the introductions were repeated. They all sat down. Zachary stared into a hexagonal china cabinet with some Royal Dutton collector's pieces in it as if that were what he had come for.

"Zachary." Mr. Peterson gave him a nudge.

Zachary looked at Mr. and Mrs. Sellers, a knot in his stomach. He shouldn't have bothered them. He should have just left them in peace. They'd dealt with their daughter's death decades before.

"You said… this was something about our daughter, Annie," Mrs. Sellers said. "I really don't understand… what this is all about. How you even know about her."

Zachary looked down at his hands, unable to keep his gaze on her face. On her sad eyes.

"I was at Bonnie Brown years ago. When she… was there."

"You couldn't have been more than a boy," Mr. Sellers said. "You couldn't have worked there when Annie was there."

"No. I didn't. I lived there. A resident. Like your daughter."

"Oh." They both considered that.

Mrs. Sellers inched forward in her chair. "Did you know Annie, then? Were you friends?"

"No… I knew who she was. Heard about her. But she was normally in a different unit than I was."

"Ah." She nodded.

Zachary found it impossible to continue. The silence grew. He couldn't even look at Mr. Peterson, afraid of being pushed into the conversation before he was ready.

"I have pictures of Annie," Mrs. Sellers offered. "Would you like to see them?"

"Yes. Sure."

She got up and retrieved a photo album. It wasn't thick. It started with Annie as a baby, looking like a perfectly normal baby, happy and healthy. Gummy smiles in faded Polaroids. Pictures with her family. But as she got older, her different-ness became more obvious. The distant gaze. Fingers screening her eyes. Limbs skinny and awkward, mottled with bruises and bite marks. Fewer pictures with her family. An occasional candid shot of her playing alone, isolated.

In the last pictures, she looked just how Zachary remembered. The thin, dark-haired girl who didn't want anyone to touch her. It unlocked a flood of memories. He had been suppressing the images for years, trying not to remember, but they were still there, as clear and crisp as if it had been just the day before.

"What happened?" Mrs. Sellers asked, her voice shaky. "Were you there?"

Zachary nodded. There was a lump in his throat and his eyes stung. He relived the outrage he had felt then, combined with the terror that if he didn't stay out of it, he would be next.

"I was in the detention unit," he said. Maybe they already guessed that part. "I kept screwing up. Getting in trouble. When they brought her in, she was screaming, kicking, having a… a tantrum, they called it. A meltdown. I don't know what triggered it."

"She did that," Mr. Sellers said. "That's why she was there. We couldn't handle her anymore."

"She managed to bite one of the guards." Zachary was amazed that the names still came to him easily, so many years later. "Berens. It was really bad. Bleeding. So after they got her into her cell, the one next to mine, they called the police. Had her charged with assault."

Mr. Peterson looked surprised at this, but her parents didn't.

"Why would they do that?" Mr. Peterson asked. "If they knew she had autism… she couldn't help it, could she?"

"They did that. Schools do it now. Call the police on little kids. Kids with disabilities. Like their behavior is criminal."

Mr. and Mrs. Sellers nodded. They must have been acutely aware of it whenever such a story hit the news.

"So the police came," Zachary glanced up at them and then stared back down at his hands. "She was still… mid-meltdown. If they'd just left her alone, she would have calmed down… wouldn't she?"

"Eventually," Mr. Sellers agreed.

"They didn't tell the cops she was autistic, just that she was violent and had assaulted Berens. He showed them the injury. Still bleeding. So when they took her out of her cell…" Zachary swallowed. He tried to just go on. It would get harder before it got easier. "They were hitting her. Punching her with their fists and yelling at her to stop fighting." A glance at their faces showed Mr. and Mrs. Sellers intent, living the story, and Mr. Peterson listening in shocked horror. "They got her down on the ground. Prone. One of them kneeling on her while they handcuffed her hands behind her back."

Zachary put his hands over his face, needing to escape from their gazes. The details of the memories didn't dim. His shoulders shook as he tried to keep his body under control.

"She stopped breathing. The cop, he got off of her and they turned her over. She started… started breathing again. She was mostly conscious and was breathing when they took her away."

Zachary rubbed his aching eyes. He opened them and looked down at her picture again. If he could just finish, maybe he would stop being haunted by what had happened.

"They never told us that," Mr. Sellers said.

Zachary nodded. Of course they hadn't told her parents. They hadn't even filed an incident report. He took a few deep breaths, again trying to calm himself. "Other cops brought her back a couple hours later, gave the staff hell for not telling anyone she was autistic. The guards put her back in her cell…"

Mrs. Sellers was crying softly. Mr. Sellers put his arm around her. "Did they hit her again?"

"No. She was quiet. But they… they put her in there, on her bunk, in handcuffs. When they found her in the morning, they took the handcuffs off before anyone got there to investigate, so they wouldn't know."

Everyone was quiet. Mrs. Sellers continued to cry, looking down at the photo album and stroking one of the pictures with her thumb.

"Sometimes when they arrest someone, and they lay them prone, with handcuffs on… it makes it harder to breathe… it's called positional asphyxia. I've researched it…" Zachary explained, the guilt weighing heavily on him. "She was in that position all night…"

"All of these years," Mr. Sellers said. "We've wanted to know why. If it really was just because she was… frail. Or if something happened. We knew about the arrest, but they said it couldn't have had anything to do with her death. Just a coincidence."

"Why didn't they tell us?" Annie's mother demanded. "Why didn't they just tell us the truth from the start?"

"They were afraid of losing their jobs," Mr. Peterson suggested. He rubbed Zachary's shoulder, watching his face with concern. "Getting sued. The institution getting into the papers and losing their funding… there would have been a lot at stake for them, if it was determined that they caused or contributed to her death. Whoever made the decision to leave her there in restraints could have ended up in prison."

"I never told anyone." Zachary gulped. "I had to talk to one of the cops who came and investigated, but… I didn't tell him she was left in handcuffs."

"You were only a boy," Mr. Peterson reminded him. "You couldn't have known how important it was."

"I *did*, though," Zachary insisted. "I knew they were covering it up. I knew it would get them in bigger trouble if the cops found out." He rubbed his eyes and arched his back, trying to loosen the tension in his shoulders. "But I was afraid to say anything. Berens… he'd beat the hell outta me if I did. I'd already gotten in trouble for making noise when they arrested her. Shouting and banging on the door. He'd already beat on me for that. I was just… I was too small to defend myself."

His face burned. For years, he'd lived with his cowardice in keeping his mouth shut. He'd told himself that it didn't matter. That it didn't make any difference. When all along, he knew her parents deserved to know the truth. He'd balked when Mr.

Peterson suggested he get in contact with them to make peace with his past.

But having gotten it out, finally letting the burden of his secret go, he felt the weight lifting from his shoulders. It was easier to breathe. He had thought that the pain in his chest was an aftereffect of the electrical shocks, but maybe there was more to it than that. The more he'd learned about Summit and the life children like Annie led, the worse he'd felt about failing Annie all those years ago.

"Thank you for coming," Mrs. Sellers sniffled. "Thank you for finally giving us the answers."

"I was worried… I would just be stirring things up."

"No. We've never been able to let it rest. Maybe now… now that we finally know…"

Mr. Sellers nodded his agreement.

Mr. Peterson patted Zachary on the back. "You did the right thing, Zachary. Maybe now, you can let the past go too."

***

"Let's go see who's at the door," Ray-Ray's mother said.

He didn't like to leave his project, but she waited, holding her hand out for him, and eventually Ray-Ray got to his feet and took her hand and went with her to the door. The actors who came to the door didn't ever want Ray-Ray, but his mother wanted him to be in the same room as she was. She said he got into trouble too fast if he was out of her sight.

"Who do you think it is?" she asked him.

"Jeremy Clarkson?" Ray-Ray suggested. Not because Jeremy Clarkson had ever come to his door. But that was who he would have liked it to be.

His mother laughed and shook her head. "What a silly boy."

She opened the door and Ray-Ray saw immediately that it wasn't Jeremy Clarkson. The man was smaller, his hair was darker, and he was not as old as Jeremy Clarkson.

"Hi, come in," his mother said in a pleased voice. She tugged on Ray-Ray's hand. "Aren't you going to say hello to Mr. Goldman?"

The name triggered a memory in Ray-Ray's brain. He blinked rapidly and tried to remember what it was.

The man he had met at Summit in a therapy session.

Give Mr. Goldman a hug.

He remembered the lines. Remembered the scene. Mr. Goldman was the man who had been kind to Ray-Ray. Had hugged him gently and made him feel safe. He had been there, in Ray-Ray's therapy session. A special guest star.

Ray-Ray let go of his mother's hand and moved toward Mr. Goldman. He stopped, facing him, and tentatively put out his arms. Mr. Goldman stepped forward and gently enfolded Ray-Ray, like two gears meshing together. Mr. Goldman patted him on the back, just like Ray-Ray remembered from the first episode. Ray-Ray did the same thing, patting Mr. Goldman on the back.

"Hey, bud. How're you doing?" Mr. Goldman said in a soft voice.

Ray-Ray recognized the script. "I'm fine, how are you?" he responded, taking care not to run his words together.

His mother made a noise of approval and ruffled his hair. "Good job, Ray-Ray. How about showing Mr. Goldman what you're working on?"

The two of them released their hugs and Ray-Ray took Mr. Goldman by the hand to lead him back to the kitchen. Mr. Goldman looked at the items scattered across the table.

"Well, this looks interesting. What are you doing?"

Ray-Ray looked at his mother. Before, he hadn't been allowed to talk about cars. When he was at Summit, if he tried to talk about cars during therapy, Sophie got mad and yelled. But his mother nodded her head, which meant it was okay.

"Taking apart a carburetor," he informed Mr. Goldman. "To clean it. See, this is the float," he pointed. "These are the jets... that's the choke."

"Wow. That's pretty cool!"

Ray-Ray looked back toward his mother. She was still smiling. He climbed up onto his chair and got back to work.

"He looks happy," Mr. Goldman said.

"He is… much happier… and he's still growing and progressing. I was always terrified that if we didn't do all of the therapy we could, everything that was available in every aspect of his life, he'd stop his progress. They always told us the only reason he was learning was because of the therapy."

"He looks like he's learning plenty!" Mr. Goldman said with a chuckle. "I don't know how to take a carburetor apart."

Ray-Ray's mother turned on the teakettle. Ray-Ray stopped and listened to it for a moment. He liked the way it ticked like a radiator when it was heating up.

"He's learning more than just how to take cars apart. He was always good at that! But his speech is improving. Social skills. It used to take hours for him to unwind after getting home from Summit. He would be so stressed out and touchy. He keeps on an even keel better now. Our home life has really improved. Before… we were talking about when he would need to start residential at Summit. He was becoming so unmanageable at home."

She paused for a long moment. Ray-Ray looked at her and saw her looking at Mr. Goldman with very shiny eyes. She touched Mr. Goldman on the arm like she might want a hug too. "Thank you. I never would have dared to pull him out of Summit before your investigation. I'm so sorry for what you had to go through, but without you, I never would have gotten my Ray-Ray back."

Ray-Ray shook his head and picked up his screwdriver, pondering her meaning as he removed the air screw.

Zachary looked around the little diner and spotted the black woman and her daughter in the back, at a table near the kitchen.

He could smell French fries and grilled cheese sandwiches. And ketchup. The good stuff.

Zachary led Margaret up to Ava's table.

"Uh… hi."

Ava had been talking to Tirza. She looked up from their conversation. "Oh! Mr. Goldman. I was watching for you, but then I got distracted." She motioned for him to take a seat across from them. Zachary slowly sat down. He gave a nod to his companion.

"Margaret, this is Ava and Tirza."

Margaret thrust her hand toward Ava before sitting down. She didn't offer to shake Tirza's hand, but gave a nod in her direction when Tirza looked up.

A slightly robotic voice came out of Tirza's computer. "Hello Gold Man."

Zachary grinned. "Hey. You got your voice back. How are you doing?"

"Fine," Tirza spoke the word aloud immediately, as if cued, then shook her head and turned her attention to her keyboard, tapping something in. "No, not fine. Hurting," her computer voice announced.

A couple of people sitting nearby turned to look at them, studied the computer and the girl, then eventually went back to their own conversations.

"I'm so sorry," Zachary told Tirza. "How can I help?"

She shook her head. "Can't… Not at Summit now… Done there… Thank you." She raised her gaze from the computer and looked at him out the corner of her eye.

"You're welcome… but I didn't really do anything to help you…"

Ava reached across the table to grasp Zachary's hand. "You did help. When I saw your video… I couldn't leave Tirza there. Not one night. Not one more session. I don't know what to do now…" She looked at Margaret and gave a helpless shrug. "I don't know what else to do."

"We'll talk it over," Margaret assured her. "There are other options. If Summit closed tomorrow, there would be places for all of their residents to go. One way or another. I'd be out a job, but nothing would make me happier." She turned her head to look at Zachary. "Not that I think they're ever going to close their doors. But at least Zachary's experience persuaded a few parents to pull their kids out. Maybe you can't change the whole world… but you've changed the whole world for a few people."

Zachary looked at Tirza, choking up. Physically, Tirza was completely different from Annie, but he could still see something of Annie in her. Maybe Annie's memory would finally leave him in peace.

There were still too many Quentins and Angels trapped in Summit or other places they were being abused.

But maybe he had made a difference for just a few.

Did you enjoy this book? Reviews and recommendations are vital to making a book successful.

Please leave a review at your favorite book store or review site and share it with your friends.

Don't miss the following bonus material:
Sign up for mailing list to get a free ebook
Read a sneak preview chapter
Other books by P.D. Workman
Learn more about the author

Sign up for my mailing list at pdworkman.com and get Gluten-Free Murder for free!

PREVIEW OF SHE WAS DYING ANYWAY

1

Zachary Goldman?"

Zachary nodded distractedly at the man with the clipboard. The movers were wrestling his couch through the doorway of the apartment, turning and angling it to get it through. He wasn't sure whether they were inexperienced or whether the door was narrower than a standard door. He hadn't expected them to have any trouble getting his few pieces of new furniture inside.

"Mr. Goldman."

"Yes?" Zachary's eyes were drawn back to the bald, sweating man in a grey jacket, who was thrusting a clipboard toward him.

"I'm here to hook up the TV."

Zachary had guessed as much from the crest on his uniform.

"Yeah, sure."

"You need to sign the work order."

Zachary pulled his eyes away from the movers again to scan the heading and the signature line of the form on the clipboard.

"This says you're done."

"I am."

"But you just got here."

"I don't need to do anything here," the man said impatiently. "All of the wiring is done in the utility closet. I'm all done."

"Oh… then I guess I need to test that it's working."

Their eyes were both drawn back to the movers as there was a crunch of the couch meeting the doorframe yet again and one of the movers swore angrily at the other.

"It is working," the TV man said. "I've tested it all out."

"But in here," Zachary motioned to the apartment. "I should test it in here, make sure it's hooked up to the right apartment."

The bald man rolled his eyes at Zachary's presumption. "Come on, buddy. I've got other jobs to do. This one has already taken longer than it should have."

Since Zachary hadn't even seen him until that moment, he had no way of knowing whether it was true, or whether it had been a two-minute hook-up. He knew he really ought to check to make sure everything was working. If he signed the work order saying that everything was done, and then ended up having to call the company to get it fixed, it would be an extra charge. He looked at the movers in the doorway, wondering how much longer it was going to be before they could get the couch in through the door, so he could get in to test the TV and make sure he was getting all of the channels.

"Uh, if you'll just wait for a few minutes…"

"Do you even have your TV unpacked yet?"

That was going to be another problem, Zachary realized. The TV wasn't even out of the box yet. In fact, it was probably still down on the truck. He couldn't remember it being brought in yet.

"No," he admitted. "Could you maybe come back after your next job? Or take your lunch break now and come back in half an hour? I'll get these guys moving and get it all plugged in…"

The man thrust the clipboard at him again. "Just sign the form, buddy. If there's a problem, you'll have to put in a call."

"But how long would it take to get you back here?" Zachary had dealt with enough utility companies to know that it could be days.

"I've done my job. You're not going to need anyone to come back. Just sign the form."

Zachary sighed and took it from him. The form was dense with fine print, and he knew he should read it all, or at least skim through it before he signed it. There was another volley of swearing from the movers, and a long creak of protest from the couch as they tried to bend it through the doorway. Zachary winced and looked over at them. He scribbled an unreadable signature on the form and handed it back to the TV guy, who took it, ripped off a carbonless copy for Zachary's records, and left without a word of thanks. Zachary went over to talk to the movers about the couch.

"We're going to have to cut it into sections," the older of the movers said, wiping his forehead with the back of his arm. "Otherwise, it's never going through this door."

Zachary looked at the damage they had already done to the doorway and the wall around it. The couch was obviously not going to fit. And he wasn't sure how anyone was going to reassemble it if they cut it up to get it through the door. He imagined the pieces sitting in his new living room forever, unusable.

"It will have to go back to the store. I'll have to get something smaller that will fit through."

The two men looked at each other, rolling their eyes.

"Sorry," Zachary apologized. "I'll call them."

At least his phone was a cell and didn't have to be wired in at the apartment. He was sure that would have gone wrong too.

The movers left the couch in the hallway as they went down to bring the next piece of furniture in off the truck. Hopefully, the bed. He could live without anything else for a few days, but he was really looking forward to sleeping on a bed again, after the months of sleeping on Bowman's couch. Not that the couch wasn't comfortable. But it was a couch. He would have his own space back, out of Bowman's way. A bed of his own. His own TV.

Zachary looked around the small apartment. He had viewed it in the evening a couple of weeks before, when the lighting had been softer, and it hadn't looked quite as dingy as it did in the late morning sun. The landlord had said that he would repaint it, but it was obvious he hadn't.

There was a tentative knock on the open door of the apartment, and Zachary pulled himself from his consideration of the merits and deficits of the apartment to turn around and see who it was. Another utility man, the landlord, the movers…

But it wasn't any of those. It wasn't another form or agreement he was going to have to sign. It was a petite blond woman. Her hair was still much shorter than she preferred it, but at least it was her own hair. It had come back in just the same as before chemo, no change in color or curl, as the doctors had warned it might. Bridget's face was filling back out so that she no longer looked sick or waifish, but like herself.

"Bridget! Come in!"

She lifted the grocery bags by way of explanation. "I brought you some things."

Zachary hurried over to relieve her of her load. He hesitated, always unsure how to greet her appropriately.

"You didn't have to do this." Zachary indicated the bags, settling on just taking them from her without any handshake or friendly kiss on the cheek.

"I figured you would be busy with all of the other arrangements and wouldn't have the time to feed yourself properly."

Zachary put the grocery bags on the counter in the kitchen and started to go through them. The fridge was already plugged in, luckily, so nothing would spoil if he put it all away.

"That was really thoughtful. I hadn't even thought about food," Zachary admitted. He ran a hand over his hair. He kept his dark hair short, so it wasn't messy even if he happened to forget to comb it when he got up, but he couldn't remember if he had bothered to shave when he got up that morning. He hadn't expected to have to be presentable for anyone. He scratched his jaw and found it was covered with stubble. Not just one day's growth but probably a few. Another of the things he didn't put a lot of thought into, especially if he was on surveillance. People didn't pay much attention to a man who was a little unclean or rough-looking. They tended to avoid eye contact, in case he might ask for money or a job.

"No, I didn't think you would," Bridget agreed. She grabbed a carton of milk from one of the bags and put it into the fridge, then proceeded to unpack the other items. Zachary grabbed a few dry goods to put into the cupboard before she could do the whole job herself.

When they were finished, Bridget turned and looked at the rest of the apartment. Most of it was visible from the kitchen.

"This is nice."

Zachary was sure that, to Bridget's critical eye, it didn't qualify as 'nice.' He knew how exacting her standards were. She would never even have considered the place for herself. But Zachary wasn't going to be doing a lot of entertaining. His needs were modest and, despite the little bit of recognition he had garnered on a couple of recent cases, his cash flow was thin and irregular, and he needed to be sure not to get anything that would be too expensive for his usual income.

"Thanks. Um... I'd ask you to sit down, but I don't actually have anywhere yet..."

"It will be nice for you to be back in a place of your own again. I'm sure Mario was a good host, but you both need your own space."

"Mario's been great." Mario Bowman really had been a lifesaver, letting Zachary come to stay with him for a 'few days' when Zachary's own apartment had burned down, and allowing him to continue to recover there until he was able to get back on his own feet again. Zachary hadn't been comfortable intruding on Bowman all the time; he couldn't imagine how uncomfortable it must have been for Bowman to have someone else in his territory, always underfoot, for what had ended up being weeks on end. "But no one will be happier than him that I'm out of there now."

The movers arrived, with kitchen furniture this time, so in minutes, Zachary and Bridget were able to sit down to visit.

"You'll have to take care of yourself," Bridget said. "You won't be able to rely on Mario to keep the fridge stocked or make supper."

"Yeah, you're right." He would have to make sure he was eating properly, something that was too easy for him to forget when he was distracted by a case or other things going on in his life. "I'll be fine. I've done it before."

"Yes… but not well."

It was strange that Bridget was there. It was nice of her to bring him food and help him to get settled, but he wasn't quite sure why she would. They weren't together anymore. She didn't have any responsibility to look after him, as she was always quick to point out. Yet, in spite of the rift between them, she kept showing up, acting like she still cared what happened to him. She had gone on and was together with Gordon Drake now. Zachary was seeing Kenzie occasionally, though they hadn't really settled into a dating relationship yet. Bridget should have just moved on and not had anything to do with Zachary.

"I'll be fine," he assured Bridget. Maybe that was all she needed. Just some reassurance that he wasn't going to end up starving or in the hospital, somehow making her feel guilty for having broken up with him.

But Bridget didn't make any move to get up and leave. She tapped a nail on the tabletop, a nervous gesture that was out of character for her. The ticking of her nail against the table ratcheted up his anxiety.

"Is… there something wrong?" Zachary ventured. "Is everything okay with you?" He had a sudden sick feeling. What if she had relapsed? What if the cancer had come back?

Bridget instantly read Zachary's expression. "No, no. I'm fine," she assured him. But her eyes filled with tears.

Zachary instantly went into full-blown panic. Her anger and criticism he was used to dealing with. Even her blame. But her tears were something he didn't know how to handle. Bridget never cried. Even when she had told him about her diagnosis, it had been with dry eyes and a flat, stoic voice.

"What is it? What's wrong? What can I do?" He reached out to her, and she actually took his hand, squeezing it for comfort. She blinked rapidly and looked up at the ceiling, trying to avoid shedding the tears that had gathered in her eyes. If it wasn't the cancer, what was it?

Bridget breathed deeply to calm herself. When she spoke, her voice was even, but she talked more slowly than usual, and he knew it was a struggle for her to keep from crying.

"I don't know if I've ever mentioned my friend, Robin Salter, to you."

Zachary flipped through his mental catalog. He was good with names. As a private investigator, he needed to be able to make connections between people quickly, and it was amazing how often a previous name came into play on a new case. Seven degrees of separation became a lot less in a smaller community.

"Not that I remember," he said, feeling bad he couldn't make any connection to the name. Someone she worked with? Was in a club or other organization with? Bridget was very social; she and her family had a lot of friends.

Bridget waved away the apology in his voice. "I didn't know her while we were together. We were in treatment together."

"Oh. She had cancer too?" Was it appropriate for him to ask what kind? Or was that impolite? Invasive?

"Yes. Ovarian, like me. Only…" There was a slight waver in her voice. She was doing her best to hold it together, but she was right on the edge. She cleared her throat and took another deep breath. "Hers didn't go into remission. It metastasized."

Zachary's stomach was a tight knot. That could have been Bridget. The doctor had warned them that treatment might not be successful. Only thirty percent went into remission. Zachary had dealt with the specter of death before, but not like that. Not looking at his beautiful, vibrant wife and knowing that she could die in a matter of months.

"And they… there was nothing they could do?"

"They tried. But she knew she was terminal."

"I'm so sorry, Bridge."

Bridget swallowed. "She died on Friday."

He squeezed her hand, wishing there was more he could do to comfort her. "I'm so, so sorry."

Bridget stared off into space. He wondered whether she was imagining her own life if things had gone differently. Her own death. What if that had been her? What had she accomplished in her life? Who would be mourning for her?

"I need your help."

Zachary blinked, surprised. Even when they were together, Bridget had not asked him for help. She had been happy to be in charge of everything. She took on extra responsibility like it was a new suit to add to her extensive collection. Even now, with the divorce well behind them, she was still bringing Zachary groceries and fussing over his health and his ability to take care of himself.

She never asked for help.

2

I don't think she died of natural causes."

That wasn't what Zachary had been expecting to hear. He furrowed his brow, studying Bridget and trying to divine her meaning.

"You said she had cancer. Terminal cancer. It had metastasized."

"Yes."

Zachary sat back in his chair.

"I want you to look into it. I'll pay your fees."

"You don't need to pay me," Zachary objected. "You're my…" He trailed off. She wasn't his wife. They weren't family, not any longer. Categorizing her as his ex didn't make it sound like a close relationship.

Bridget didn't seem to notice his awkwardness. "Nobody else thinks anything of it. Her family, her boyfriend, not anyone. Or at least, if they do, they aren't saying anything. But I know it wasn't natural. It wasn't her time."

"Sometimes people go before they are expected to," Zachary pointed out. "Pneumonia, or an infection, or just because they gave up."

"She hadn't given up. I had just talked to her. She wasn't ready to go. She was still fighting."

"Chemo can be very hard on the body." He remembered the doctor talking to him and Bridget about how difficult the treatment could be. That for some people with very advanced or aggressive cancers, it was better to have a few months with good quality of life than to eke out a few more in complete misery.

"I know that," Bridget's voice was getting harder the more he protested. Losing that vulnerable, teary edge and growing angry. He could deal with her anger better than her tears. "But I saw her, Zachary. She wasn't ready to go. She wasn't!"

Zachary nodded slowly. "Okay. So, what is it you think happened? You think they made a mistake in her treatment? An accident?"

"Maybe."

Zachary scratched his jaw, thinking it through. He didn't have any big cases on the go. Just the routine insurance claims, cheating spouses, background checks; the kind of cases that were his bread and butter. Routine work he could survive on. As long as Bridget's case didn't take up too much of his time, he could afford to take it on as a favor. If it ended up taking up too much time, she was prepared to pay him. More than likely, it would just be a few inquiries to find out what had happened and then he could put Bridget's mind at ease.

"Are you sure you want to do this, Bridget? It could just end up making you feel worse, keeping it fresh. It might hurt Robin's family and friends and cause resentments."

Bridget nodded. Her jaw muscles were tightly clenched, but otherwise she gave no sign of her deep emotions, smiling pleasantly as if they were discussing the weather. "I realize all that, but… I think it's important."

"Is it what Robin would have wanted? I mean… she was dying anyway, would she really have wanted to make a big deal over it?"

A flush started to creep up Bridget's throat.

"You don't think it's important?" she demanded. "You think that those few months aren't worth anything? That they can just be written off? Our time here is important, whether it is years, or months, or days. No one has the right to take them away from us."

"Okay. I just want to make sure it's really what you want. When someone starts poking around in a case like this, people can get pretty worked up. You might not think that anyone would care, you think that everyone else would just want to know the truth, but it can cause… really bad feelings… even threats of violence."

"I'm prepared to deal with that." The rosy flush had risen all the way to Bridget's ears. She was steamed, but she was holding back because she wanted Zachary to take the case. She knew that if she exploded, he could simply say he wouldn't take the case. He wasn't obligated.

But he would take it, even if she did blow up at him. He would always do any favor she asked of him.

"So, will you? Will you look into it for me?"

"Yes. Email me all of the information you have on Robin and the hospital or treatment program and I'll see what I can find out. I just wanted to be sure you knew what you were getting into."

Bridget's shoulders dipped and her jaw relaxed. "Thank you, Zachary. You don't know what this means to me."

He allowed himself only a fleeting vision of her expressing her gratitude to him in other ways. Of her softening toward him and realizing how good they were together, how important they were to each other.

But that wasn't why she was there. That wasn't why she had come.

There was a knock on the open door, and Zachary startled, jerking his head around to see who was there. For a split second, he worried that it would be the landlord, upset about the couch sitting in the hallway and the damage to the doorframe and wall.

But it was Mario Bowman, smiling at them. He was balding, over-weight, and always looked a little seedy when he wasn't wearing his police uniform. But he was a devoted friend who had gone above and beyond the call of duty to help out a man who was hardly more than an acquaintance at the time. Zachary's respect for the cop had only grown as they had gotten to know each other better. Bowman was one of the good guys. One of the best.

"I thought I'd get a start on these boxes." Bowman was leering as if he'd just caught the two of them in a heated embrace. "If you two don't mind being interrupted."

Bridget was on her feet before Zachary, letting go of his hand and stepping over to greet Bowman with a peck on the cheek. "Mario! What a delight to see you again! I'll bet you're happy to be getting rid of this scoundrel."

Zachary made it belatedly to his feet, feeling off-balance for just a split second before he managed to gain his equilibrium. While it appeared to everyone but his physical therapist that he was fully recovered from his last couple of 'accidents,' Zachary was acutely aware of every movement or reaction that took a microsecond longer than it used to. Those instants frustrated him, and all the more when he was the only one who noticed them and everybody else thought he was overreacting or imagining things.

Bowman looked at Zachary with an expression of affection. "Well, to tell the truth…" he trailed off, letting the phrase hang for a moment, "yes, nothing would make me happier than to see the back of him."

He gave Zachary a rough hug around the shoulders to show that he meant no ill will toward Zachary. And Zachary knew it was true, Bowman would be happy to see Zachary out of Bowman's apartment, but even happier to know that Zachary was safely installed in a place of his own.

"So, shall I start bringing things up?"

"Yes, sure," Zachary agreed. "There really isn't much though."

"Not much." Bowman rolled his eyes at Bridget. "It's amazing how much one person can acquire in the space of a few weeks."

He slapped Zachary on the back and headed back out into the hallway to go get the things he'd brought over in the car.

"It isn't that much," Zachary repeated to Bridget, his face warm. When he had moved in to sleep on Bowman's couch, he'd had nothing but the clothes on his back, which weren't even all his own. He hadn't even had a wallet or any means to pay for anything else. But Bowman and others had chipped in to get him clothes, a suitcase, and what other little necessaries Zachary needed until he was able to access his bank account and credit card account, and then to get the settlement money from the insurer so that he'd be able to get established again. He had a new laptop and some photographic equipment, a few files for the cases that he'd worked on since losing everything, his clothing… but it really wasn't more than would fit in a couple of suitcases.

He followed Bowman down to the car and bent over to pick up a suitcase, looking into the car. "What's all this?"

Bowman picked up a couple of boxes, carefully stacked and balanced. "Just a few little things."

Zachary lugged his suitcases, trying to figure out what else Bowman had packed. There couldn't have been that much more than would fit in his suitcases. Bowman had shooed him out of the apartment early that morning, telling him that he'd better be ready well before the first workers were scheduled to get there, and that Bowman would pack everything up and take it over.

Bridget was still there when they got up to Zachary's apartment. He hadn't been sure whether she would stay around or if she would take the first opportunity to disappear. She took the box that Bowman had stacked on top of the one he was carrying and set it down on the kitchen table to look through the contents. Zachary looked down at an assortment of dishes, sheets, and towels. He looked over at Bowman. A bachelor himself, Bowman didn't exactly have a lot to give away.

"Just a few things I wanted to get rid of," Bowman offered with a shrug. "I mean, you're going to need all those sorts of odds and ends, and my place is getting cluttered."

"You didn't need to do that."

Showing no hint of being self-conscious, Bridget started to remove the dishes and find the appropriate places for them in the kitchen. When Zachary looked at her with his mouth open, looking for a reason to object, she just shook her head.

"Why don't you go unpack your clothes?"

"Uh… okay," Zachary agreed, and took the suitcases into the bedroom to get a start on them.

***

Zachary was exhausted at the end of the day when everyone was gone, and he was left in his new apartment all alone. He had furniture, other than a couch. The TV and internet were both working, and his various possessions and the donations from Bridget and Bowman were all neatly put away. The apartment felt sparse and empty, but it was a start. After years of being a foster kid barely able to hold on to the one possession that really mattered—the camera given to him by Mr. Peterson—he was used to starting over with nothing. And he knew that he would start to collect new possessions at a rate that would have alarmed Bridget had they still been living together. She never could understand his need to hold on to absolutely everything. Like a grandparent who had lived through the depression, Zachary knew what it was like to want. Parting with anything, no matter how small and insignificant, was difficult.

It was probably a good thing he didn't have a couch, so he couldn't lie down and go to sleep in front of the TV in the living room like he had been doing at Bowman's house. Doctors had always told him that was poor sleep hygiene and that he wouldn't really get the REM sleep he needed to be alert and mentally healthy. It would be his first night sleeping in a bed in months, and he was looking forward to being able to stretch out and not worry about running into the ends of the couch or falling off the side as he had several times.

It was no surprise that when he lay down to go to sleep, he was not the least bit sleepy. His brain whirled around and around, going over everything that had happened during the day, analyzing it, thinking of all of the things he should have said and done instead of what he had. What kept returning to him over and over was the conversation with Bridget about Robin Salter. He probably should have said no. He should have at least been more resistant and given Bridget a day or two to think about it before agreeing to help. The more he looked at the problem, the more obvious it became that it was a minefield, with no safe way across. If he didn't find any evidence that it was not a natural death, Bridget was going to be angry and think that he had not been trying hard enough and had not done a good job. If he did find evidence that the hospital had covered up a mistake or something else, she was going to be angry about Robin's life being cut short before her time was up and she wouldn't have anyone to vent to about it except for Zachary. There was no one else behind her on her mission to find out the truth, so that put Zachary directly in the crosshairs either way.

What if she didn't accept his findings? What if the police or the doctors didn't? What if he had suspicions but couldn't prove anything?

Zachary got out of bed and wandered out to the living room. He turned the TV on and began to pace, trying to silence the arguments going around his head and to get into a rhythm. He checked out the fridge, but he wasn't really hungry, and despite the fact that Bridget had filled it with food, nothing appealed to him. He would have to make a start on it the next day, because otherwise, a few days down the line, things were going to start going bad and he wouldn't be able to keep up with them.

His body was exhausted before he started, so it was no wonder that he quickly tired of the pacing and had to sit down. He had an easy chair, but he wanted to lie on his side rather than recline and was too antsy to stay in the chair.

He ended up lying on the carpet where the couch should be, a throw pillow between his arm and his head, watching inane infomercials on TV until he fell asleep.

Order *She Was Dying Anyway,* Book #3 of the *Zachary Goldman Mysteries* series by P.D. Workman can be purchased at pdworkman.com

ABOUT THE AUTHOR

Award-winning and USA Today bestselling author P.D. (Pamela) Workman writes riveting mystery/suspense and young adult books dealing with mental illness, addiction, abuse, and other real-life issues. For as long as she can remember, the blank page has held an incredible allure and from a very young age she was trying to write her own books.

Workman wrote her first complete novel at the age of twelve and continued to write as a hobby for many years. She started publishing in 2013. She has won several literary awards from Library Services for Youth in Custody for her young adult fiction. She currently has over 50 published titles and can be found at pdworkman.com.

Born and raised in Alberta, Workman has been married for over 25 years and has one son.

Please visit P.D. Workman at pdworkman.com to see what else she is working on, to join her mailing list, and to link to her social networks.

If you enjoyed this book, please take the time to recommend it to other purchasers with a review or star rating and share it with your friends!

facebook.com/pdworkmanauthor

twitter.com/pdworkmanauthor

instagram.com/pdworkmanauthor

amazon.com/author/pdworkman

bookbub.com/authors/p-d-workman

goodreads.com/pdworkman

linkedin.com/in/pdworkman

pinterest.com/pdworkmanauthor

youtube.com/pdworkman